Veronica Bennetts is a musician, teacher and writer whose career spans composing, writing, directing and teaching. Studying Music, English Literature and Education at Cambridge, she also holds a Master of Education degree from Liverpool University. One of her particular loves has been seeking to provide creative opportunities for young people in order to stimulate them to express themselves imaginatively. She has written and compiled many performing arts works (music, story and lyrics) and until recently has been Director of Education for Performance Arts for an international Theatre Arts franchise.

She is deeply interested in children who have been damaged or who struggle from the impact of early life events. Whilst undertaking some training with the NSPCC she learnt more about the tenacity and courage that characterise many of these youngsters. The insights gained have led indirectly to the writing of her debut novel *Twisted Threads* and the subsequent two novels in the trilogy *Love's Tangled Tapestry*.

Veronica has four grown up children, lots of grandchildren, and very importantly, two golden retriever dogs. Her late husband was the Bishop of Coventry. She now lives in Chertsey and devotes as many hours as she can to her passion for writing.

*Love's Tangled Tapestry*

A Trilogy

No. 1

*TWISTED THREADS*

Veronica Bennetts

_____

_____

*Love's Tangled Tapestry*

A Trilogy

No.1

*TWISTED THREADS*

Vanguard Press

VANGUARD PAPERBACK

© Copyright 2023
**Veronica Bennetts**

A CIP catalogue record for this title is
available from the British Library.

ISBN 978-1-80016-593-9

*Vanguard Press is an imprint of
Pegasus Elliot Mackenzie Publishers Ltd.*
www.pegasuspublishers.com

First Published in 2023

**Vanguard Press
Sheraton House Castle Park
Cambridge England**

Printed & Bound in Great Britain

In memory of my beloved husband,
Colin Bennetts

My grateful thanks are due to all who have read the draft of *Twisted Threads;* in particular to Sarah Bennetts, Martin Kuhrt, Christa Hook and Kate Wright for their hugely valuable feedback, and to Stephanie Manuel for her unfailing support and encouragement.

*PART ONE*

# Chapter 1
## 1955

Bruce Connor stared out of his bedroom window in disbelief at the scene unfolding before him in the street below. He was mesmerized and appalled by it in equal measure. At the tender age of twelve, he had come to the sad conclusion that he hated his father. What he was witnessing now simply served to reinforce that conviction.

It was a sultry Sunday evening, with the day's fierce heat still hanging in the air. Suddenly, cutting through the stillness like a razor grating on glass came the sound of violent shouting from Bruce Connor's furious father. It was immediately followed by agonized shrieking. James Connor, age thirteen was running down the road in terror, hotly pursued by his bellowing father. Albert Connor was known in the neighbourhood for his temper although no one had witnessed any physical violence from him towards any of his four children. Those who knew the nature of the man had their deep suspicions about the goings-on within the four walls of his house.

Bruce, upstairs, was shaking with fearful anticipation at the fury he saw in his father's clenched fist as he shook it violently, his chase nearing its destination — the running boy — with all the menace of a horror movie. James, terrified, continued to run down the road. Albert Connors shouted with all his might.

'Stop, boy!'

In his upstairs room, Bruce was on the edge of panic. What was the punishment to come for James? Would it be a severe beating for disobedience, or something worse? James skidded to a halt on the pavement and turned to face his father, who said nothing, but held up a large sketch pad. Slowly and systematically he began to rip the thick pages from it, tearing each one almost ritualistically into small pieces in front of James' face. He then scattered them onto the pavement, never taking his angry eyes off his son. Bruce, watching, saw his brother cover his head in despair as the pictures he had worked on so painstakingly fell to the ground like thick pastel-coloured confetti.

'No, Dad, no, *please* don't,' James pleaded in agony.

This act of barbarism towards James was a far deeper punishment than a beating could have ever been. Bruce knew that. What he could not fully comprehend was the far-reaching consequence it would have. Nevertheless, fear for his brother seemed to penetrate the very marrow of his bones.

Undeterred, Albert Connors continued to rip the thick pages out, until all that remained in his hands were the two covers of the sketch pad.

'That'll teach you, you wretch of a boy.'

Grabbing James roughly by the scruff of the neck, he bellowed in his face,

'You were meant to be *mending your bike*, not doing your airy-fairy drawings. Now pick up every piece then come inside.'

This was James' only crime. His passion for his art had obliterated in his memory the order from his father.

Albert Connor stomped back down the road, a bull of a man with a stocky, square frame and a jutting out chin. Before he reached the house, he shouted back,

*'And get a move on, you stupid namby-pamby wimp.'*

James sank to the ground, anguished, and began to finger the shreds of paper. These were his precious sketches that he had been compiling for a year now into a collection — all wrecked because he had failed to mend his bike. He tried in vain to place some of the pieces together. They were mainly soft pastel and charcoal drawings — pictures of people, animals, birds, trees, moths, and most precious of all, a head and shoulders portrait of his mother he had spent weeks on and was going to give her for her birthday.

From the window, Bruce saw his younger brother weep over the fragments, knowing it was a lost cause to try to salvage any of his work. Ever since he was a small boy James' instinct had told him that his father despised him. For a start, he was sandy-haired and small for his age and too slender for his own good — "a good-for-nothing bag o' bones" his father often repeated. James was, everyone said, the spitting image of his mother. His father, on the other hand, was dark and hairy, with balloon-shaped muscles in his upper arms, and shoulders the width of a battering ram.

James had a rare talent for artwork, particularly sketching, and would spend every spare minute up in his room working on the latest picture for his portfolio. For his father to have destroyed virtually his entire collection in one fell swoop was something from which he was never to recover. It was not only the sketches his father had trampled on; James knew his father was illustrating in vivid terms just how much he despised his younger son.

Bruce, in his bedroom, suddenly unfroze and leaped swiftly into action. He began to jump down the narrow staircase two steps at a time to help his brother. At the same time, out of her bedroom ran an older girl, the boys' sister. Sadie was fourteen. Dark and strong, her appearance and nature were the opposite of her younger brothers. Sadie adored James most particularly out of her siblings, and such was her empathy for her sensitive brother that she felt her father had been trampling over her own feelings as well as James' and his pictures. The two children had always been very close.

Sadie reached her brother, who was now curled in a foetal position on the still warm pavement.

'I'll help you, Jamie. We'll soon get this done.'

Sadie began collecting up the paper fragments, putting them into the abundant pockets of her navy-blue school gymslip.

'I'll see if we can salvage any of them,' she said soothingly to James. 'Our father is a pig and I hate him.'

'And I hate him too,' whispered James through his tears.

When they reached the front door, their mother Rosa, a delicately made woman, was waiting for them. She said nothing, but scooped James up into a huge hug, put a hand out in gratitude to Sadie, and led her stricken son indoors.

'Did you see what Dad did, Mum?' asked Bruce, joining them at the front door.

Rosa looked questioningly at her children.

'Don't even *ask,*' said Sadie angrily to her mother. 'He's only gone and ripped up Jamie's artwork, the mean and nasty bas—'

'Sadie!' said her mother weakly. 'Don't use a word like that about your father!'

Sadie scowled.

Bruce was bold when it came to defending his siblings.

'Mum, why do you always stick up for Dad? He's a bully and we all hate him.'

'What did you say?' bellowed their father from the shed. 'Just *what* did you say?' he repeated, coming into the room and twisting Bruce's ear with an oily hand.

'One day you'll pay for this,' muttered Bruce under his breath. 'You just wait!'

Albert Connors gave Bruce's ear a further agonisingly hard twist, shook his fist in the boy's face and returned to the shed and James' bicycle. Rosa poured orange squash for the children and produced a plate of comforting, warm homemade biscuits, speaking in soothing tones all the while.

'There, there. No harm done. No harm done,' she crooned. 'Your daddy didn't mean it.'

Albert Connor returned to the kitchen within five minutes.

'Well, I've done it for you, you little tyke,' he said gruffly to James, who was still quietly sobbing, white-faced. 'It just needed the chain put back on. I suppose that was too much for your precious hands, was it?'

He paused, taking stock of the situation, and saw the reproachful, wounded eyes of his wife staring at him.

'If you'd have mended your own bike, none of this would have happened. It's your fault. Learn to do as you're told, boy,' he said more softly, his temper dissipated and his wife's eyes continuing to subdue him.

Sadie's face was red with fury. She went up to her father, not intimidated by his manner, and spoke angrily to him.

'Dad, how could you destroy his sketches? How *could* you? You're a cruel and mean man.'

Albert Connor momentarily looked as though he was going to hit his daughter, but then unclasped his thrusting fist and swiped her head with the oily cloth he had been using.

'I'll thank you to keep your big nose out of it, *Miss* Sadie Perfect,' he retorted, tilting Sadie's head upwards roughly. 'Or *are* you so perfect?' he sneered in an undertone.

'We all hate you, Dad,' Sadie screamed behind her as she pounded upstairs.

Albert followed in hot pursuit, inadvertently putting oily fingerprints on the walls as he went. He caught up with her on the top step and suddenly, changing his mood, fondled her buttock briefly.

'*Don't* do that,' shouted Sadie viciously, turning round and glaring at him.

'Why not?' retorted Bert. 'You're my daughter!' Then, changing the tone of his voice to a whisper, 'Anyway, you know you like it.'

Sadie ran into her bedroom and locked the door.

'Mum, why don't you say anything?' said Bruce, exasperated. 'You could at least stick up for James.'

'There's no point,' she replied wearily, resigned to the fact that she would never get the better of her bullying husband. Time and again she had toyed with leaving him, taking the children with her, but knew she had nowhere to go. Anyway, she was in the early weeks of another pregnancy, which complicated matters further.

An uneasy peace finally settled on the home, with Albert wallowing in a long soak in the bath, Rosa darning socks and Bruce, in his bedroom as ever chronicling events in a thick, red notebook. James was deeply grieving over his destroyed artwork and quietly hatching a dark plan, while little Connie, the youngest child, was putting colourful beads on a thread to make a necklace, outwardly unperturbed by the arguments around her which were a familiar feature of the household.

What no one knew was that Sadie was upstairs packing a suitcase.

Later, she wrote two identical notes, one to James, the other to Bruce. She waited until both boys were asleep (which was gone midnight), then slipped the notes under each of the boys' pillows.

*"Jamie. Brucey. I'm leaving. I must. I'll think of you often. I'm sorry. Tell Mum that I love her very much. Look after Connie. Love always, Sadie xx".*

\*\*\*

There was huge consternation the following morning. Bruce showed his mother the note. Bert initially dismissed the disappearance of his daughter as 'a teenager indulging a fantasy' but became more worried as the hours turned into days. Rosa, her heart bursting with panic and pain, visited the police station to report Sadie as a missing person, and Albert toured the neighbourhood and beyond every day in his blue Ford Consul car, often taking Connie with him to provide an extra pair of eyes.

If Albert Connor had any feelings of guilt or remorse over the showdown with James, and Sadie's involvement in it, he didn't show it. He outwardly dismissed it as an irrelevant family tiff. How he felt inside was anybody's guess.

Rosa was twelve weeks pregnant and fearful of what the acute anxiety might do to the baby she was carrying. She had already had two miscarriages since Connie, who was now six, and for her this was a longed for and carefully safeguarded pregnancy. Every baby was precious in Rosa's eyes, and despite all the practical implications of another mouth to feed, she had greeted her missed period with hopeful anticipation that there might be a fourth child on the way and she would manage to carry it full-term.

She read and reread Sadie's note, finally deciding that for the sake of the baby she was carrying she must accept that her eldest daughter knew what she was doing and would keep herself safe. She noticed that Sadie had taken all her savings, which over the years had amounted to a reasonable amount, so at least she would have money to support herself until she came home in a few days' time.

However, much to the acute heartache of Rosa, Sadie never returned.

\*\*\*

Rosa Connors, the children's mother, came from a talented background and was the youngest of six children. Her father was a professional musician, an expert clarinettist, but despite his considerable musical gifts, had made very little money from his profession. Somehow the family scraped by. Rosa's mother had been a nurse.

Creative gifts had been inherited by two of Rosa and Albert's children. James had his grandmother's artistic talent (her pictures adorned their walls) and Bruce, his younger brother, was demonstrating distinct musical talent. This was illustrated by the dexterous way he had taken to playing the clarinet bequeathed to him in his grandfather's will.

Interestingly, artistic gifts seemed to have bypassed Sadie, the eldest daughter of the Connors family, but what she lacked in creative ability she more than made up for in practical skills, and generally had a pragmatic approach to life even at the age of fourteen. Rosa relied heavily on Sadie for help with the household chores. It was too soon to tell with little Constance, known to everyone in the family as "Connie", aged six, if she would turn out to be artistic or more like her older sister. Rosa thought that her little daughter's drawings and doodling seemed to indicate some promise.

Albert Connors discounted his boys' gifts as being no earthly good, and as he had expressed so viciously to James, too 'airy-fairy'. He was an extremely grounded and practical man. He had learnt carpentry after he was demobbed from the army at the end of the First World War but saw making tables and chairs and sideboards as a necessary evil rather than at any time fulfilling a creative purpose. Everything he made was solid, without patterns or inlays, stained dark brown and painted over with several layers of thick varnish — strictly utilitarian and suiting the stringent post-war years. However, they were beautifully made and underneath the harsh protective layers clearly the work of a master craftsmen. Orders for them came in thick and fast. His business was growing.

Rosa maintained that Bert, as she called him, had not always been the gruff, bullying man he was now. Born in 1900, he had been one of the physically mature and strong lads who had joined the army at the tender age of fourteen. He was enlisted prematurely by a less than scrupulous sergeant at a time when the army had put out desperate calls for troops. The boy Albert had therefore been in the trenches in the First World War during the Battle of the

Somme and had witnessed grotesque and inhuman sights, including that of his best friend's head being blown off in front of his eyes. This was the one and only event he had ever recounted to Rosa, and afterwards he wept and shook in her arms for more than an hour.

Thereon in, he sealed up his emotional life. He locked away memories of events so that they festered within his psyche for years and damaged him profoundly, and in turn his entire family. Rosa knew instinctively that the suppression of these feelings and thoughts meant that Bert's psychological damage and trauma had been sublimated. Consequently, they surfaced in many other ugly forms. Despite witnessing the bullying and anger, therefore, that Bert directed at his sons in particular, Rosa showed leniency towards her husband on the grounds that he was a severely damaged man who had witnessed unimaginable horrors to which no boy of fragile teenage years should ever have been subjected.

Rosa's apparent submissiveness was largely a learnt skill for her survival, having been taunted mercilessly as a child by several older brothers. She had found that the best way to deal with what she regarded as these quintessentially "male" traits was to say nothing at all in response.

Rose met Bert when she was twenty-one and he was forty. Her brothers teased her mercilessly about the age gap.

'Making love to your daddy!' one would say in a singsong voice.

'Snatching baby from her cradle, then?' taunted another.

And, more offensively,

'Hey Rosa. You'll never manage him. He'll be too old and big and hairy for you!'

Gestures and guffaws of crude male laughter would follow. When they met Albert Connors, however, one by one they were silenced by his intimidating and powerful presence, and the way he could speak out a well-timed sentence in his booming voice and silence them in an instant. The boys' taunting gradually turned into a genuine fear for their youngest sister as they could see that Albert had the all the makings of a monster.

'Paper tigers all of them,' Bert used to say reassuringly to Rosa. 'Don't worry about those bullies. You're *mine* now.'

Rosa would look up gratefully and give him everything he wanted. In her eyes he was her saviour.

# *Chapter 2*

Bruce Connors, Rosa and Albert's second son, was a complex boy. He was used to being severely punished by his father for the slightest misdemeanour. Bert assumed his son would go into the army, as he himself had, and did everything he could to "toughen him up". He was outraged when the boy showed distinct leanings towards pacifism even at the tender age of twelve. Bruce surreptitiously circumvented his father's opinion on the matter and persuaded his mother to let him join a local Quaker group, finding the silence and lack of pressure for expression a comfort. He was a solitary boy and the group suited him, although he had not yet formed a set opinion regarding the possible existence (or not) of God.

Albert was incandescent with rage when he learned about Bruce's strange choice of activity. As a punishment, he confiscated his son's precious clarinet, took out its reed and hid it, together with the "spares", thus rendering the instrument useless. Bruce was ordered not to play it again under his father's roof.

In the middle of the night, however, Bruce would creep to the cupboard in his father's workshop and take out the clarinet. He would run his fingers along the dark mellow wood, depressing the silver metal keys and polishing them carefully one by one.

One evening, Bruce's father found him with the clarinet and snatched it from the boy, replacing it with his own unloaded rifle which he had secreted from the Army as a rather grizzly souvenir. Bert thrust it harshly into Bruce's hands.

'This is what boys of your age should be practising with, not a *clarinet!*' he spat out the word. 'What earthly use will that be when there's another war?' he snarled.

Like his mother, Bruce rarely argued about anything. He was terrified of his father's anger, but generally stifled his feelings in front of him, learning to cry silently, stifling his sobs of despair and punching his pillow furiously repeatedly in frustration. He longed to shout and kick at his father but mostly he remained silent and afraid. Moreover, he hated himself for his cowardice and occasionally found the courage to challenge Albert over issues, but in the end, he caved in under the verbal cruelty of his father.

Albert made the boy polish the rifle incessantly throughout that night, setting his alarm and checking him two hourly with military precision until Bruce could see the first rays of sun falling on the gun.

Bruce knew that his mother desperately missed her elder daughter Sadie, who had helped with everything in the house including bath times with Connie. His mother looked perpetually worn out as she sweated over the ancient boiling copper wash tub, (Albert refused to buy her a twin-tub washing machine, saying no one should trust these "new-fangled" ideas). The four children inevitably made copious amounts of washing, even though they wore their navy-blue school knickers and grey/white liberty bodices and vests all through the week. Bruce watched his mother poking the bubbling garments and sheets down into the water with wooden tongs, then lifting the heaving weight of dripping clothes, flopping them down by the mangle, and finally expertly flattening them through the wringer one by one for the cleansed uniforms' silent weekly torture. Bruce helped his mother as much as he could to compensate a little for the absence of Sadie, so often went to bed exhausted.

Bruce by now had been told Rosa was pregnant with baby number five, so that was even more reason to do what he could for her. He was dimly aware that she had lost two other babies. He loved his mother deeply. Sometimes, when the other children were in bed, he would clamber onto her knee, twelve years of age, and lean his head on her chest as she sang to him and stroked his hair as she had done when he was small. This was the sweetest time of the day for him. All was well with the world when he was curled up on his mother's lap.

Every night, Bruce covertly read old library books under the covers of his bed, using a tiny beam of torchlight. He loved it when the house was silent and everyone was asleep. He gave himself generously to Connie during the day, following Sadie's example by rarely becoming impatient with her demands, but night times, reading and writing under the covers in solitude and peace, were *his* times.

Bruce had found out that his mother was deeply wronged by his father, and Bruce had the evidence. This was the secret reason, in addition to the bullying, the rages and the confiscating of his clarinet, why Bruce loathed his father. One night, Bruce had realised to his horror and disgust exactly what kind of a man his father was. He had crept from his bed as he often did to check on his clarinet. He sat in the darkness fingering the silver keys silently and aching to hear the sombre, velvet sounds that it should have been making. Instead, he heard grunts and soft moans from the next room. This was the spare room that Great Aunt Edith always had when she came to stay. It was kept like a new pin and dusted daily in readiness for the occasional appearance of his somewhat formidable aunt. The room reminded Bruce of a shrine, with the patchwork counterpane that smelt of mothballs acting as a shroud. On the walls were framed Bible texts made from cross-stitch which were framed in dark wood: *"'I have searched you and known you,' says the Lord"*. Bruce didn't find that a very helpful text. He did *not* want God, or anyone else for that matter, knowing how dark and venomous his thoughts were towards his father, how he fantasised about his having a fatal accident of some kind, how he wished him dead.

As he polished his clarinet, Bruce listened carefully to the sounds coming from the room next door. Instinct told him that he should not be hearing all this — these were private sounds. He did not care for them at all. He pressed his ear to the wall and heard the rhythmic grunting grow louder, interjected by soft, female sounds. He crept to his bedroom door, wedged it open, tiptoed out and looked through the split in the door that led to Great Aunt Edith's room. There, he saw his father, nightshirt raised, the crack of his backside showing, counterpane dishevelled, thrusting down on his little sister Connie.

Connie was whimpering softly, moving her arms around slightly, her head on one side, her fair hair splayed over the pillow. Her face was screwed up with a look that told Bruce that she was enduring pain. His father eventually let out one last moan and flopped down onto Connie. She bore his whole weight without a murmur.

With a perfected sense of timing Connie at last said softly,

'Can I get up now, Daddy?'

'Yes, get up lass. And remember, *our* secret. You know how much your daddy loves you, don't you?'

He disentangled himself from her, wiping himself on a corner of the counterpane.

'You can get your barley sugar from the jar, but quietly, mind. You're a good girl. What are you? Daddy's *good* girl! Say it, Connie.'

'I'm Daddy's good girl.'

She tottered unevenly to the door. Bruce crept silently back to bed. He lay there aghast. Connie passed his door and peeped in, her fair hair tousled and her face flushed.

'Bruce. Brucey! You awake? Your torch is still on.'

'Connie! What are you doing up?'

'Nothing,' she said, wide-eyed, innocent. 'What do you think I'd be doing?'

'You tell me.'

'I needed a toilet.'

'You all right, Connie?'

'Yes.'

'You sure? You'd tell me if anything was wrong, wouldn't you, or if anyone was hurting you? You would, wouldn't you, Connie?

'Course I would.'

'Do you want to come in with me, Connie?'

'No thanks, Brucey.'

'Better get back to bed then.'

'Night Brucey.'

'Night Connie.'

Bruce lay staring up in the darkness. A huge pit of fear and pain had opened in his stomach. He felt sick. He knew without a shadow of a doubt that his father had no right to be doing what he *was* doing to his sister. It seemed to hurt her. Bruce understood next to nothing of the human sex act, even though he was twelve, but he had watched farmyard animals mating and something now resonated darkly inside him. His father's thrusting reminded him of them. It made him feel sick. Sweet, innocent, six-year-old Connie, smelling of mothballs, with her hair dishevelled and her nightdress damp, was learning fast to look her brother straight in the eye and lie for the sake of a stick of barley sugar.

Bruce suddenly heaved, reached swiftly for the ancient chamber pot under his bed, and was violently sick into it.

\*\*\*

Two months later, Sadie still had not returned despite days of police searches, door-to-door enquiries and frantic notices pinned on tree trunks along the pavements in every one of the surrounding roads. Rosa continued to grieve and weep for her eldest daughter, and only the baby visibly growing and moving inside her gave her a modicum of comfort. She was now well into her fifth month and dared to believe that she might go full term with this pregnancy.

'Sadie will be home for the baby,' she told herself. 'She was so excited about it when I confided in her.' She knew that if only Sadie would come home, she, Rosa, could cope with anything.

Another month passed. Albert regularly used little Connie mercilessly for his own gratification. James became more reclusive and increasingly withdrawn; Bruce mainly suffered in silence and sought solace in his writing and music.

Still Sadie did not come home.

Evening after evening during that unusually hot and dry summer the setting sun bathed the front door of the Connors' with rosy light. Anyone sauntering past for an evening stroll once the day had cooled might think there was nothing particularly extraordinary about the semi-detached house in South West London, but behind the closed doors Albert Connors continued the abuse of his family unchallenged with disastrous results for each member of his family.

# *Chapter 3*

Bruce left school at fifteen with the sorrowful burden of family abuse and tragedy weighing him down in a way that was reminiscent of Christian's great load in *A Pilgrim's Progress*. Soon after Sadie had left, he witnessed two traumatic and tragic deaths in his family and carried a sense of profound loss and guilt with him into adulthood. Some years after he left school, he finally unburdened himself to expert ears, but the legacy of his father's cruelty left him a scarred man.

A highly intelligent boy — top of the class in fact — he had been made to leave his academic studies by his father. His earnings were needed to supplement the family income. Being allowed to keep one quarter of his meagre pay for helping his father's growing business meant that Bruce could afford one clarinet lesson a week. Having a continuing passion for the instrument, combined with a natural aptitude for sight reading music, at the age of seventeen he was invited to take up a place in the prestigious county symphony orchestra as lead clarinettist.

Bruce had avoided being called up for national service by one year, for which he was heartily relieved. He knew that if someone stuck a bayonet or a rifle in his hand, he was very unlikely to find the courage to use it ever. Furthermore, he resonated with the Quakers' core belief in peace and pacifism rather than the taking up arms in a war; however, he knew now with certainty that he did not believe in God, especially after this invisible and altogether implausible 'being' had allowed such tragic events to unfold in his family in such a short space of time.

Bruce would have left home and fended for himself, but always the well-being of Connie was uppermost in his mind, so he endured his father for her sake. The saving grace in his life was the orchestra. He was never happier than when working to find the best sound that he possibly could from his clarinet, or tackling a tricky orchestral part, and he loved the collaborative atmosphere of the symphony players.

It was there that he met Clara.

Beautiful, striking Clara, playing her violin in the orchestra, made eyes at Bruce over her music stand from the very first rehearsal. She was the leader of the second violin section, and as such had a decent view of Bruce Connors, especially in the slow movement of the piece, when the conductor waved his arms much less vigorously. In truth, Bruce was a marked man. Clara had decided by the second rehearsal that he would be hers and she need look no further. After all, he had all the requirements: good-looking, with a strong square jaw, a head of thick brown hair, an engaging smile, playing the clarinet superbly, and above all, holding the promise of her longed-for escape route from home. For several months she had been determined to move out from her elderly parents' home and had promised herself to fall in love with the first eligible and handsome male who crossed her path.

Bruce Connors would do very nicely even though Clara knew she would have to wait a few years. Immediately attracted to his qualities of understated humour, together with a certain calm that she sensed in him, Clara found in addition that he was physically alluring. It certainly would not take much at all for her to fall in love with him, she decided.

Clara had taken home a variety of suitors, none of which was approved by her parents. Her mother had produced Clara when all hope of ever having a child seemed lost. She was the apple of her parents' eyes, the focus of their whole existence and spoilt beyond anything remotely reasonable. No one, of course, was good enough for their daughter. Clara thought, however, that in her parents' eyes, Bruce Connors might be different. She estimated that he would appear to them, to use their language, "a thoroughly upstanding and decent young man".

The difference between Clara's motivation and Bruce's was that for Clara, certainly at the beginning, it was a calculated decision to woo him, whereas for Bruce, it was a hopeless falling in love at first sight.

For the next few rehearsals Clara used every flirting technique she knew to secure Bruce's affection, although she did not have to work very hard. Bruce watched for the catlike green eyes that regularly flashed across at him, and then would immediately hide themselves behind the music stand. In shyness, and because of a complete lack of experience of the repertoire of tantalising female games, he always averted his eyes and with cheeks reddening and burning hot, would try to concentrate on the music.

'Bruce. Wrong notes *again!*' growled the conductor. 'What's wrong with you? Concentrate! There's a concert in two weeks, *if* you care to remember. This isn't like you. Buck up your ideas!'

After the rehearsal, Clara came up to him. 'Now, Brucey, wrong notes again!' she mimicked. 'You weren't concentrating, were you?' She smiled. 'Tut, tut, naughty boy!'

He found her teasing irresistible. A passion rose in him whenever he met her. He was both shocked and thrilled at the level of physical desire he had for her.

Clara was a proficient violin player and singer, but she was a naturally gifted dancer. Her elderly parents did not approve of what they called the "shameful flaunting" of her body but she had not been deterred. She left school at fourteen, worked in an office counting figures laboriously, and like Bruce with his clarinet, earned enough money to pay for dance lessons in the evenings. Clara felt alive in a way that thrilled her when she danced. The life within her changed and leapt as she was transformed from everyday office girl to graceful, beautiful woman — wrapping the space around her effortlessly.

She was indeed very beautiful. Her finely chiselled features were delicate and her flowing chestnut hair gleamed with spun gold lights in the shafts of sunshine that poured through the dusty rehearsal hall. She was a beauty and she knew it. She was proud of the way she had steadfastly pursued her dream and vain about her slender figure — the reward of years of eating *just* enough to keep her the right side of a disorder. Clara was the envy of many young women. They all kept a close eye on their men when she was around.

Bruce would plan opening sentences to ask her out, writing them down in a scrawling hand and rehearsing them. He would think about her day and night, and always — always — see the magnetic green eyes flashing an exciting invitation above her music stand, round the conductor, over to Bruce and straight into his heart.

He need not have rehearsed the opening sentence to her. After the concert, Clara, in a black dress that shimmered and clung, moved close to him. She softly poked her violin bow in his ribs. 'Don't you think it's about time you asked me out, Bruce? What's keeping you?'

That was it. Romance blossomed, although Clara's head was fully in control of the situation. She found Bruce shy but strong in the kind of way that made her feel safe. Bruce's first kiss with her sent everything in him whirling and dancing inside. He simply adored her and became her devoted slave.

At the age of eighteen, Bruce started an apprenticeship in London with a famous firm of violin makers and restorers. His employers sensed in him a passion for the medium of wood, and a musicality that gave him a sensitivity towards the stringed instruments he was learning to repair. One of few things that Bruce had to thank his father for was teaching him fine carpentry skills to an unusually high standard.

During the two-year period of Bruce's apprenticeship, his relationship with Clara blossomed and deepened. Clara began to develop a real love for Bruce, although it was always within her framework of self-absorption and putting her own needs and dreams before his.

At the age of twenty-one, Bruce asked Clara to marry him, and she readily agreed; after all, it was already a foregone conclusion in her game plan. She made it clear to Bruce before they married that children were not on her agenda, nor ever would be. Dancing was her life, and a baby would be more than an inconvenience; it would be a major disruption and a tragedy in her eyes, ruining her figure and her career.

Bruce wanted nothing in the world as much as to consummate his marriage and be able to express with his body his desire and adoration for Clara. For two years he had dreamt of being intimate with her and finally making her really his — of showing her his lifelong commitment.

Sadly, however, Bruce was a deeply damaged young man. His childhood years of lying in his bed in agony as he listened to his father's grunts in the next-door room as he abused his daughter, had taken their toll. Buried deep inside him there had grown an unacknowledged fear and loathing of the male sexual act. Although not conscious of it in any way, he found it repulsive and abusive.

Despite his complete passion, both emotional and physical, for Clara, he could not enter her beautiful body on their wedding night. There were tears and apologies, with bewilderment on both sides. With every subsequent attempt at love-making an insistent inner voice warned him that this was violation, that he must not abuse Clara, who, like his little sister, was so perfect and beautiful.

Night after night, Clara would fling herself to the edge of the bed as Bruce failed to consummate their marriage despite increasingly desperate attempts. She cried in frustration and humiliation as he wept bewildered and bitter tears. Bruce's father, in his greediness and brutishness, had wrecked his son's chances of happiness and left him a legacy of sexual failure.

When they returned from a brief honeymoon in the Cotswolds, their marriage unconsummated still, Bruce prayed that *this* time, in the security of their own home, he would be able to show Clara how much he loved her. Clara, for her part, set the scene in the bedroom with candles, soft lights and her most seductive nightwear. But her faith in her ability to allure him began to fade as each time the result was the same. Now when Bruce wanted most to spill his love into his wife, he heard the grunts of his father and saw the innocent eyes of his sister. Clara and he were both left unfulfilled and wretched, nursing their individual thoughts of failure.

Lovemaking in their own home proved as disappointing as in the five-star hotel four-poster bed of their honeymoon.

Thereafter, Bruce worked obsessively hard in a thousand different ways to compensate Clara for his inadequacies in the marital bed. He treated her as a precious china ornament, a toy doll, pandering to her every whim, running errands for her, buying expensive gifts and indulging her in every way possible. Clara became impossibly spoilt by Bruce, but the endorsement that she craved most of all had denied her. She became increasingly demanding and tetchy, treating him with distain, dismissive of his attempts to make her happy. She was bored and despairing and selfish and his impotence made her despise him.

In time, Clara realised it was no good waiting for Bruce to prove himself as a man. Certainly there would be no children. That was one relief. She made the decision to focus entirely on pursuing her own life as a dancer, merely treating Bruce as a comfortable companion and stooge. The subject of sex became taboo, with both nursing their individual wounds secretively and silently. They still slept in the same bed at night, but physical contact on Clara's part was minimal. Clara showed increasingly profound irritation at everything Bruce did and was. The more he tried to please her, the colder and more indifferent towards him she became.

Clara shared with her one close friend Jane the predicament of her marriage. She wept as she recounted her feelings of worthlessness.

'Not *your* worthlessness, Clara. It's *his*. Why don't you have one last try and if it doesn't work, leave him. You don't want to be stuck in a sexless marriage.'

'It's not as simple as that, Jane,' replied Clara. 'You see, I've learnt to love him. It's not just the sex. 'It's what it…' she struggled to find the right word. 'It's what it symbolizes. The togetherness. The union I suppose I mean.'

'Oh come on, Clara. You need a good going over. It's not so much a "union" or "togetherness". It's a basic drive. We're all animals at heart,' she laughed.

Clara shrugged. She knew what Jane meant, but for her it certainly was not the whole story.

She decided she would have one last attempt to woo her husband.

That night, she took out her ivory wedding gown from the wardrobe, ironed the voluminous skirt — that took her over an hour — and put the delicate silk dress on, tying a bright red sash around the waist. It still fitted perfectly. If anything, Clara had lost weight.

She waited in the bedroom to hear Bruce's key in the lock.

'Clara. Clara,' he called. 'Where are you?'

'Up here Brucey,' she called back.

She stood at the top of the stairs, a vision of white and red, hands on hip, chestnut hair flowing.

'Oh Clara. You look wonderful. Your wedding dress!' He ran up the stairs and took her in his arms.

'Brucey. Play for me,' she said, reaching for his clarinet and thrusting it into his hands. 'That gypsy tune, you know. The "Habanera" from "Carmen".'

'What, *now?*' he enquired.

'Now,' she commanded.

Bruce flung his bag on the top stair, took up his clarinet, led Clara into the bedroom like the Pied Piper and started to play, at first slowly and then increasing in speed. The warm tones filled the bedroom and Clara began to dance. She slowly untied the red sash from her dress and began to swing it around voluptuously, bullfighter-style. Not Carmen, but Clara, the femme fatale.

'Faster, faster; Clara commanded. Bruce ran his fingers expertly over the keys, playing the music, swinging the instrument in time to its rhythm, leaping and falling, dipping and rising, and watching her intently all the while. She danced on, gaining momentum as the music began to build to a climax. At its peak, Clara slid onto the bed and began to pull the dress off her shoulders and down, down.

Bruce placed the clarinet on the chair carefully and knelt beside the bed, as if worshipping the image in front of him. He wanted her so and was ready for her. He leapt up and held her tightly, entering her and making her gasp, but filling her with hope at his power and readiness. Then it happened. The old familiar feeling of despair and anguish ate into him as he felt himself collapse inside her. He moaned. Clara cried in frustration.

'Come on, Bruce, come *on*.' But his sister Connie's face filled his vision and he too cried out, 'No, *No*. Go *away*!'

'I'm so sorry, Clara,' he sobbed. 'I love you so, I do, I do. Please forgive me. I'm sorry, so sorry, so sorry.'

They lay holding each other for several minutes. Finally Clara turned away.

'Please get me a glass of wine, Bruce. The "Chardonnay".'

Bruce leapt up immediately to do her bidding, and so it continued, with Bruce forever compensating in a hundred different ways for his inadequacy.

***

At the very first audition attended, Clara was accepted into a London West End musical theatre company. She was exceptionally talented, but even so found herself in the chorus, dancing and singing. But it was an opening. Bruce became increasingly side-lined in her life, despite his undiminished love for her. Her growing coldness and indifference left him feeling guilty and alone.

# Chapter 4

The first encounter between Clara Connors and the new theatre chaplain Oliver Lockwood took place at the theatre during a meeting Oliver was holding for new cast members. Anyone scrutinizing their first encounter with each other would have noticed an unspoken synergy between them.

Oliver Lockwood had been a student of philosophy at Cambridge University but changed courses midstream to study theology. Oliver always said that he had been drawn into the Christian ministry whilst running as hard as he could from it in the opposite direction. As a teenager he had heard a sermon which turned the wartime slogan "Your Country Needs *you*" into "Your God Needs *you*".

Oliver did not return to that church for many weeks, unable to face the direct challenge that God seemed to be making to him. The words ran through his head more frequently and with greater urgency as time went on. "Your God needs *you*", "Your God needs *you*".

When Oliver was a young child, his mother and father had insisted that he went every Sunday, to Sunday school, even though they themselves were not churchgoers. The Sunday roast finally served, and the laborious process of washing up and cleaning the oven accomplished, his mother packed him off down the street towards the church, with threepence in his pocket for the collection. Afterwards, he would run home proudly clutching stickers given out by the teacher, a reward simply for attending. The stickers intrigued Oliver. They had an anaemic-looking bearded figure on them, clad in white: *"Jesus the Good Shepherd"*, *"I am the Light of the World"*, *"I am the Bread of Life"* and other unfathomable statements that God apparently was making to Oliver through these pastel rewards.

There was always chocolate cake at home on a Sunday. Oliver felt it compensated a little for the dreary hour he had to spend listening to Miss Poppy, who had whiskers on her chin and a mesmerising wobbly pimple on the end of her tongue, and who spoke in a droning voice about the love of God. God was rewarding Oliver's patient attendance with chocolate cake.

Yet, as Oliver later used to say with a smile in his testimony of faith, Miss Poppy had indeed sown her seeds of faith in his heart and he was unfailingly grateful to her.

At Cambridge University Oliver found God speaking to him once more. This time it was through the dynamism and fervent passion of a rotund and reputedly eccentric preacher at the high church in the town square, rather than Miss Poppy with the hairs and the pimple. *God works through the most unlikely vessels*, Oliver mused.

Oliver found the figure of Jesus presented to him by the rotund vicar compelling and nothing like the insipid Jesus figure on the stickers he had collected at Sunday School. This Jesus sounded as though he could set the world on fire through his messages. Oliver knew from the thumping in his heart and the heat that spread throughout his body on one occasion during a particularly passionate sermon, that he simply could not keep running away or turning his back on what was obviously a calling. He *must* respond.

The principal and his team at theological college were initially dubious about taking Oliver. He was regarded as rather a free spirit, with his overlong dark hair and his calf length flowing black coat making him look like a cross between a giant bat and an Oxford don. Furthermore this rather gaunt-looking character was into *Drama*. However, they had the insight to see that Oliver had a passion for theology and a genuine desire to serve God, and that he fervently believed that he had been set apart for this purpose. After much consultation, the selection board decided to take a risk and offer him a place.

Oliver took a vow of celibacy at his ordination, not because he was forced to, or because it was expected of him, but in his zeal he felt he wanted to offer *everything* up in the service of God, even his sexuality. The bishop had asked him during his preordination interview whether this desire for celibacy was a safety net in case 'Um, yes, well — are you — um, in case you turn out to be — er — "that" way inclined — batting for the other side as it were?' A pause, then he whispered, '—You know — "Queer – Gay"'

Oliver almost laughed out loud. Instead, he simply said respectfully, 'No it's not like that at all. It's something I think I should do for God.'

It had not been a difficult vow to keep. If ever Oliver was tempted by the call of the flesh, he would keep these thoughts at bay by having an ice-cold bath every morning to admonish the flesh. However, the fact of the matter was that Oliver had never fallen in love.

His first curacy was in a small market town, in the parish church of St. Bede, where he learned of the prejudices of folk, and of the open door of hospitality, and how curates were required to eat lots of rich tea biscuits washed down by numerous cups of weak tea. Once, visiting an elderly lady of the parish, he noticed that the tea he was handed had a thick layer of dust floating on the top. Seizing the opportunity while his hostess was topping up the teapot with boiling water from the hob, Oliver quickly christened a large plant of indeterminate variety with the offending tea.

'More tea, Vicar?' the old lady asked as she hobbled in, teapot lid rattling precariously on top of an old blue and white striped china teapot.

'I'm all right, thank you Mrs Lamdin.'

'Oh, come now, Vicar, one cup of tea won't sustain you through an afternoon of visiting,' she said, the teapot wobbling dangerously as the tea finally found its destination, half in Oliver's cup, most of the other half in his saucer and a few drops on his cassock.

On another visit, Oliver asked to be shown to the lavatory of the parishioner he was visiting. The visit had been long and tedious, and Oliver's bladder was overly full from a third statutory cup of tea.

'Can I just use your convenience, please, Miss Bird?' he asked.

'It's outside, Reverend. Mind the step.'

Oliver picked his way to the end of the garden, where he found the lavatory inside what amounted to be a broken-down shed. Desperate by now, he hastily locked the door inside, lifted his cassock and began to undo the buttons of his flies beneath. He looked up. There in front of him was a large picture of biblical words made from cross-stitch which seemed to leap out of the frame with a warning: "'I will go before you,' says the Lord".

*Oh no you won't!* thought Oliver. *Not on this occasion.*

Oliver disliked parochial church council meetings — "P.C.C.s". He would pray before every fortnightly meeting, 'Lord, quieten my heart and help me serve my flock.' St. Bedes, Oliver decided, warranted a shake-up. It needed to move into the twentieth century. The weekly litany and communion services were strictly 1662 *Book of Common Prayer*, and woe betide anyone who deviated from it.

Enough was enough. Time to coax everyone into the twentieth century. His patience was wearing thin.

The PCC meeting opened in prayer — the usual one, praying that everyone would be open to the will of God and the moving of the Holy Spirit. *Hmm. Some seem more open than others*, Oliver mused.

He had been preparing his speech. He stood up, cleared his throat, looked around at the sea of faces, some expectant, others resistant. It took all his courage to stay on course and put his proposal to what now suddenly seemed a threatening mob.

'Thank you everyone for coming. I won't beat about the bush. Christmas is coming and instead of the usual nativity play I am proposing that we take on something just a little bit different — a bit of a challenge you could say.'

He could feel his audience freeze.

'I have found an excellent play called *"This Jesus"*. It's very inspiring and has scope for plenty of players, including one special part for someone who feels they could take on the role of Jesus. It tracks the main points in His ministry.'

That was it. Looking back, Oliver realised that it was as if several wild cats had been let out of a bag in one go.

'A *person* playing our Lord?'

'That's blasphemy.'

'Vicar, I'm amazed. You a man of the cloth as well!'

'We can't have that.'

And so it went on.

Oliver calmly commented that they had used Sonia Taylor's three-week-old baby as the baby Jesus in last year's nativity play. What was the difference? It was still representing Christ in human form.

'We cannot have a grown man playing Jesus. It will offend the weaker brethren,' said the church warden piously. 'Jesus would be offended.'

Oliver, normally a mild man, felt an anger rise inside him.

'So you know the feelings of our good Lord, do you, Ken? Most of us must be content, after much prayer and fasting, to see through a glass darkly when it comes to seeking out the will of God.'

There was silence.

Old Mrs Tenby slowly put up her hand.

'Father, perhaps we could represent the figure of Jesus with a light rather than a real person?'

'Yes, a candle moving instead of him speaking.'

'Or a bicycle lamp under a cloth, then there'd be no fire risk. I'd be prepared to lend mine.'

Oliver began to speak.

'So you think a bicycle lamp representing Jesus is less blasphemous than a human being, do you Frank?'

'Well yes, in a manner of speaking. I do. He was the Light of the World, after all.'

The meeting eventually closed with the PCC unanimously voting that a bicycle lamp, wrapped in a cloth, should represent the Light of the World and all spoken words of Jesus would be cut.

The following morning, Father Oliver wrote his letter of resignation to the Bishop, saying he really felt there was no longer a place for him in the parish of St. Bede. He had tried long and hard, backed by prayer and fasting, to soften the hearts of the congregation and to point out that there were sometimes other ways of doing things than their own, and a fresh vision would be exciting. But had failed miserably.

He began to scour the advertisements in *The Church of England Newspaper* for vacant posts, preferably other than in a parish. He always turned to the back page first.

The non-parish jobs requiring an ordained person were usually found there.

*"Theatre Chaplaincy Vacancy".*

*"A theatre chaplain is required to undertake the cure of souls and the pastoral care of all actors, actresses, onstage, offstage, backstage and front of house. The suitable candidate will have a breadth of vision, a friendly personality and demonstrate an ease with people of all faiths and none. He will welcome and embrace different expressions of faith and serve as a wise listening ear to all those burdened by their concerns".* Location: Richmond upon Thames.

Oliver dropped the paper into his lap and stared unseeingly into the room. After a few seconds, he picked it up again and read the advertisement slowly aloud to himself. His whole body became adrenaline-filled and electric with excitement. Did ecclesiastical posts such as this *really* exist: "Breadth of vision" — "Embrace different expressions of faith" — "All faiths and none".

Picking up the phone, he telephoned the number on the advertisement.

Engaged.

Oliver banged the receiver down. He made himself a cup of coffee, read the advertisement several times once more, and redialled.

Engaged still.

Oliver hung on — and on. Transferring the receiver into his left hand, he grabbed a notepad and began writing a list of why he thought he might be a suitable candidate for the job:

"Frustrated by the confines of the parish, no longer able to cope with narrow attitudes to worship and faith which give rise to feelings of worthlessness and inadequacy".

No.

He scribbled thick lines through his notes. That certainly wouldn't do. There had been much kindness shown to him in the parish and there were some wonderful people within it. Think positively. He scribbled again:

"I am ready for a new exciting challenge. I believe all people to be welcomed within the embrace of the open arms of a generous God. I will find different ways of supporting people of all faiths and none. I am excited by the prospect of being able to exercise a sensitive approach within a theatrical setting while preaching the gospel"

Better.

'Hello. Ecclesiastes House. How may I help you?'

'I would like to know more about the post you are advertising in *The Church of England Newspaper* for a theatre Chaplin, please, at Richmond — upon — Thames'.

'Yes, well, I must tell you firstly that we have had a flood of applicants. You are the seventeenth applicant so far and the advert has only been out since last Friday.'

It seemed Oliver was not alone in wanting a change from parish life.

***

Oliver was shortlisted for the post. He was one of six. As the interview day approached, he decided to confide in his bishop, the Right Reverend Timothy Hermes, who was new to the diocese. This bishop was an artistic and sensitive man whose passionate hobby was watercolour paintings. He fitted neither the common stereotype of a bishop drawn up by folk who had little contact with the real church, nor of Anthony Trollope's "Barchester Towers" ilk.

'Come in, Oliver. Nice to see you.'

'Thank you for seeing me, your Grace.'

'Not at all. It's a pleasure, Oliver. And please drop the "My Grace" bit. Go ahead and talk to *me,* rather than the role,' he smiled.

The bishop took in the half-smiling figure moving towards the chair: not handsome, but with an appeal of sorts; tall, but not overbearing, hair dark, skin tanned. His appointment at St. Bedes had been a risk, but he had followers, and they weren't all the young and pretty spinsters of the parish.

'He'll appeal to my wife,' the bishop surmised. Her type.

He rang a bell. A warm, smiling woman appeared in a few seconds.

'Could you manage tea, darling? Oliver, it is tea, is it, or would you prefer coffee?'

'Tea would be great. Thank you.'

'Margaret, this is Oliver. Oliver, Margaret. I'm not sure you've met before. You were in hospital when Oliver was ordained.'

'I hope you're fully fit, Mrs Hermes?'

'Quite fit now, thank you, Oliver. Just a minor op.'

As she left the room, Margaret gave an almost imperceptible nod of approval to her husband.

Her husband smiled. 'Just as I thought,' he said to himself.

Over a decently brewed cup of tea, not too milky, and a slice of homemade Victoria sponge cake, Oliver filled the bishop in about his desire to leave the parish, showing him the advertisement.

The bishop was thoughtful. After a minute, he looked Oliver firmly in the eyes.

'Oliver, I know everyone will be desperately sad to see you go. I have had wonderful reports of the work you have done at St. Bede's, but I sense it has been an uphill struggle for you. But never doubt that you have changed lives there.'

'I do doubt it, bishop. I think that for every one person who has listened to me there may be another half a dozen I may have driven away.'

'Driven away?'

'In a way, bishop, yes.' Oliver thought about the Christmas play in particular.

'Well, I can't accept that Jesus wants us to be bound up in old traditions to the exclusion of accepting possibilities for change. Jesus was about breaking with accepted traditions, wasn't he? The creative spirit surely is expansive, exciting, daring... wanting us to take risks and...'

Oliver stopped suddenly. He was becoming too fired up about things. But the bishop broke into a smile.

'Oliver, I think you should apply for this post. Don't lose the fire in your belly. Stay exciting and excited. You could just be their man.'

They both sat quietly for a few moments. The new bishop read the notes that had been handed on to him about Oliver from the previous bishop. Finally he looked up. He clasped his hands together, cleared his throat, and for a moment averted his eyes from Oliver.

'There is one other matter I'd like to talk with you about and for you to consider. It's — er — rather personal, but I feel compelled to speak about it.'

'Yes. Your Grace — bishop?

'Oliver, I read that you made a vow of celibacy when you became ordained.' The bishop looked down, cleared his throat once more and stirred his tea again.

'I wonder if that vow has been tested in your parish very much? I believe your congregation is mainly on the elderly side.'

Oliver stared at the bishop. He could think of one or two occasions when he had asked God to help him honour his vow in the face of temptation — for a start the nubile seventeen-year-old girl with the too-tight tee-shirt which distinctly showed her nipples. She had offered to run a youth club and seemed to need to talk her ideas through with Oliver more times than was good for his soul.

'If you are offered the theatre chaplaincy, I wonder if you have thought about this aspect of your ministry?'

'Could you enlarge on that, bishop?'

'The theatre is full of expressive artists who often have youth on their side and enjoy and embrace freedom in all its forms. If I understand the theatre correctly it is about exploring and breaking boundaries. Look at Shakespeare. Romeo and Juliet were hardly conventional young lovers, were they?'

Oliver realised what the bishop was getting at.

'Oliver, your vow of celibacy was self-inflicted — I'm sorry, I should say "self-imposed". It can always be rescinded you know.'

'I don't envisage a need for that, bishop. I'm absolutely committed to the celibate life. I made a vow to God eight years ago and I will not break it. Ever. I believe it to be something I feel God requires of me as an individual. I can't explain it more than that.'

"Ever" is a long time, Oliver. What would happen if you found yourself rather alone — lonely — going through a valley of depression, for example? Bunyon describes it as "The Slough of Despond". It happens. There is nothing like a true soulmate at those times, you know, and a good marriage can glorify God.'

'I don't doubt it,' replied Oliver.

'Or you fall in love, Oliver?'

'I won't let that happen.'

There was silence. Oliver had much to learn. Eventually the bishop broke the silence.

'I hope you know I'll always be here for you. I think a lot of you, Oliver. You're an honourable young man.'

'Thank you, bishop. That is very good of you — very kind. He glanced at his watch. 'I must go now if you will excuse me. I must take the "Pleasant Sunday Afternoon" meeting at church.'

'Ah, the challenge of the PSAs! Yes of course you must go and take up your cross, Oliver,' he said, laughing. 'But just think about what I have said and don't ever be too proud to ask for help should the need arise. Life has a way of surprising us. And you know, whatever your convictions about not falling in love, the heart can be slow to learn.'

'Sorry?'

'The heart is slow to learn.'

Not quite understanding, Oliver got up to go. 'And please thank Mrs — um — your wife — for the tea and cake. Very nice. Much appreciated.'

'Not so fast, not so fast, Oliver.' The bishop gently put a restraining hand on his shoulder. 'A quick prayer.'

Oliver bowed his head, ashamed of what he had overlooked.

*'Father protect and bless your servant, Oliver. Give him wisdom and keep him on the path of righteousness, and lead him not into temptation, but deliver him from evil — and that goes for both of us, Lord. Amen.'*

'Amen.'

'Amen.'

Oliver left not quite knowing whether he was mildly affronted at the bishop's intrusion into his private life, or grateful that such a man had cared about him and had been brave enough to speak out. One thing was certain, Oliver was going to like the new bishop.

# Chapter 5

After several rigorous interviews, Oliver was offered the post of theatre Chaplain. He accepted it with great pleasure.

Six weeks later, he arrived at the theatre, was led by a diminutive caretaker down a labyrinth of passages and through several scruffy rooms backstage to reach, finally, what was going to become his study.

The walls of the room were painted dark green onto which were pinned at random angles pictures and photographs of past performances. Across one of the corners was an old three-seater brown leather settee, beautifully comfortable, Oliver discovered, although cracking with age. There was a battered-looking desk with a modern bright red swivel chair across one corner and an ancient kettle on a cabinet across the other, together with a couple of stained mugs on a tray. Oliver opened the cupboard underneath to find a flood of small individual plastic milks tumbling out onto the floor.

*At least there are no pale green cups and saucers,* thought Oliver, patiently picking up the milk. He had detested the sets of regulation green crockery that had adorned the parish kitchen at St. Bede's. At one PCC, Oliver had suggested that they might invest in some colourful mugs, but the idea had gone down very badly.

Extravagant and unnecessary. *Just like Mary Magdalene's precious ointment,* Oliver had mused. *Extravagant and unnecessary in most people's eyes.*

Oliver picked up a note that had been deliberately wedged under the blotter on his desk. Opening it, he saw that the writing was flamboyant and sprawling,

"Be very happy, Rev. We're not a bad bunch here and we're looking forward to meeting you. Nick. Resident Director".

*Nice,* thought Oliver. *Very nice.*

That afternoon he designed a large notice to put in the actors' coffee lounge.

*"I'd love to meet you all. Please come and introduce yourselves tomorrow afternoon at five p.m. before your warm-up for the evening rehearsal. Coffee, tea and chocolate digestives provided. Warm wishes, Oliver Lockwood (Chaplain)".*

*A bit informal? Not informal enough? Should he say wine instead of tea and coffee? "Warm wishes" — or "God bless you"? No. Not "God bless you",* Oliver decided. He hoped and trusted from the bottom of his heart that God would bless them, but it might sound a bit "churchy" at this stage.

Oliver bought the provisions and laid out the stained and motley selection of mugs that were in the coffee room cupboard. He filled the urn with water, put the chairs in a circle and waited. Five came and went. Five-thirty, likewise. Just as he was about to abandon the whole idea, he heard a group of people laughing and chatting as they ambled down the corridor.

Oliver estimated that about a dozen people wandered into the coffee room together, most — women and men — in black rehearsal leotards, trousers and tops.

'Hi Rev, sorry we're late. Had an emergency rehearsal. Understudy in tonight.'

'More are coming,' said one.

'Only for the biscuits!' said another.

'We're all nosey about you, Rev. Last Chaplain left under a cloud. All very hush-hush.'

'Oliver, isn't it?'

Another group came in and soon Oliver was filling more coffee mugs with boiling water from the temperamental urn.

*A nice atmosphere already*, thought Oliver. *What a friendly bunch.*

He thought of the parish, thanked God quickly for it, and thanked Him again for giving him a fresh chance to spread the gospel a fresh way.

'What are your plans, Rev?'

'Where were you before?

'Are you married? Have you a partner?'

'Have you much theatre experience?'

Oliver answered their questions clearly.

'What about the God thing, Rev? Are you going to try to convert us?' said one student, slightly curling his lips.

'I'll leave that to God,' Oliver smiled. 'Meanwhile, I'll just be here to support when needed. My door will always be open. Anyway, I have a lot to learn from *you,*' he said. 'Anyone started this term, like me?'

A few hands went up.

'Well, good luck to you and be happy,' said Oliver.

Folk began to drift away. Oliver's eye was caught by a rather interesting and beautiful young woman who was sitting in the corner.

'Hi. Are you OK?'

The head turned slowly, the long chestnut hair moved, and a pair of green, catlike eyes looked up.

'Yes, yes, thank you. Quite OK. It's just a bit of a shock to the system — so many confident people,' she said. 'I thought I was confident but this lot seem really, *really* sure of themselves.

'I doubt they are,' said Oliver. 'We're all fragile underneath, aren't we? I know I am. Scratch us and we bleed — particularly in a new environment.'

'I suppose so,' she said, getting up.

'Well the door is always open, should you want to talk. May I ask your name?'

'Clara,' she replied, 'Clara Connors' and with a ripple of hair she was gone.

# *Chapter 6*

Clara returned to Bruce each night. She became thrilled by the work in the theatre. The constant rehearsing suited her, and the preperformance adrenaline rush never failed to set her alight so that she could give of her dynamic best when the curtain went up. She had little joy in going home. especially as bedtime was never anything more than a peck on the cheek, a companionable curling up and a sleepy 'Goodnight.' Bruce now seemed to avoid anything intimate. *Fear of failure, I suppose,* thought Clara, but she never made any advances herself. She was slowly but surely drawing apart from Bruce.

Bruce, for his part, knew he might be in danger of losing his beautiful wife to her new life. He was pretty sure that she would never be unfaithful, but all the while he could not satisfy her physically, he knew there was a deep hunger in her that remained unfulfilled.

Bruce felt that same hunger. He had never been able to consummate the marriage. Nearly, sometimes, but never fully. He cursed his father repeatedly. As an impressionable pubescent boy, he had watched his father, a bulldog of a man, thick set and full of muscle, covertly eyeing his sister Sadie's friends when she occasionally dared to bring them home. He had seen the way his father would brush up against their skirts. He saw his hands being over-familiar with them and he had known the abuse that was taking place with his beautiful little sister. When his older sister Sadie sat reading, Albert would move up behind her and put a hand down the front of her blouse saying he had "a perfect right" to see how his "little chick" was developing. Bruce saw how his sister stiffened in loathing but said nothing.

Bruce was appalled by his mother's reaction, or rather, non-reaction. She seemed strangely blind to what went on. Occasionally, when Sadie protested, she would meekly say, 'Leave the child alone, Daddy.'

And "Daddy" would reply, 'Mind your own business, Rosa. I have a perfect right. She's my daughter.' Whether his mother turned a blind eye for the sake of peace or was afraid of her husband's bullying and violence Bruce was not sure, but Rosa continued to act as though she had not seen, did not know what was going on under her own roof. Bruce was scandalised but had no idea how to deal with it.

He was a mild boy in temperament, a kind and sensitive boy who looked for the good in everyone. He was generally patient, but he had what he knew was a fatal flaw in his psyche which he managed mostly to keep under lock and key. He had his father's vivid temper which could flare up within seconds of provocation.

One night, after he had lain next door listening to his father's grunts and Connie's submissive sounds, he waited until she had returned to her bed and was asleep. On such nights as these, his mother would take herself off to the couch downstairs. Bruce could never make out whether in fact she knew what went on, or whether it had become part of the marriage ritual to sleep apart every so often.

Bruce summoned all his courage and entered his father's bedroom. His father lay in bed with a satiated half-smile on his face. *I'll wipe that off,* he thought to himself. *How dare he look so pleased with himself.*

He crept up to the bed and before his father had a chance to react, Bruce started pummelling him with all his might. With each blow he yelled at his father:

'How — dare — you — wrong — my — sister! You — disgusting — old — man.'

With each punch, Bruce hit harder and harder, and at that moment would have gone on until — well — he dared not think about the consequences but breaking free his strong father rose and took the boy by the scruff of his neck and hurled him against the wall. Bruce was up. He grabbed the empty chamber pot from under the bed and swung it violently at his father. It caught him on his mouth and immediately blood spurted out. Bruce cowered in the corner, his anger spent and shock waves flooding over him.

'Mother, Rosa, come here! Quickly!'

Rosa came rushing to the bedroom door. 'Daddy, whatever's happened?' She looked at Bruce, who had his head in his hands.

'It's all right, Rosa. The boy has had one of his fits — over nothing. It's just his filthy temper. No provocation.' The blood poured out copiously.

'Get to bed, Bruce,' shouted his mother. 'How dare you hit your father?' She went to the bed and held her husband, then pulled a pillowcase off the pillow and began to stem the bleeding.'

'It wasn't about nothing, Mum. *Open your eyes*!' he shouted.

Bert, bloodied and bleeding, staggered to his feet and cuffed the boy hard around the face and ears.

Bruce's nose started bleeding and he rushed out of the room.

Later, Rosa found him in his bedroom.

'Do you want to know what happened, Mum?'

'You lost your temper, son.'

'Yes, but do you know why I lost my temper?'

'You mustn't speak ill of your father, Bruce. I know he's not perfect, but…'

'Not *perfect*?' Bruce shouted. 'He touched up Sadie and now Connie, Mum. What are you going to do about it?'

Bruce looked at his mother. She had tears in her eyes and was shaking her head.

'Get to bed, Bruce. There are things you don't understand. Your father had a terrible childhood and a very bad war.'

'What's that got to do with everything he does now, Mum?'

'I can't go into it. I'm tired. Now stop all this talk. Goodnight Brucey. Try not to get blood on the sheets.'

From that day on, Bruce realised it was no use saying anything. Bewildered, he went out of the room, but his little sister Connie was waiting for him. She said nothing but put her arms around him.

'Have a lick of this, Brucey,' she said, thrusting the barley sugar towards him. 'It's nice. Daddy always gives me one after…'

'After what, Connie? Say it!'

'After Daddy's been.' She struggled to find words. 'After he's stopped.' She looked up at Bruce with her wide, innocent eyes.

'But he's always nice afterwards.'

Bruce stroked her head. Somehow he managed to hold back his tears for his damaged sister.

'Go to bed now, Connie.' Bruce followed her in, tucked her up and kissed her goodnight.

'Goodnight, sleep tight—'

'And mind the bugs don't bite,' added Connie.

Bruce, aching in body and soul, curled up, foetal-shaped in his bed and wept himself to sleep.

\*\*\*

Bruce lay remembering these bitter episodes as he waited for Clara, who was late home. The show had gone badly and unexpectedly wrong in one scene. Nick, the Director, normally known for his unruffled manner in a crisis, was angry. She related this to Bruce when she arrived home.

'Right. Act One, Scene Five. Disaster. Rubbish. What happened?'

Various members of the cast started to give explanations.

'That's enough!' he shouted. 'Get in position to run the scene again.'

Cast members moved desultorily into their starting points for Act One, Scene Five.

'And Clara. Don't think I didn't notice. What *were* you doing during the last verse of the song? What happened?'

'Nick, I'm sorry. My shoe…'

'That's no excuse. Now let's have it perfect, or we stay here all night. From the top of Scene Five. Action.'

The emergency rehearsal went on for over three hours.

Clara had emerged from the theatre tired and humiliated. She thought Nick had reckoned her work, but it did not seem so tonight. She had missed the last bus, so hailed a taxi. The driver insisted on taking her on his "short cut", which was nothing of the kind. She finally arrived home ready to tumble into bed. No shower, no teeth, just bed. Bruce was already there, his head propped up on the pillow. She sank down beside him.

'Clara, where've you been? It's twenty-five past one'.

'Emergency rehearsal,' said Clara. 'Don't go on.'

Suddenly, all the anxiety, all the worry, all the guilt Bruce felt over Clara erupted.

'Go on? I'd like to know what you've *really* been up to. Who is it? Nick?'

'Bruce!' said Clara. 'Don't be so utterly ridiculous!'

'Ridiculous! *Me* — ridiculous?'

'Yes, you're crazy making innuendos like that.'

'Making innuendoes like that?'

Clara sat up.

'Don't keep repeating my words,' she said, exasperated. 'Leave me alone, Bruce. I'm tired'

'Tired from what, exactly?'

'Shut up, Bruce.'

'I won't shut up. Be careful, or I'll give you what for,' he replied.

Clara's patience snapped.

'You'll give me "What for?",' she taunted. 'Chance would be a fine thing. I'd like to see you! You haven't given me "what for" since the day we married. You're not a real man Bruce,' she shouted. 'You just can't manage it, can you?'

Clara had lit the blue touch paper. Bruce ripped off his pyjama bottoms, pulled her legs down the bed, bumping her head fiercely off the pillow, and began to straddle her.

'No Bruce, no,' Clara screamed. 'Leave me alone. How dare you! *Leave me alone*!'

But Bruce, as if possessed, continued pressing into her. He was roused and he was violent.

Clara knew how to get the better of him. Breathily, she snarled,

'This is rape, Bruce. I tell you; this is rape. You're no better than your father.'

Bruce. who was a few seconds away from what he had longed to achieve and never could, withdrew rapidly from her. He stumbled to the door, slammed it hard as he left, and just as he had done as a child, curled up foetal-shaped and sobbed into his pillow.

Clara lay staring up at the darkness. She was incandescent with internal rage. She was incredulous at

Bruce's behaviour, but most of all she was drowning in guilt and remorse. Yes, she had moved away from him.

In the morning, Bruce, going downstairs to let Midas out, found that Clara had gone, even though it was an hour earlier than she needed to leave for rehearsals.

Bruce made himself a cup of tea and sat brooding.

'Where do we go from here?' he asked himself. After a few minutes of staring into space as he sipped his tea, he said out loud,

'I need help.'

Midas barked at the door.

'Come on then, Midas.' Midas, gold fur rippling, eyes shining rushed in, smothering Bruce with kisses.

'Where would I be without you, boy?' he said. 'We'll go for a walk as soon as I'm dressed.'

Midas pulled at Bruce's pyjama bottoms with soft golden retriever teeth.

'Hey, Midas, don't do that! These are new.'

Looking down at the trousers, already recently torn, Bruce thought about how he had ripped them off furiously last night, pulling his wife down angrily and punishing her physically. He felt sick.

Ashamed, he went into his study and took a copy *Yellow Pages* from the bookshelf. He searched under "C".

*"Counsellors and Psychotherapists"*

He ran his thumb down the list

*"Dr. Sonia Hamilton. Experienced counsellor and psychotherapist. Specialist in emotional, sexual and behavioural difficulties.'*

'I'll ring her as soon as I get back,' he promised himself, even though the thought filled him with dread.

'Come on, Midas, just a quick one this morning.'

Midas, bounding with happy energy, pulled on his harness.

'Steady Midas. You're growing out of this one, boy,' said Bruce. 'Soon time for a black one instead of this puppy red.' He remembered how he and Clara had scanned the harnesses in the pet shop, thrilled with their bundle of pale gold and decided that a red one was best for a puppy.

'Next time, we'll be choosing a pram, please God,' murmured Bruce.

Clara had looked up at him with a mixture of despair and distain.

'Hmm. Well something's got to happen before then, Bruce.'

Bruce had turned away with the familiar pit of despair in his stomach.

'It will, Clara. It will. I promise,' he had said.

That was two years ago and there had been what seemed like a thousand failures since then.

Midas smiled up happily at his master, eyes shining, tail wagging. It was impossible to stay in quite such a pit of despair with such a joyful dog gazing up at him.

*Thank God for dogs,* thought Bruce, *No reproaches, no moods, just unconditional love.* He bent down and patted Midas vigorously on the back as they raced along.

## Chapter 7

Oliver Lockwood found himself a flat near the theatre. The rent was prohibitive and took three quarters of his monthly salary. After all, this was Richmond upon Thames. Oliver enjoyed the fact that its ceiling was beamed and an interesting shape, even though it had a tiny sitting room, a small bedroom and a diminutive kitchen. He scoured the charity shops and found Indian woven drapes, one or two Moroccan pots, an old, squishy brown velvet three-seater sofa which was going for a song, and a few colourful cushions which vaguely coordinated with the drapes. He certainly had his mother's artistic eye for making marginally promising items look something special. He had a childhood memory of watching his mother try pictures in various positions on the wall, while his father patiently followed her with hammer and nails until she finally was happy that she had found exactly the right position for it. On more than one occasion his father had painted over a room not twice, but three times before his mother was satisfied that she had the "right colour" on the walls.

When Oliver had finally satisfied the Cat Rescue Centre that he would neither neglect nor abuse a cat, he paid a few pounds to buy himself a six-month-old tabby cat from the centre. The cat was called simply that: "Cat".

Cat slept on his bed, walked over the kitchen surfaces, hated the cat flap, stole food if it was left around, meowed incessantly and generally made his presence felt. Oliver loved him.

One Saturday, Oliver realised that Cat was in fact a "she" despite the information he was given from the rescue centre. One particularly cold morning, she was missing. Oliver eventually found her, after much calling and searching, hidden in the compost heap at the bottom of the tiny yard. She was not alone. Six tiny kittens were latched onto Cat's milk supply. Cat herself was purring loudly.

'Oh I'm so sorry, Cat,' he said. 'Out on the coldest night so far! Aren't you a clever girl?' He gently lifted Cat and her kittens into a box and brought them into the comparative warmth of the flat.

When he went to work at the theatre the next day, he put up a notice:

*"Due to unforeseen circumstances I am now the owner of six kittens. If you would like to put your name down for one, please see me. Come and choose your kitten. Oliver".*

Oliver began preparing for the Sunday service in the small theatre chapel. He had renamed the chapel "The Multi-faith Centre". Despite this inclusive gesture and rewriting services to pay respect to other faith beliefs, very few students ever came. Perhaps eight or nine on a good day.

*Am I watering down my faith too much or am I paying respect to all those who find God in another way?* thought Oliver. It was the endless question he asked himself. The parishioners of his last parish had seen everything in black and white terms. Was he turning faith into wishy-washy grey? Heaven forbid!

Oliver also held group discussions on a Friday lunchtime which he named "Agnostics Anonymous". These were better attended than the services, and Oliver wrestled with the many of the difficult questions that the students threw at him. *Why was it so much easier to argue on the side of there being no God,* he always asked himself. The problem of suffering was the stumbling block. No doubt about it. Always was, always will be. Most of the objections from the students to faith were always on the same theme: "Why does God allow suffering"? How many books had Oliver read on the subject? How many times had he prayed with people who were recently bereaved? And yet there were never any satisfactory answers, were there?

The most helpful thing that Oliver could do was to quote lines from a hymn:

*And when human hearts are breaking under sorrow's iron rod,*

*Then they find that self-same aching deep within the heart of God...*

He felt he could leave it at that. It didn't explain things, but it kept a loving God firmly in the centre of things, and Oliver knew he had seen lives transformed by faith in Christ.

\*\*\*

Clara saw Oliver's notice about the kittens on the board. It was the excuse she had been waiting for: to see Oliver on a one-to-one basis. She knew she needed forgiveness for her attitude towards Bruce. She had a kind of faith, although she fitted more into the Agnostics Anonymous Group than the Sunday morning worship. She told herself she was not a bad person; just nursing a grievance about her marriage.

She knocked on Oliver's theatre study door and waited. Soon, the door opened wide.

'Hello Clara,' said Oliver. 'Nice to see you. Come in.'

Clara sat down and averted her eyes.

'Coffee?'

'No thanks.'

'Tea then?'

'I won't, thanks.'

'Did you want to talk?' said Oliver gently.

Clara tossed her hair back.

'I've come about the kittens.'

'Oh yes,' said Oliver, not quite understanding his feeling of disappointment.

'Can I just say that I've watched you dancing and I really think you should apply for a lead in the next show, Clara. You're made for *West Side Story,* you know. There's so much dance in it. The *America* scene for a start. You'd make a wonderful Anita.'

'I'll think about it,' said Clara, knowing that to be cast in a role was beyond a dream, having only been in the company a few months.

'But let me tell you about the kittens. There are three tabbies, two black and white and one ginger. Not sure what sex they are. I got my own cat hopelessly wrong,' he laughed.

Whether it was the warmth of Oliver's study combined with the comfort of the old leather sofa, or whether it was Oliver's utterly open and generous manner that gave Clara courage was something she pondered on afterwards.

'And — there are other things,' she said.

'Happy to see if I can help. I can certainly listen. Are you up for that?'

'That depends on how broad-minded you are, Rev.'

'I'll cope,' he smiled back.

Oliver looked at Clara. There she was, lithe, catlike, with striking chestnut hair the colour of shining autumn conkers which she tossed back impatiently, and with *the* most compelling eyes, but the eyes were full of something other than their usual vitality today.

Clara had not planned to tell Oliver anything about her marriage. She had come about a kitten hadn't she?

'Everything is completely confidential of course,' said Oliver.

'Yes, yes, I'd assumed that,' replied Clara.

Silence. Then suddenly Clara began to sob.

'I'm so sorry. I've never done this before. I'll go. How embarrassing for you.'

She rushed to the door.

Oliver stopped her. He put his arm across the door and gently steered her back onto the sofa and sat next to her.

'Clara, trust me,' he said. 'I'm here to help.'

Clara had begun by wanting a priest — Oliver — to take her through a prayer for forgiveness, but somehow it was difficult to begin.

'I have a good husband. He's kind, he's gentle, he is a *good* man. I've been horrid to him. Very mean, cruel, actually. I can't cope any longer with my feelings.'

'Were you provoked?' said Oliver quietly.

And so began the great unburdening. Clara spoke in whispers, wiping her tears every so often. Oliver resisted the urge to take her hand as he normally would have done. Clara spoke of Bruce's impotence, of her sadness and impatience, of his father's secret life with Connie, Bruce's sister, and finally of how, two nights ago, she had called his father a paedophile. When she reflected on this later, she was incredulous that she had told Oliver so much.

Oliver was silent. The gas fired occasionally spluttered and popped. Clara continued to wipe away tears.

'Well, that is an accurate word for your father-in-law, isn't it?'

'Yes, but Bruce has never acknowledged that openly. I should never have said it.'

Clara began to cry once more. Oliver put his arm round her. Her hair smelt of apples and his stomach lurched. He left the sofa and returned quickly behind his desk, shocked by the feelings she had unwittingly stirred in him.

'I think you need a few sessions to unravel all this,' he said. 'Not with me, but with a counsellor. You see, I think you need someone who has specific experience of this kind of thing — a marriage guidance counsellor or — er — a sex therapist. But one thing I do know is that you must not blame yourself — certainly not mainly, at any rate. It has been a hard road for you.'

'Yes,' said Clara. 'I understand. I'm sorry I let go.'

'Don't be silly,' said Oliver, moving swiftly over to her once more. He took her hand. 'You see, there are some things that are better dealt with by a professional in the field.'

Clara suddenly got up and stamped her foot.

'That is exactly what I *don't* want: some professional "know-all" finding answers for me.'

'That is not what counsellors are trained to do,' replied Oliver gently. 'They are trained to listen and help find your own answers.'

She looked at him fiercely.

'I thought that is what *you* were trained to do. Didn't they teach you anything at theological college? Thanks for nothing "Father",' she said mockingly. She moved to the door. 'Oh and forget the silly kitten. They're tatty specimens anyway, to be honest.'

And she was gone. Hair that smelt of apples swished angrily like a horse's mane in full flight.

Oliver picked up two of the kittens and held them close to his cheek. He had no idea where he had gone wrong, but he knew that the kittens, tatty or not, were beautiful to him.

# *Chapter 8*

Oliver didn't see Clara in the building for weeks. He avoided the rehearsal room and went about with a heaviness inside himself, not only because he had not been able to "reach" her or help her in any constructive way, but because she had somehow ferreted her way into his emotions.

Eventually, he looked out for her, and with feigned innocence made enquiries about her. Her absence acted like quicksilver in Oliver, forever changing his mood unpredictably and rapidly.

He despised himself for his sudden instability. This was not how a priest was meant to be. A priest should be steady, calm, stoical in demeanour and most of all, emotionally stable.

Oliver had never felt like this before. There had been a girl in the sixth form at school, who had flashed her eyes at him during break times and made opportunities to talk with him. Oliver supposed, yes, he had to admit, that he "fancied" the girl at school. He had always hated the word, but it seemed to describe his stirrings for her, even though he did not actually like her.

With Clara it was completely different. He had resonated, albeit briefly, with her inner self. She had shared something intensely personal and painful with him, and he had let her down. He went over and over their final conversation and hated himself for mentioning counselling to her. That was clumsy. But then, what had she come for if not for some kind of pointer as to steps she might take to understand the situation with Bruce?

Clara, meanwhile, blotted the whole scenario out of her mind by learning a great deal of the script of *West Side Story*, even though the auditions weren't for three weeks. Inside, she was embarrassed at how she had behaved, and longed to be able to take back her confession and start to heal again from her outpouring. It had cost her dearly, and it had not had the outcome she hoped for.

'And what was that?' she asked herself. 'What exactly *was* that'? Had she some secret, unacknowledged agenda regarding her visit to this quietly charismatic pastor? She didn't allow herself to answer that question.

The day of the auditions arrived. Nick the director approached Oliver.

'Hey, Rev, I'd like you on the audition panel, please. Neil has gone down sick and we really do need another bloke to keep the balance. Could you do it for us? It'll be most of the day.' (Neil was the lighting designer).

Oliver thought quickly — about Clara. He knew he couldn't face her.

'If you don't mind, I'd rather not, Nick. I'd — I'd be a very poor substitute,' he said hesitantly.

'On the contrary, Rev, you'd be great: calm, non-judgemental, rational — and there to pick up the pieces of the quivering wrecks. It's your pastoral duty,' he said, with a mischievous smile.

Oliver had no choice, put like that.

'OK. Well, just fill me in with who we are seeing.'

And there she was. Last but one on the list. Clara Connors.

\*\*\*

Clara, as Oliver inwardly predicted, proved to be head and shoulders ahead of the other actors in her audition. She had a natural ability to communicate on stage — in all the three elements of dance, drama and singing. She chose Maria's *I Have a Love* as her audition song. Nick wrote on his pad simply,

'This is it.'

At the end of the auditions, Nick invited everyone to share what they had scribbled down on the paper, without adding anything verbally.

'Mesmerizing. She'll do.'

'Tender. A good Maria.'

'Not bad, in fact good.'

'Outstanding.'

'Must have.'

'Yes.'

It came to Oliver's turn.

'What have you written, Rev?'

Oliver did not look up. He doodled on his paper, his face burning.

'Rev?'

'Oh, yes, well I haven't actually written anything.'

'Nothing? Did she make no impression on you?'

'I was too moved to write anything at the time,' he stumbled. 'But yes, she was everything you have all said: "Brilliant." He struggled for normality in his voice. 'Could someone pass the water jug, please?'

As one body they stared at Oliver curiously. Was he unwell? Did the song have a "history" for him that caused this strange behaviour?

He gulped the water, pulled himself together and spoke briskly, 'I'd say she gave the most convincing interpretation of the song. There were one or two others who came close, but in my opinion, Clara Connors has the edge on all of them.'

He shut his book decisively.

'I must be going now… lots to do. I won't stay for the casting if you don't mind. I've given you my opinions. Bye all. Good luck with it.'

Oliver exited swiftly, went straight to the gents' toilet and sat on the seat with his head in his hands, shaking.

\*\*\*

When Clara arrived home that evening, Bruce was putting the finishing touches to a casserole of beef for supper.

'Well, how did it go, darling?' he said, taking her jacket from her and hanging it on the peg.

'I was very nervous,' replied Clara. 'There were six on the auditioning panel. I couldn't read their faces. Especially not the chaplain's — Oliver. He just looked down all the time. No eye contact whatever.'

'Hmm. Strange. Why was that I wonder, because you're very compelling when you're singing, *and* when you're not!' he added softly, coming over and gently twisting a lock of her hair around his finger.

'I don't know. Bad manners I call it, not to even glance up. Very disconcerting.'

'Perhaps he was borne away on a tide of emotion by your singing,' Bruce replied teasingly, returning to the hob and reaching for a large serving spoon, and being nearer to the mark than he realised.

'I certainly don't think *that* would be the case,' said Clara.

'What about the rest of the panel?'

'No idea, really,' Clara replied. 'They were all pretty inscrutable.'

Bruce served casseroled beef onto two plates that had been warming in the oven.

'I'm sure you were brilliant,' he said. 'Wine darling?'

'Yes, definitely. Lots!'

Bruce filled Clara's glass with red wine then went to the cupboard and brought out a second empty glass, placing it by the side of her full one. He filled it up.

'There you are,' he said, 'Lots it shall be. Two full glasses.'

They ate and drank in an agreeable silence. Finally, Clara said,

'That was tasty. Thank you Brucey. Nice wine. What was it?'

'Nothing very special, but it was on offer.'

'Get a case of it, Brucey. I like it.'

She poured herself a third glass of wine.

Bruce watched her. *I adore everything about her,* he thought.

'Dare I?'

'Clara, come over on the sofa.'

She hesitated for a minute, knowing it was a prelude to something else, but she got up, swayed slightly and sat down next to him. He began slowly to stroke her arms, her hair, her skin. 'I love you, Clara Connors. Come here.'

He pulled her closely into himself and very gently began overtures of lovemaking. Clara did not resist. She felt mellow and folded her body into his.

After a few minutes, things followed the well-worn pattern: at first passionate and desperate, then halting, tentative, disappointing and finally despairing.

After the encounter was over, Clara said,

'It doesn't matter Brucey. It's never going to happen, is it? I love you anyway. It's not as important as it was. Let's just accept it.'

'All I know is that you are my life,' said Bruce quietly.

Clara got to her feet.

'Yes, well, as I say, it doesn't matter. It's become a *non-issue.* Anyway, I've got my career now,' she tossed back at him as she began to clear the dishes and blow out the candles. 'I'm going to bed now. I expect you're staying down to do the washing up, aren't you? Thanks for a nice meal,' she added offhandedly. 'Try not to wake me when you come up Bruce. I've had a gruelling day, and another tomorrow. I'll leave your pyjamas on the landing — oh, and don't forget to order that wine.'

Bruce didn't answer but continued to despise himself as he always did. He straightened the sofa cushions and made for the kitchen.

It was anything but a non-issue to him.

\*\*\*

The next day, Bruce went to the local doctor — an elderly gentleman who was long overdue to retire. He looked at Bruce over intimidating half-moon glasses. Bruce haltingly and with great embarrassment explained his predicament.

'Look old boy, try not to fret. It's very common. Stress, usually. One day there's be a pill for it I dare say. But you're young for this to happen.'

He drummed his fingers on the desk, thinking, and finally looked up.

'Do you want children, Mr — um—' (He looked down at his notes in search of Bruce's surname). 'Mr Connors?'

'Well, yes, I do. Clara is ambivalent about it. I'd love a child, but it's much more important for me to make Clara happy. You see—' Bruce looked down and pushed back his mop of brown hair. 'I feel such a failure, Dr Spencer.'

Doctor Spencer coughed and looked rather out of his depth.

'Quite honestly, I can't imagine Clara with a child anyway. She's rather wrapped up in herself and her own desires, don't you think?'

Bruce rose in Clara's defence.

'With respect, Dr Spencer, that is not for you to say. Anyway,' he continued more softly. 'It's out of the question with my problem, isn't it?'

'At the moment, obviously. I'll refer you to a sexual behavioural psychologist, see if they can sort you out.'

'Sorry, I'm not really familiar with the term.'

'No, you wouldn't be. It's a comparatively new thing. Psychology is defined as "the scientific study of behaviour". We need someone to study yours.'

'I know.' Bruce felt patronized. 'I don't exactly want anyone to study my behaviour in this area!' Bruce blushed.

'No, no, of course not, not literally. I've read quite a few recent articles about the male's inability to perform. A psychologist will try to find out *why* you can't — um — er — function properly when you love your wife so much. They'll ferret around and ask you lots of questions. For example, "is there anything in your past that might be causing this"?'

Bruce knew the answer without having to put himself through lots of psychoanalysis. What he needed were some strategies to move forward.

'It's a bit of a mystery I'd say, Clara being so beautiful,' he added, showing in one fell swoop he had no insight whatsoever into the situation.

'And,' he added under his breath. 'Her being rather enticing.'

He looked up at Bruce.

'I'd keep her under lock and key if she were mine, particularly with your kind of problem.'

86

'That is *not* a helpful thing to say, Dr Spencer,' said Bruce angrily. 'You're clearly out of your depth. Please refer me to the behavioural psychologist as soon as possible.'

With that, he marched to the door and turned.

'I'll thank you to keep those kind of observations to yourself, Doctor. And for your information, I have no need to keep Clara under lock and key. I trust her completely.'

'Hmm. Very foolish,' Dr Spencer muttered under his breath as Bruce slammed the surgery door shut.

Bruce had just about managed to keep hold of his temper with Dr Spencer. He hoped to goodness the sexual behaviourist or whatever he was called had a bit more insight and professionalism about him.

*\*\**

A week later, Bruce walked through a gate in the iron railings and mounted the concrete steps to The Hospital for Nervous Diseases which had a small department devoted to behavioural psychology. The waiting room was bleak, with grubby cream paint on the upper half of the walls and dark bottle green lincrusta on the bottom half. Bruce had a sudden vivid memory of sitting on the stairs of his childhood home and denting the pattern on the lincrusta wallpaper with his finger nail as his father shouted at his mother downstairs. The more his father shouted, the more viciously Bruce would dent the pattern.

Bruce wondered what a behavioural psychologist might look like. A strange looking man with wild, white hair? No, that was such a caricature. Perhaps a younger dapper doctor whizz-kid with an overconfident air? His stomach churned.

After about ten minutes, the door of the waiting room opened.

'Bruce Connors, please?'

Doctor Hamilton stood framed in the doorway; not tall, and with reddish hair sleeked down and parted at the side, a warm and friendly voice, of average build, with large, black-rimmed glasses. Dr Hamilton was a woman.

'I'm here to try and help,' she said with a smile, guiding him into her surgery.

Bruce was invited to take a seat opposite a large and threatening desk. He stared at her, and suddenly realised how rude that must appear.

'I'm so sorry. I somehow wasn't expecting a — a—'

'A woman?' Dr Hamilton said, laughing. 'Yes, there are a few of us around now, thanks to Anna Freud. We're a rare breed at the moment. It's still rather a male preserve, but you know what? We are gradually getting there, after all, we've come through the swinging sixties!' she smiled.

She pulled her chair out of the desk well opposite and brought it round to sit nearer Bruce.

'That's better. Never did appreciate too much of a barrier between doctor and patient, but I do have a bolt hole in case we come to blows,' she said, laughing again.

He liked her immediately. She was old enough to be his mother, but her warmth and vitality made her immediately accessible. Bruce felt himself relaxing.

'It's good you've come Mr Connors. It takes courage. Shall I call you Bruce?'

'Yes of course, and your name is?'

'I'm Sonia Hamilton and I'm here to see if we can find a way forward for you. Doctor Spencer has written to me about you. He doesn't say much, except that you have difficulties of impotence.'

Bruce winced at the term. No one, least of all himself, had admitted to that label.

'Yes,' she said, seeing his expression. 'It's an ugly word, but it's better to come to terms with what we are dealing with straight away, don't you agree? No use skirting round things and taking up ten minutes of an all-too-short appointment, is there? I must reassure you that although these problems are stubborn, nothing is totally insoluble. It's a surprisingly common problem.'

Bruce immediately felt something like reassurance. She poured two glasses of water. Putting one down for Bruce, she continued:

'Bruce, I wonder if you could start by telling me about yourself a little — where you grew up, about your home life and so on, so I have a clearer picture of you?'

She had lit the blue touch paper within a few minutes of his arrival into her office.

*What my home life was like,* he thought. *Where do I even begin?*

He'd never spoken about it to anyone except Clara, and then not in too much detail.

'I lived in South West London,' Bruce started. 'In a reasonably sized semi-detached house in a suburban street.'

'What about your father?' said Sonia Hamilton. 'Tell me about him.'

Bullseye in one. Where on earth could Bruce start about the man he loathed with every fibre of his being?

He remembered in intricate detail all the writing he had done in his red book many years ago. He had the dates and times of particularly bad scenes at home but needed no prompting regarding emotional content and feelings. Those were indelibly etched in his memory for life.

## *Chapter 9*

A day later, everyone at the theatre was gathered in the casting room, waiting for the cast list notice to go up. All clamoured around as Nick pinned it on the wall. Clara was unanimously cast as Maria, the lead, by the auditioning panel. The others congratulated her, mainly effusively, a few offhandedly, while one or two turned away, nursing their own agendas.

Oliver stood at the back of the room, watching. Clara had seen him and flew towards him waving the paper in her hand.

'I got it,' she said excitedly. 'I got Maria!' 'Can you believe it, Rev? I'm so excited!'

'I'm so pleased for you,' Oliver said. 'Well deserved. Your song at the audition was marvellous,'

'Oh thanks, Rev.' Her smile faded a little. 'By the way, I'm sorry if I was rude the other evening. Can we forget all that? I wasn't myself. Out of order, wasn't I?'

'I expect I was clumsy. Yes, let's do that. Just forget it. No harm done?'

'No harm done,' she said, briefly putting the palm of her hand on his chest and smiling up at him.

Oliver felt a thousand volts of electricity shoot through him. In one moment, he knew absolutely that he was captivated, smitten, ensnared by his feelings for this woman.

'Now,' continued Clara. 'About that kitten. I *do* want one. I'll keep it in my room with a dirt tray. You would see to it sometimes if my rehearsals went on a bit, wouldn't you? Just keep an eye out for it?'

Again, she touched him lightly on the chest. Again the electric charge.

Oliver was quiet, overwhelmed by Clara's presence. She was so exciting, glowing, so full of electricity and terrifyingly beautiful. A temptress.

'Come and choose a kitten then. Even though they're tatty specimens,' he added, giving her a mischievous half-smile. 'Come round tonight.'

Oliver could have walked away then, could have made an excuse and not seen her so soon, while he was still capable of rational thoughts. But everything in him was screaming to spend more time in Clara's company. He found her irresistible. He knew if he did see her that evening, then he was escalating forward into something that might be difficult to control. Stop now. Now!

She arrived that evening and Oliver led the way to his room, opening the door on the now squealing kittens, who staggered semi-blindly over to his feet. Clara scooped two of them in her arms and nestled into the green sofa by the fire stroking them. 'They're so sweet,' she murmured, her head buried in their fur. She kissed each one lightly.

Oliver watched, mesmerised. What was it about this woman?

Clara's rich hair hung low over her face and the kittens. Oliver felt his whole body lurch, as though it were turning inside out. There was still time to stop. But slowly, slowly he crossed to behind the sofa and hesitatingly began to smooth Clara's hair back from her face, holding it loosely into a bunch at her neck. *Stop now,* the voice inside warned. *You are in danger zone.* The trouble was that Clara did not resist, He very gently pulled her head further back and bent forward and kissed her slowly and softly on the lips. Clara shook her head free.

'What are you doing?' she said.

'I'm so sorry. I shouldn't have done that. I really shouldn't. You're so beautiful, that's the trouble. It's your fault,' he whispered. 'Please forgive me.'

She put the kittens down unceremoniously and turned around, kneeling up on the sofa, and cupped his face fully in her two hands. 'No you shouldn't have done it,' she said. 'A man of the cloth and all!' She looked up at him with soft, soft eyes. 'All right. I forgive you,' she said.

They were silent. Neither moved. Then:

'Oliver, is *this* what you want?' She pulled him round to the front of the sofa.

Then everything became as in a slow-motion dream — gentle hands caressing, lips searching, bodies lifting, the minimum of clothes shed and finally the curving seamlessly into each other.

Tenderness. Urgency. Excitement.

And finally: fulfilment, joy, incredulity, wonder, whispered phrases of gratitude from each to other.

Several minutes later, when the euphoria began to subside, there crept feelings of disbelief, guilt, bewilderment and the realisation in both the enormity of it all.

'I must go,' said Clara shakily.

Clara untangled herself rapidly, put the hastily taken-off garments on, half-threw the kittens into their bed and left the room without turning back.

Oliver was motionless. He sat staring into space for minutes. His vows had been broken as easily as the garments shed, his ideals and promises and years of careful control relinquished in an instant.

But oh, the wonder of it.

Clara. Clarus. Bright. Clear. All-consuming.

Her light burned within him like a fire.

\*\*\*

'I've been to the psychologist today, Clara. I'm going to do something about all this,' he said, briefly sweeping his hand downwards.

'Oh, gosh, yes,' replied Clara. 'Of course you have. Sorry. I forgot. I've been a bit wrapped up in things today.' *Understatement of the year,* she thought, as she threw her duffle coat over a chair and kicked off her shoes. Avoiding any eye contact with Bruce, she felt as if her infidelity was plastered all over her in luminous paint. Her body was still alive within her from her encounter with Oliver.

'Have you heard if you've got a part yet?'

'Yes. I've been cast as Maria.'

'Wonderful,' he twirled Clara off her feet. 'So you read that vicar's body language all wrong, then, didn't you?'

Clara said nothing. On the contrary, she had read the vicar's body language correctly.

'How did *you* get on Brucey? Was he any good? Helpful?'

Bruce told Clara that his "homework" for the psychologist ("A lady, surprisingly") was to write down everything that he could remember about his father during his childhood years. After some gentle probing, followed by quite a long discussion, Dr Hamilton had decided that this was the first avenue for exploration — to see if there were any behavioural issues in Bruce's father that may have had a bearing on the way he brought up Bruce and influenced him.

*Hmm. Just a few,* thought Clara.

Clara went to bed early that evening. Once on her own, she could hardly marshal her thoughts and her feelings, so all-encompassing was the confusion. She relived it all. On the one hand she knew the most wonderful thing had happened to her — something she had longed for with Bruce for so long and that had never been accomplished. She had always blamed herself in some way for his failure. What exactly was she doing wrong? Was she an incompetent partner for him? Undesirable even? Now she had proof that she was sexually attractive and capable of giving herself completely. She felt alive, awake, cherished. She hugged these things to herself, still excited and amazed by the encounter.

On the other hand, she felt guilty, ashamed, appalled at herself, incredulous at how it had all happened so easily, and very frightened of the implications of this outpouring of desire for Oliver on her future with Bruce. Sleep was very far away.

She hugged her knees and her secret to herself.

Bruce stayed up late into the night, thinking and writing. His memories were crystal clear but he used his red book to confirm that his memories were accurate. Sometimes he could hardly bear to read the notes he had made as a child. They were simply too painful.

He scribbled furiously.

He recorded how his father Bert would grab his mother and fondle her roughly while she was cooking; how once she turned on him with a hot metal spoon, held it against his face screaming

'I've told you before, *leave me alone! Stop mauling me'*.

'It's my right, damn you woman,' his father had shouted back, grabbing her wrist and bruising it in the process.

Pressing her hard against the sink he kissed her roughly as she leant further and further back.

Bruce felt immense sorrow as he wrote that Sadie, his lovely elder sister, seemed to have disappeared off the face of the earth. The police had recorded a verdict of "Lost Person".

He recorded how his youngest sister Connie had innocently shared with Bruce how their father would take her for a walk with their dog Patch down by the canal, and in the seclusion of the shaded path — always the same spot — how he would kiss her on the lips "long and hard".

'Why do you let him?' Bruce had asked, through clenched teeth, distraught at the thought,

'He's bigger than I am,' replied Connie. 'And anyway, I just pretend he's a prince and I'm a princess. It's romantic.'

'Connie, you mustn't let him,' urged Bruce, cupping her face in his hands and looking earnestly at her.

But Connie just shrugged her shoulders and replied, 'It's OK Brucey, I don't mind.'

Bruce had wanted to tell his mother what Connie had said, but every time he started, he would look at her defeated face and somehow know that it would only make matters worse for her, so he never did.

He recorded how he decided to accompany Connie and his father the next time she was taken out with the dog. They walked in silence by the canal while Connie chatted brightly. His father obviously resented Bruce's presence and was more than a little suspicious as to the reason.

'This is where we stop, Daddy. Look, Brucey, by this tree.'

'What are you doing suddenly coming down here with us, boy?' Bruce's father questioned aggressively. 'Why aren't you at home helping your mother, you lazy good-for-nothing.'

Bruce wrote in his notes how occasionally he would bring a friend home from school with him. He related how his mother was always kind and attentive and baked special scones for them, often his favourite cheese ones.

But if his father came into the room, within seconds he was demanding in his booming voice,

'You got a girl, then, lad? If not, why not? Don't be like Bruce here,' he would add. 'The day he brings a girl home I'll put out the bunting. Something wrong with the boy,' he added, muttering. 'Like the other one.'

Inwardly, Bruce vowed he would *never* bring a girl home. He didn't trust his father's wandering hands and eyes. He had witnessed that with his eldest sister Sadie before she left home. She only once brought a friend home, and the confused girlfriend found herself within minutes on Bruce's father's knee. 'To show we're friends,' he would say, running his hand up her thigh.

'Don't do that, Daddy,' his mother Rosa would say wearily. 'I've told you before. They don't like it.'

'She likes it all right,' he would reply. 'Don't you, lassie?'
The girl would half-smile wanly. No one was strong enough to take issue with him, and so his disgusting ways continued.

Worst of all, branded like a hot iron in Bruce's memory, were the noises coming regularly from next door in the night time, and Connie's return to her own bed with a stick of barley sugar after the deed was done.

Bruce reread his notes and was consumed with despair. No one would believe any of this. His mother and his sisters were beautiful in his eyes and to be protected, and he was impotent to shield them. That was what agonised him so.

But the deepest and darkest family secret that was never ever talked about was regarding his older brother James. Sandy-haired and anaemic-looking, James was a quiet and reclusive teenager who found integrating with anyone at school difficult. He was a lonely boy and his mother worried about him constantly. She would put little notes in his bread and luncheon meat sandwiches for lunch time saying, "Remember I love you, Jamie Boy". Or "Always here, son". "All my love, Mum". She alone knew how much her son struggled with life.

"Jamie Boy" held a secret close to his chest. He and another boy had quietly and without fuss declared their love for each other, kissing on the lips and shyly having a quick feel of each other in the alleyway behind the school. These were forbidden feelings in James' eyes, and always he was haunted by what his father would say if ever he found out.

Bruce continued writing into the night. It was as if he was on fire with the memories, and his anger burned brightly within him.

He recorded how Albert, his father, had little time for James. If Bruce, with his sensitive temperament, was a failure in his father's eyes, then James was doubly so. He often goaded the boy. 'Are you a man or a mouse, James? Let me see your muscles, boy. You're puny. Goes with that pale hair. You're no son of mine, I swear. Man up, boy. Show some guts.'

That evening, as they were sitting down to an all too familiar supper of stewed scrag end of lamb and mashed swede ('cheap but nourishing,' his mother often said),

Albert attacked James with a catalogue of his failures. Bruce wanted to defend his brother, but as Bruce recorded in his notes, he was too terrified and too much of a wimp (to use his father's word), to face the punishment his father would deal out to him, and so he remained a coward. This cowardice, as Bruce perceived it, was to haunt him for the rest of his life.

Bruce stopped writing. It was getting late into the night, but he knew he must write the final passage before he ducked out of it. He continued.

"After this latest burst of verbal abuse from my father at the meal table, James acted on the plan he had clearly meticulously worked out in his head. While my family and I were downstairs finishing supper in the one room that my father would allow to be warmed, James, between the main course and the pudding, slid off his chair and crept upstairs. He tied together the three school ties he must have gathered from my siblings' rooms and fastened one end with a tight knot to the coil of the light socket. He made a large loop in the other end of the ties, placed a chair under the light coil, stood on it, put the loop around his neck, kicked the chair away and hanged himself".

\*\*\*

The remainder of the story was too painful for Bruce to write in the first person, so he decided it would have to be in narrative form. Every now and again, however, he lapsed into the first person and the writing became painfully disjointed in parts. Bruce stopped frequently to blow his nose. He stared into the distance, his heart full of unbearable pain as he recalled events.

In his red book, he had simply recorded,

"James died tonight".

\*\*\*

He continued with his writing for Dr Hamilton:

"A few minutes elapsed before Albert, noticing the boy's absence, boomed, 'Now where's that wretched boy? He didn't ask permission to leave the room.'

'Daddy, leave him alone,' said my mother. 'You get at him too much. The boy can hardly breathe for criticism from you.'

'Get at him? *Get at him?*' shouted my father. He pushed his chair back from the meal table, knocking it over with a bang. 'I'll thank you to leave the disciplining to me, woman,' he shouted furiously. 'That boy's a failure,' he added, with which he thundered up the stairs.

My mother quickly followed him, afraid of what he might do to the boy. In effect, though, his father had already done it.

Albert stopped dead in his tracks in the doorway. The boy's body, finally still, hung limp, his head lolled to one side, his tongue flopped out and his face was mottled red and blue.

Father blindly reached his hand out for Mother, but she pushed him away and sunk to the floor in the deepest unspeakable anguish.

'This is you, this is *you*,' she sobbed, but Father was flying down the stairs for a kitchen knife. He thrust one in my hand too. 'Follow me,' he barked.

'Can I have a knife too?' asked my little sister Connie. 'Why are you giving Brucey one and not me?'

'Stay down Connie,' my father instructed, but as he and I ran up the stairs, my curious little sister followed.

Once James had been cut down, my mother stroked his head in agony while cradling her pregnant belly with the other, as though protecting the unborn child from the pain and grief. The police were called, questions asked, details taken, an undertaker arrived and James' body was taken away in a temporary black coffin, leaving us all in the darkest place I have ever known.

The letter James had left my mother told her about his "wrong kind of loving" for the boy at school, as he described it, and pleaded with her in writing not to tell his father. She never did, of course, but some years later she came up to my room, woke me gently and unburdened herself as she read the letter to me. I held my mum for a long time in my arms as she broke her heart and shed a river of tears into my shoulder for her eldest son. My tears mingled with my mum's as we clung to each other with wet cheeks through the night".

\*\*\*

Bruce sent what he had written to Doctor Sonia Hamilton, as requested. She opened the envelope at the end of a long and tiring working day, deciding that she would read its contents in the morning. However, she skimmed the first page and with increasing horror, reread from the start to the end.

Dr Hamilton was not given to tears or becoming emotional over her patients, usually remaining at a distance from them in terms of empathy. That was part of the training ethic. It was no help to them, she had decided herself a long time ago, to become emotionally involved. That was unprofessional. What she always tried to work with was a sympathetic, but cool head, a considered detachment. She called it her "subjective objective" approach.

By the time she had read a page, she felt her eyes filling with tears. How grievously this family had been treated by one man, how he had ensnared them, trapped them, through his damaged psyche. His poisonous tentacles had ensured that none of his children came out of their childhood unscathed. Poor, poor Bruce Connors. This would take a great deal of painstaking unravelling.

She decided she would ask for the rest of what he needed to write before seeing him again, so that she had as full a picture as possible, so she wrote to him to that effect.

\*\*\*

The funeral of James was a dreadful affair. Albert had insisted that he wanted to make the coffin himself. A carpenter by trade, he nevertheless was overruled for once by his grieving wife, who angrily said James deserved a coffin with satin lining in, not some "botched effort made from spare bits of wood". Albert's grief was subjugated by feelings of intense anger and aggression, and it seemed he was less aggrieved with himself than the world in general and his son in particular. His wife did not seem to understand that making a coffin for James might be an important step for him to take.

Rosa held in her heart an unspoken longing that somehow Sadie would hear about her brother James and come home. But she never did. It seemed she had simply vanished off the face of the earth.

There was no outwardly obvious self-analysis or reflection in Albert. He appeared not to ask himself questions about *why* his son might have taken the action he did. He became more and more angry and at the same time increasingly morose. The entire family was frightened to speak to him and replied only in monosyllables when addressed.

A minister took the funeral service with little reference to God, at Albert's request.

'Don't want any of that rubbish,' Albert had warned him beforehand. 'And *no* hymns.'

'What exactly is your problem, Mr Connors?' the minister had asked, shaken by the ferocity of the instructions he had received.

Albert gave him such a black, angry look, and the minister, noticing his white-knuckled clenched fists, decided to take the line of least resistance and quietly eliminate almost all reference to God in the funeral service. His clerical colleagues and he at a monthly meeting recently had observed that funerals were a prime time to preach "The Word" as people were generally receptive and hungry for comfort and guidance, but on this occasion — definitely *not*.

Bruce, at the tender age of eight, had been to his grandmother's burial, and as he stood looking down at the gaping hole, had thought what a dreadful thing it was to abandon coffin and body in this way. He had been fond of his gran and found tears rolling down his cheeks. His mother had quietly moved round to his side and put her hand in his as they watched the slow, slightly swaying descent of the coffin into the ground.

Although he had been sad at his gran's funeral, everyone knew it was the natural order of things, and at the age of eighty-three she had "had a good life" as people kept reassuring the family.

But this was completely different. This was his brother, who he had kicked a ball and played five-stones and jacks with, who had heard him reading his first book aloud, helped him with his spelling, and to whom he had clung when his parents' arguing threatened to turn into physical violence. This was *James* being lowered into the ground, having found life quite simply too much.

He looked across at his mother. She was broken with grief and tears and had turned away from Bert. He was tight-lipped and pale. Bruce surreptitiously moved around the circle of mourners to where his mother was standing, half bent, her hands clutching her belly. He slipped his hand into hers and she briefly gave him a small smile.

When handfuls of earth had been thrown onto the coffin, Bruce's mum whispered to him urgently,

'Brucey. The baby. I think it's coming away.'

Ten minutes later, an ambulance swung through the wrought iron gates of the cemetery, driving as near as it could to Rosa, who was lying on the ground with a pool of blood around her feet and legs and her skirt drenched with violent red.

'When's the baby due?' she was asked by one of the ambulance men.

'Not for another three months,' Rosa whispered.

'Sorry love,' he replied.

She was lifted gently onto a stretcher and driven away.

\*\*\*

It had been an extremely painful journey for Bruce to record these tragic happenings, but eventually he managed to conclude his writing for Professor Hamilton.

"My father never moved, neither did he say a word to my mother, never threw earth onto the coffin or whisper a goodbye to his eldest son but as I looked at him, I saw a tear slowly trickle down his set jaw. He turned and watched the disappearing ambulance, then he drew out his pocket handkerchief which my mother had starched for him that morning and slowly waved goodbye to the ambulance, then to his dead son in the freshly dug grave.

The baby had been another boy, so on one dark day, my mother had lost two out of her three sons. I felt a terrible weight of responsibility on my shoulders simply to stay alive for the sake of my mum. There must be a limit to how many times a heart can be broken."

# Chapter 10

For the next two days after his encounter with Clara, Oliver was nowhere to be found. Various actors knocked on his door, then slipped notes underneath. The cleaner said she couldn't get in to do the room, but she could hear the kittens meowing piteously from inside. It seemed Oliver had simply taken off without telling anyone.

Clara began rehearsals the next day and "doctor theatre's medicine" as she called it, prompting the powerful flow of adrenaline, worked its magic, leaving her feeling elated. She knew only too well that she had a mountain to climb in terms of remembering both stage directions and script, learning songs and practising choreographic steps. but she loved every minute of the process.

*I must find him,* she thought at the end of the rehearsal. *See if he's all right, apologise* (but what for, a rebellious voice inside said — for love?), *draw a line under things and then try and act normally. See how he is. Simply see him.*

Clara hadn't been able to eat since their encounter. She sipped coffee and water but her stomach was too knotted with the intoxicating mix of high emotion and longing that threw her completely off course. At the same time, the drum roll of guilt and betrayal rumbled on deeply and relentlessly inside her.

She slipped a note under Oliver's door which read simply,

"Oliver. Can we talk? I need to see you".

Oliver on impulse had taken a train to see his sister in Edinburgh. It was Morag who always rescued him when the threads of his life became twisted. She was single and the head of the village primary school and always knew what to do in any situation, especially where her younger brother Oliver was concerned.

Oliver arrived unannounced, but the moment Morag saw him, she knew he was in difficulties. Oliver explained that he'd "run into a bit of trouble" at the theatre. His sister was wise enough to know that if Oliver needed to talk further, he would in his own good time. He never did this time, so she just kept on feeding him with everything he liked best — shepherd's pie which was more mashed potato than meat, scones laced with cream and raspberry jam, homemade chocolate cake hastily put together, and a large dish of apple and blackberry crumble and custard. Comfort food. Oliver slowly began to relax. She was a gem of a sister, all right, and Oliver knew it. What he didn't eat she would pack up for him to take back. Morag was a firm believer that whatever else might fail, there was always good food to help make things feel better. Her ample waistline was testament to her philosophy!

On his return after a couple of days, Oliver rapidly sifted through the notes posted under his door and found the one from Clara that he had both longed for and dreaded. He ripped it open.

"Oliver. Can we talk? I need to see you".

'Yes, oh yes please!' Oliver said aloud.

Suddenly he was aware of the kittens and their mother yowling piteously and rubbing against his legs. The kittens were hungry and their mother looked scraggy and scrawny after her two-day fast.

'Oh poor Cat. How could I?' said Oliver as he opened a large can of cat food and put the entire contents into Cat's dish. He then opened a can of evaporated milk and poured the creamy liquid into two saucers, added a little warm water and placed the kittens around the saucers, poking their noses gently into the milk.

'There you are little ones. I'm so sorry,' he said, stroking their bony spines gently as they began to lap hungrily.

The next morning, Oliver left a note in Clara's pigeonhole where she gathered her mail.

*Clara. I hope you are all right, Can you come round to my flat tomorrow after rehearsals to talk? Yours, Oliver.*

There was nothing in the note to indicate the turmoil of his feelings. *Play it cool now,* he resolutely thought.

She arrived the following day. He greeted her formally as he opened the door.

'Hello Clara. Good to see you. Thank you for your note.'

'Thank you for responding,' she replied, equally formally.

Then, quite suddenly, he took her in his arms and held her very close.

'I'm so sorry, Clara.'

Eventually Clara pulled away and looked him directly in the eyes.

'Sorry for what?' she said. 'Doing what came naturally?'

'Too naturally,' he replied. 'But it mustn't happen again, must it?'

'No,' said Clara. 'It mustn't. You a priest and me a married woman. Not quite "the bishop and the actress" but not a million miles short!'

'I'm thinking I must resign,' said Oliver. 'I can't cope with seeing you around and I feel I've let God down.'

'Let *God* down!' Clara said with indignation. 'He shouldn't have brought us together if he didn't want us to do anything about it! After all,' she teased. 'I've always been led to believe that we won't be tempted more than we can stand.'

Standing taller, Oliver became the priest,

'No, that's theologically not quite it.' he said. 'Corinthians 10, verse 13:

*"He will not let you be tempted beyond your ability, but with the temptation he will also provide the way of escape, that you may be able to endure it".'*

'Don't quote the bible at me,' she said, suddenly furiously, her green eyes flashing. 'It's too late now. You didn't think of that on your brown sofa, did you? What are you saying — that your way of escaping me is to leave? Can you blot me out just like that?'

'Never,' replied Oliver softly. 'I think I fell in love with you the first time I saw you.'

Clara moved closer to him again and put the palms of her hands on his chest. Oliver felt the electricity.

'*Please* don't leave, Oliver. I promise I'll keep out of your way. To be honest, I can hardly face Bruce and I feel guilty as hell too.'

'Guilty as hell,' said Oliver. 'That's an interesting concept.'

'*Oliver*!' Clara shouted. 'You may be a priest to the world, but to me you're warm flesh and blood and passion and a whole lot more besides. Please don't leave.'

'We must promise to keep out of each other's way,' said Oliver.

Suddenly Clara was defiant again.

'Oh don't worry. I certainly won't be thinking of *you*. I'll be *far* too busy with Maria. It won't be an issue,' she said tossing her head again.'

'It will for me,' said Oliver quietly.

'Right that's sorted then,' said Clara, ignoring his comment. 'I'm off.'

She left, slamming the door as she went.

A moment later she was back banging on the front door. Oliver opened it.

'But it was nice, wasn't it, Vicar?' she said in a childlike voice, irresistibly flirtatious, and before he could answer, she was gone.

Clara. Cirus. Bright, Clear, all-consuming.

*And infuriatingly mercurial,* thought Oliver.

Clara danced off down the street with apparently not a care in the world, reached the corner, turned it and then crumpled in a heap, sobbing out loud.

'Damn you, damn you, *damn you,* Oliver Lockwood. I wish I'd never set eyes on you.'

The next few days were torture for them both. All Clara longed to do was burst into his room, fling her arms around him and hold him for a very long time. Oliver, by the same token, yearned with everything in him to feel the warm embrace of Clara and simply to love and protect her. Was that such a big deal?

*Yes,* he concluded, it was a huge deal and not worthy of him. She was a married woman and he was deeply committed to his vow of celibacy — or at least, he *was.*

For several weeks the two made sure they did not set eyes on each other. Clara concentrated all her efforts and passion into her part as Maria. She avoided the emotional self-harming of thinking of Oliver when she sang *There's a place for us.* When she went home, she made sure she was extra loving to Bruce. Yes, she truthfully did love him, but was slowly realising, as thousands of people before, that it might be possible to love two people at the same time. Differently, but equally. And the realisation hurt and confused her. The threads of love could become very tangled!

Oliver, for his part, believed fervently in praying and fasting as a means of subduing the will of the flesh and attempting to see the face of God more clearly in the situation. It had helped him in the past, but this time after a little while of prayer, the only face he could see was

Clara's and the movement he sensed was not that of the Holy Spirit but of Clara's thick chestnut hair rising and falling as he gently ran his hands through it.

He banished the image again and again, but it stubbornly refused to obey.

Bishop Hermes had said that his door was always open to Oliver, so with a degree of trepidation Oliver found himself walking up to the imposing door of the bishop's large, austere house. The secretary answered the door and Oliver explained that he needed to see the bishop urgently.

'Have you an appointment?' enquired the secretary, not unkindly.

'No I haven't, but I really do need to see him. Urgently.'

'Well, I'm afraid he's…'

'Ah. I recognize that voice. Oliver Lockwood, isn't it? Come in,' said the bishop, appearing suddenly from his study, swinging his half-moon glasses in one hand and holding an opened book in the other, his thumb marking the page.

'I was just preparing a talk for tonight, but it can wait. You sounded — er — troubled. Thank you, Mavis,' he said to his secretary. 'Could you arrange for some tea to be sent to my study please?'

'Of course,' said Mavis. 'Shall I rearrange your next appointment, bishop? You won't have time to finish your preparation otherwise.'

'Thank you. That would be kind.'

Mavis disappeared — a well-dressed picture of middle-aged efficiency bustling back to her office.

'It's marvellous having a good secretary,' said the bishop. 'She practically asks me if I have got a clean handkerchief when I go out!'

Tea arrived within a few minutes, bringing a welcome relief to Oliver from the everyday pleasantries exchanged about his work and so on.

Finally, the bishop looked straight into Oliver's eyes.

'Come on, Oliver. Spill the beans. What's this urgent call all about?'

Blushing furiously, Oliver began to tell his story. The bishop's gaze did not leave him. Oliver began to talk about his feelings in a way he had rarely done before. He eventually stopped.

'You see, bishop. I'm agonised over this. I don't know how to think of my love for Clara as a sin, and yet sin it is.'

The bishop came over and held Oliver's two hands in his for a long time.

'There is not one of us who hasn't agonised over a problem of this magnitude, Oliver. It doesn't have to be a sexual sin, it can be the sin of selfishness, greed, envy, falling far short of what we know we should be. Do not beat yourself up so much that you are no earthly good to yourself or anyone else. Sexual misdemeanours *are* contrary to what is best for you, but you have a calling, Oliver — don't forget that, and your celibacy was self-imposed.

'Yes, I know.'

The bishop slowly turned back to his chair and began to swing his glasses again.

'It's a great pity you had to fall in love with a married woman,' he said, showing distinct sternness for the first time. 'Remember, it's Clara's husband who is the real victim here. He is the wronged party.'

Oliver said nothing.

Finally the bishop said, 'Do you think it might be helpful for you to speak to him?'

Oliver stood up.

'Definitely not, bishop. I can't think how that would help. It might relieve *me* (or not), but it wouldn't help him, would it? Why dump my burden on him?'

'Because it is very much his business. This is his *wife* we're talking about. You and Clara have committed adultery.'

Oliver winced at the word. 'Yes, and I couldn't be sorrier. I'm so ashamed I have given in so easily to temptation. But—' he spoke softly. 'I fell completely in love with her. I've never known anything like it.'

Just then, thinking the bishop was still preparing for his evening meeting, his wife came in, slightly bent from a grey cat immovably draped around her shoulders.

'Mrs Hermes. How are you?' said Oliver, dragging himself away from his introspection and rising to shake her hand and stroke the purring cat.

'He's nice. What's his name?'

'Boy Blue,' replied Margaret. 'And it's a "she". We got it wrong! She's a blue Burmese and knows everything, including how to hold on for grim death whenever she can.' She laughed. 'She's like a limpet.'

'She's a beautiful creature,' said Oliver as he tickled the cat under her chin. 'I got my cat wrong too. Only realised when "he" presented me with six kittens!'

'Oh what fun!' Mrs Hermes laughed. 'Have you found homes for them all?'

'*No*!' the bishop almost shouted with a laugh. 'No, no, *no* Margaret. We have *enough!*'

Mrs Hermes mimicked a child's pout.

'Spoil sport! Anyway, It's nice to see you again, Reverend Lockwood. May I ask to what do we owe the honour? Or is that private?'

'Margaret and I share everything unless I am specifically told that a subject is confidential,' explained the bishop. 'But I think on this occasion, Margaret, we'll assume Oliver's problem *is* confidential, darling,' he said gently, without in any way putting his wife down.

'Yes, yes. Totally understood.' I'll leave you to it, but Oliver... I can call you that, can't I? if you ever want a blue Burmese let me know. I am in contact with the breeder. I'll leave you to it then,' she said breezily with a wave as she left.

Oliver liked her. She seemed rather a free spirit in the strange ecclesiastical world she found herself and clearly did everything she could to normalise its roles.

'Boy Blue is one of four,' said the bishop with a tinge of weariness 'The other three are upstairs. She can't resist furry creatures. She'd fill the house with them if she had her way,' he chuckled.

'Now, Oliver.' The bishop returned to the subject hastily. 'Only you can decide whether to share your misdemeanour with Clara's husband and ask for his forgiveness.'

The bishop swung his glasses, thinking hard.

'But of course that does rather dump Clara in it,' he reflected. 'Maybe it might be a case of "Least said is soonest mended," but Oliver.'

The bishop looked stern again,

'*Don't* allow yourself to get into a situation where it could happen again. It mustn't. To repeat it knowingly *would* classify as a very grave short falling. However hard it may be, you must keep out of Clara's way.'

'I know that absolutely,' replied Oliver.

'If it happens again then we must consider a defrocking due to the adulterous nature of the relationship.'

'I know,' replied Oliver. 'Please could we pray?'

They had a short time of prayer. Oliver made for the door.

'Thank you, your Grace, for your time, and for your understanding and advice.'

'It is good to see you again,' replied the bishop. 'I will visit you at your theatre some time.'

Oliver turned the door handle.

'She must have been some girl, because you are a man of principle, Oliver,' he said with just a hint of a mischievous smile.

***

Rehearsals began in earnest for *West Side Story*. The company had just twelve weeks before taking it to the stage, so everyone was under the familiar performance deadline pressure.

That was just how Clara liked it. She loved the feel of the adrenaline running fast and free through her body. She rose to the challenge of mastering Leonard Bernstein's demanding songs accurately and quickly. Once they were learned by heart, she knew she could then concentrate on the choreography that embellished them. While others were still holding scripts in their hands (much to the frustration of Nick the director), Clara was word perfect within two weeks. She loved everything about "West Side Story".

She became fascinated and enthralled by the richness of the music and the classical feel to the work, even though it had been advertised on the posters as a "Musical". Nick had explained to them at the beginning of rehearsals that somehow the work straddled opera and musical theatre, forming a bridge between the two, and therefore would hold a unique place in the musical history books. He aimed to pay respect to both genres through his creative interpretation.

Clara was given individual singing lessons with the musical director Matt, whom she regarded as "sheer musicality on legs" as she described him to Bruce. He seemed able to turn the most unpromising singers into something approximating tuneful and he found Clara 'A dream to work with,' as he said to Nick during one of the breaks.

Matt was, as Clara said to Bruce, 'batting for the other side,' so Bruce simply delighted in hearing her reports of his musical wizardry without feeling threatened in any way.

The tragedy of the story appealed to her too. She had always regarded *Romeo and Juliet* as her favourite play, and here it was, in the most amazing musical form. *There's a Place for Us* was to remain her favourite song from the work and she had finally managed to sing it without thinking all the way through about Oliver. The performance process was a wonderful displacement activity as far as she was concerned.

Four weeks into rehearsals Nick was beginning to show signs of stress.

'How can I work artistically with you when you are still on the bloody book?' he shouted. 'I'm not talking to *all* of you' he said, looking at Clara. 'Just *most* of you. Off the book by Friday or some of you will find yourselves *replaced*!'

Six weeks on, all performers were being shaped into Nick's vision of the show. He had long consultations with the set designer, who had various creative ideas, and the lighting designer, who relished the thought of putting his creative fingers round such a dramatic and dynamic show.

During those weeks of rehearsal, Bruce and Clara drew closer to each other as they each shared their separate experiences — Bruce his therapy sessions and Clara her rehearsals. Bruce, on the advice of his therapist, made no advances of a physical nature towards Clara other than giving her a warm kiss and friendly hug now and again. Both were happier that way. The pressure was off them for the time being, and they were the happiest they had been for a long time.

At seven weeks into rehearsals, everyone agreed (some reluctantly) that Clara was promising to be stunning in her performance. She gave everything of herself to the rehearsals and found herself falling asleep early in the evenings when she curled up in front of the television and was often in bed by nine o'clock.

Just before the eighth week into rehearsals, Clara began to feel sick.

\*\*\*

Bruce's next significant assignment for his therapy sessions with Dr Hamilton was to write down and reflect upon his mother's role in his childhood — what sort of a mother she was, how Bruce regarded her relationship with Albert her husband, how his mother related to her children, and so on. Dr Hamilton knew that the only way to begin to help Bruce was to examine the layer upon layer of deep hurt and damage that his unhappy home life had inflicted on him. Her aim was to try to help him untangle some of the dark threads of his childhood that were still trapping him.

She regarded Bruce as one of her most challenging patients. Rarely had she heard of such a total disregard for his own family than that of Albert Connors. Inside herself, when Bruce was struggling during sessions to talk about his father, Dr Hamilton had needed to call on all her professionalism again to prevent herself from comforting him with a hug or a soothing word. Her heart hurt for the damage that had been inflicted on Bruce, and her anger burned on behalf of the decent and honest man she saw seated in front of her who struggled to find the words to describe his broken childhood. She had seen these kinds of situations before, but never one of quite this magnitude.

Bruce found it almost as painful to write about his mother as it had been for his father. Rosa Connors had been a submissive wife in the main and had rarely stood up to Albert Conners' persistent bullying. For most of the time she had silently averted her eyes as her husband fondled daughter Sadie's friends or shouted aggressively at his sons. However, little Connie could do no wrong in her father's eyes. After all, she was the provider of pleasure for him several nights a week.

Rosa noticed Connie's increasing pallor and the way she would fall asleep at mealtimes. She worried about her youngest child but had no knowledge of the abuse that was taking place, excepting one occasion, when her suspicions were raised. When Rosa was shaking out Connie's crumpled winceyette nightdress before putting it in the boiling copper washtub for its fortnightly wash, she noticed that the back of it was damp and slightly sticky. She had no idea what the damp patch was all about, but her stomach nevertheless lurched inside her.

When Connie came in from school, swinging her satchel but pale and tired, Rosa gave her a drink and a freshly made jam tart, asked how school was and then broached the subject.

'Connie love, why would your nightie be damp and sticky? Did you have an accident?'

'No mammy' she said indignantly, 'I don't wet the bed any more. I'm *six!*' And she stamped her foot.

'Can you tell me how it was then?' asked her mother gently.

Connie averted her eyes, suddenly embarrassed.

'Come on, darling, you can tell your mummy can't you? I won't be cross.'

Connie hesitated.

'It might be sticky from the barley sugar Daddy gives me after… after…'

Rosa immediately went to her child and put her arms around her, trying to subdue the fear that was rising in her own chest as well as Connie's.

'After what, Connie love?'

'Daddy says it's our secret and I'm not to tell you.'

Suddenly she ran out of the room crying, 'Don't ask, Mummy, don't ask. It's Daddy's secret. I promised I wouldn't tell.'

Rosa did not question Connie further. She knew that to give her fear a voice, or to hear answers she could not cope with, meant that somehow the situation might became a reality and she would have to face her husband and challenge him. She was terrified of him and deeply feared his anger and the fallout from the discovery. Better the devil you know… but… this was her *daughter.*

Years later, Connie had related all this to Bruce. Bruce had never shared with his mother what he heard night after night coming from Great Aunt Elsie's bedroom. He thought it might kill her.

Bruce referred to his notes from years ago, and continued scribbling, the painful memories now tumbling over themselves to be expressed. He wrote down the deep anger he felt with his mother for not being brave enough to find a voice; how furious he was when his father bullied his mother and she did very little to retaliate; how he still couldn't accept that Sadie had gone for good, and most of all how his beloved brother James had been driven to take his own life because of his father's bullying and his mother's weakness, not to mention his own.

What a terrible mess.

Bruce came to the part in his notes which was most difficult of all to share. The pain and anguish which rose in him, just as it had when recounting James' death, threatened to block his memories and silence his pen. He forced himself recall how one warm summer's evening, he and his mother had been sitting on the concrete ground in the yard in the late sunshine, leaning their backs against the wall and drinking some of his mother's homemade lemonade. She bought fresh lemons from the market and made the lemonade for special occasions. This occasion was her birthday. She was to be forty.

It was a mellow time. The two seemed to have a special bond and understood each other without the need for words. Bruce was Rosa's godsend, sent from the angels, she used to say: her only son now.

Albert came swaying perilously into the garden from his workshop, clearly drunk.

'What's all this, then? You didn't tell me there was homemade lemonade, Rosa,' he slurred.

'You've had enough to drink as it is,' she said darkly.

'You didn't wish Mum a happy birthday either,' said Bruce. 'It's a special one, Dad, but you never remember. Why don't you? It makes her so unhappy.'

'Just listen to "Mummy's boy" talking!' sneered Albert as he lurched towards Bruce. 'Mind your own business, boy. What do you know about how she feels?'

'But Dad, it *is* my business,' he protested, finding a voice. 'She's my Mum.'

Albert raised his fist angrily to the boy, his face florid and twisted with drink,

'I said mind your own...'

In a flash Rosa was on her feet and putting herself between husband and son, arms held up in protest, just as Albert's fist came crashing down towards the boy. It punched Rosa hard in the stomach and she reeled backwards, hitting her head on the stone wall as she fell.

'See what you've done now, you stupid boy,' said Albert in a fury. 'Caused your mother to fall because you don't know how to keep your big mouth shut.'

Albert knelt beside Rosa, whose head was bleeding copiously.

'Well don't just stand there — get a cloth Bruce. Can't you see your mother's hurt?'

'Don't worry, Brucey,' said Rosa weakly, as she saw her son's frightened eyes. 'A little blood goes a long way. I'm sure it's not as bad as it looks.'

'You should learn not to interfere,' said Albert angrily to his son. He put an arm around Rosa and spoke more gently. 'I never meant to hurt you, love. You got in the way, you silly woman.' He put his hand on her knee and patted it. She pushed it away.

Rosa leaned her head against the wall. The initial sharp pain was beginning to subside into a deep throb. Bruce ran back with a piece of moistened lint and held it on the wound.

'All right, Brucey. Thank you, lad. Don't worry,' Rosa whispered. It's nothing that a sit-down won't cure. Now run along and call Connie for supper. I'll be fine in a minute.'

Albert helped Rosa to her feet and in a few minutes she was inside and slowly preparing supper. Albert, subdued, helped her lay the table. He was a hard, bullying and often unkind man but he hadn't meant to hit Rosa on this occasion — especially not on her birthday. He loved her in his own rough-hewn fashion.

They all had the usual plain supper, but afterwards Rosa produced a homemade chocolate birthday cake covered in butter icing and chocolate buttons which she cut into slices for the family. Connie devoured her slice eagerly, and asked for another one, but Bruce had lost his appetite from the afternoon's events. He noticed that throughout the meal his mother repeatedly put her hand on her forehead. She was in pain, he knew, and she hardly ate anything, but Rosa never ever made a fuss.

The next morning she stayed in her dressing gown to prepare breakfast, which was unusual. She was generally up at the crack of dawn, fully dressed and doing the chores.

'Mum, are you all right?' asked Bruce as he kissed her good morning.

'I've got a bit of a headache, son. That's all.'

Rosa slowly, slowly turned the eggs in the frying pan and carried them to the table. The next minute, without warning, she slumped by her chair and onto the floor and began shaking violently, her eyes rolling.

'Mummy, Mummy' stop it,' yelled Connie. 'Mummy!'

'Don't worry Mum, I'll run for the doctor', reassured Bruce, inwardly terrified. 'Connie. Stay there.'

Connie was left on guard to watch over her shaking mother. Very soon, puffing but pale, Bruce was back and ran upstairs to wake his father from his drunken hangover. Albert stumbled to his feet, dragged his trousers on and somehow staggered down the stairs calling, 'Rosa! Rosa! I'm coming, love.'

The three of them crouched around Rosa, trying to hold her shaking limbs steady. Albert wept over her. They remained there for minutes, frozen and silent with fear, until the doctor arrived.

Breathing rapidly, Bruce related to the doctor how his mother had banged her head the previous evening. The doctor looked very serious, pronounced she had suffered a seizure, and phoned for an ambulance.

'How did it happen?' the doctor enquired of Albert while they were waiting for the ambulance.

Albert shuffled and shrugged his shoulders, avoiding eye contact with the doctor.

'One minute she was standing up and the next minute she'd fallen.'

'Do *you* know how it happened, young man?' the doctor asked Bruce.

His father stared menacingly at him.

'No, doctor,' whispered Bruce, the colour rushing back into his cheeks. 'No, I don't.'

For once Connie was totally silent as she nervously twisted the hem of her dress. The doctor drew his own conclusion. He knew the violence of Albert Connors, but the family's conspiracy of silence was like an insurmountable barricade.

Rosa was carried out on a stretcher, leaving the children clinging to each other while Albert stumbled up the ambulance steps. She never reached the hospital but suffered a massive brain haemorrhage from her head injury. Despite the efforts of the ambulance crew Rosa was pronounced dead on arrival.

"My Mum's death affected me deeply" were Bruce's final words on his notes. Dr Hamilton read them and said out loud,

'And that — is the understatement of the year.'

## *Chapter 11*

Oliver Lockwood had spent several days mulling over what the bishop had said, reflecting on it, praying, and trying to decide whether he should resign his post as theatre Chaplain. He loved the work and was grateful to find he was suited to it. Several students had turned to him for pastoral advice, while other showed a real interest in exploring faith issues further. His weekly Agnostics Anonymous Group was usually full even though they were initially held during the intensive rehearsal period before the show went up. ("Went up". Oliver had fast learned the language of the theatre). He changed the meetings from the evenings to early morning — eight a.m. to be precise — and much to his surprise and delight more than a dozen folk turned up regularly.

The theatre chapel was full to bursting every Sunday morning now. Oliver knew he had found his calling in this setting. He was honest with the actors about the problems of faith, never ducked any difficult questions, and became admired throughout the company for his honesty and integrity.

He had deliberately avoided all contact with Clara, despite burning to see her again. He knew what the bishop said about not allowing himself to get into any compromising situations was right. He had not set eyes on her more than fleetingly in the distance for about four weeks since his visit to Bishop Hermes.

The opening night was in a week's time. He decided to allow himself to creep into the back of the stalls on the night that they took it to the stage (another phrase Oliver had learned).

Meanwhile, Clara continued to work tirelessly on her part and in rehearsals. She had a growing nausea and knew her body wasn't working normally — no monthly episodes now to worry about, thank goodness, nor the debilitating pain for twenty-four hours that usually accompanied them. She decided that the sickness was nerves and that her body's malfunctioning was because she had lost so much weight during rehearsals. Her mother had always told her that if the weight dropped off her the first thing that would disappear would be her "monthly curse". Her mother always liked her "well covered and bonny".

The week before opening night was a difficult one for Clara. She found that her body felt heavier than usual when she danced, and when trying on her costume for Maria, she noticed that she could barely do up the buttons of the bodice. Slowly the realisation dawned on her that she might be pregnant. She was horrified. But could it have happened from just one occasion? Surely not! She knew many women who waited months to conceive. She knew it could not be Bruce's.

So — it must be Oliver's.

Clara was appalled at the thought. She could not face even thinking about it, and every time the nauseous feelings rose in her throat, she lied to herself about the cause. Please God, *no*.

Four nights before the show found Oliver in the back row of the stalls, semi-hiding behind a pillar, but determined to see Clara without being seen himself. She performed well. It came to the song *I Feel Pretty* to which the choreographer had put vast amounts of upbeat dance. Clara had rehearsed it strenuously and mastered the routine with both a high degree of skill and artistry.

Quite suddenly, Clara felt on the point of collapse and rushed out into the wings.

'Sorry, sorry,' she waved to the conductor in the orchestra pit.

The conductor stopped the orchestra, baffled. This had never happened before, and Clara had always behaved with supreme professionalism. Nick raced up the side steps of the apron front stage and said to the cast with increasing panic,

'Anyone know what's the matter with her?'

One of the cast, Miranda, had already run offstage following Clara to see if she could help. She found Clara hanging over the sink, being violently sick.

'Oh you poor thing. Have you got a tummy bug? Or are you up the duff?' she asked, laughing. 'Come on, Clara. Quick as you can. You must get back on stage otherwise you'll kibosh everything.'

Clara grabbed some toilet tissue and wiped her mouth. She felt dreadful. Her legs seemed to cave in under her as she tried to walk.

'I — I can't yet. Give me a minute. Go and tell them I won't be long.'

Nick paced the stage nervously, the cast began chatting to each other, the musician started retuning and playing snatches of the music as they waited. Oliver just about resisted the temptation to rush down to the steps to see what the matter was with Clara.

Within a few minutes, Clara was back onstage, worryingly pale, but saying she was fine.

'Back to the top of the song, please,' said Nick. The conductor relayed the message to the musicians, who found the page again, and he raised his baton.

All seemed well, but just as they reached the second verse, Clara collapsed spectacularly, with a thud, centre stage. Oliver could not help himself. He rushed down, leapt onto the stage and knelt by Clara.

'Clara, Clara! Sweet one, what's the matter?' followed by his command 'Call an ambulance someone.'

'That won't be necessary,' said the stage manager in an ultra-calm voice. 'Clara's been overdoing it. She needs to rest. I suggest you put her understudy in, Nick, and let's call for her husband. Rev, can we get her to your room? It's quiet there. You'll keep an eye on her, won't you?'

Clara lay on Oliver's sofa, gradually recovering. Oliver stroked her head.

'Don't worry, Clara. It's nothing that a good night won't put right.'

'It is, Oliver,' she said in a whisper. 'I think I'm pregnant. '

\*\*\*

Bruce was at home in his workshop. He was beginning to establish a reputation with his instrumental repair business. Having inherited his father's carpentry gift, his studies in London on how to make and repair musical instruments was reaping its reward and he was finally making a decent-enough living from it. The morning he was called to the theatre found him counting horses' hairs from a tail that hung from a hook in the corner. He was about to re-hair a violin bow.

Bruce cursed the ring of the telephone at that moment. He had reached one hundred and ten in his counting and needed another eighty to ensure the violin bow was just the right weight and tension. He never ignored the telephone, however, because it was possible it might herald another commission.

'Is that Bruce Connors? Hello. It's the stage manager here. I don't wish to alarm you unduly but your wife has collapsed on stage during the rehearsal. She's come round now, but we think you should collect her. She's not feeling very well at all. She's resting in the chaplain's room now. Just follow the arrow at the main entrance.'

Bruce raced for his car keys, took them down from the hook, dropped them in his hurry, cursed, picked them up and drove his grey Ford Popular at top speed to the theatre. He parked, followed the arrow to the chaplain's room, knocked and waited.

Oliver came to the door, and the two worried men stood face to face in the doorway. Oliver wanted to avert his eyes as he looked into the honest blue ones that were gazing questioningly at him.

'Come in. You must be Bruce. I'm sure you've been worried by the message.'

'You're the Rev, aren't you? Clara has spoken of you often. Good to meet you.'

'Good to meet you too. I'm Oliver,' he replied, shaking hands with Bruce. He felt like Judas — a traitor, betraying Bruce not with a kiss but a handshake.

Clara was lying semi-curled on the sofa, with a plastic bowl poised on a small table beside her. She was very pale.

'Clara. Darling. You've really been overdoing it. What exactly is the trouble?'

Clara didn't look up.

'There's a sickness bug going round,' she whispered, not daring to look at Oliver. 'It would be just my luck to get it. I'm praying it will go quickly.'

'Let's hope so. I bet Nick is in a state.'

'He'll have to pull in the understudy,' said Clara.

'Come on now, Clara, think positively. These things can be over in twenty-four hours.'

Clara gave a furtive sidelong glance at Oliver, whose face was a picture of inscrutability.

'Thanks so much for holding the fort, Oliver. I'm sure Clara has been well looked after. Come on darling.' He held his hands to Clara and gently pulled her up. 'Let's get you home to bed.'

Clara looked at Oliver briefly. 'Thanks Oliver. I'll see you tomorrow.'

'I do hope so,' replied Oliver. 'And so does the rest of the cast.'

Bruce had to stop the car twice on the way home for Clara to be sick. There was nothing she could do to control the nausea that kept rising inside her. She had heard about morning sickness, but this had come on very suddenly, and seemed to be about every half an hour throughout the day.

*\*\**

'Shall I phone the doctor?' asked Bruce when they arrived home.

'No, no, *please* don't Bruce. Just let me rest upstairs. I'm sure it will pass soon.'

But it did not pass. Clara was up several times in the night, vomiting, and in the morning felt light-headed and dizzy. Bruce phoned the doctor without her knowing, asking him to come round and see his wife. He then phoned Nick.

'I'm very sorry, Nick, but Clara is unwell. There is no way she will be able to rehearse today.'

There was a long silence on the other end of the line. Finally, Nick spoke.

'If she doesn't come in today, I'll have to put her understudy in. It's the tech tomorrow and the dress the day after,' he said. 'In today, or I'm afraid it's out of the show.'

'She's mortified,' said Bruce.

'We all are,' replied Nick. 'Clara is irreplaceable in terms of her performance. But needs must. It's tough on us all.' Finally, grudgingly, he said, 'Give my best wishes to

Clara. Tell her to get well soon. Keep me posted, Ask her again if there's *any* chance she could make it for this afternoon.' The phone clicked down.

Doctor Spencer arrived quickly before his morning surgery; a pompous little man who knew everything and had a nasty habit of sucking his teeth when he was thinking. Bruce led him upstairs to Clara. Clara glared at Bruce, furious with him.

'I'll wait outside, Doctor. Clara, it's the right thing to have done. I'm sorry I went against what you wanted, but you're ill.'

The doctor asked Clara some questions, gave her a quick examination, felt her abdomen. He sat for a second, sucking his teeth.

'Clara, this is an extreme case of morning sickness. A few women can have it very violently. You're already dehydrated. You must drink lots because it won't go in five minutes.'

He sat on the edge of the bed, looking at her and sucking his teeth again.

'I didn't know you were pregnant.'

'Neither did I until yesterday,' said Clara weakly.

'Well its good news, isn't it? Your husband's sessions with the therapist I referred him to have obviously done wonders,' he said smugly. 'You've conceived very quickly considering he was only referred, what was it, two or three months ago? Very satisfying, very satisfying,' he muttered to himself. 'Dr Hamilton *will* be pleased, and I clearly did the right thing referring him,' he said. 'Now, come along to my clinic on Wednesdays and we'll set you up for the birth. A home birth would be…'

Clara grabbed him by the arm, startling him. 'Doctor Spencer, please don't say anything to my husband. I want it to be — to be — a surprise.'

'Very well. Your secret is safe with me,' he smiled patronizingly.

The doctor met Bruce on the landing and gave him a knowing pat on the back. 'Not to worry, Bruce. She'll be fine. But she has a bad dose of sickness, so no treading the boards, I'm afraid. But well done, well done, my boy. Didn't take you long to sow the seed!' he laughed.

'Sow the seed?'

'Er — sow the seed of doubt — in the director's mind,' he said, flustered. 'You said you phoned him, didn't you?'

'Yes, poor fellow. It really has left him in the lurch.'

'All for a good cause,' the doctor replied. 'Keep me posted Bruce.'

Bruce shut the door, perplexed by the doctor's strange remarks. He went up to the bedroom, but Clara was feigning a deep sleep. Bruce crept out and went to the corner shop to buy his wife some flowers.

\*\*\*

Bruce was due for another session with his therapist that afternoon but assumed he would cancel it to care for his wife. He put the flowers in a vase and crept into Clara's bedroom. Clara was sitting leaning against the pillow looking fragile. Bruce sat on the edge of the bed.

'How are you now, Clara?'

'No worse, thank you. I'll be in for rehearsals tomorrow whatever happens. Thank you for the flowers.'

'It's a bit of a paltry selection at the corner shop, but they're just to say, "I love you",' said Bruce.

'Bruce, isn't it your session with Dr Hamilton today? You must go. I'm OK. I've got everything I need, and I just want to sleep now.'

'If you're sure,' replied Bruce. 'But I'm happy to cancel.'

'No. Go,' replied Clara, longing for some space to process the enormity of what was happening to her.

She lay back and tried to fathom out what her next step would be, but nausea and fatigue overwhelmed her and in between bouts of vomiting, she slept deeply.

\*\*\*

'Bruce, what you have shared with me so far is very helpful,' said Dr Hamilton, moving from her desk to sit a close but comfortable distance from him. 'It is also very brave. I think we may be able to move on soon to some practical therapy. It will be aimed at helping you to manage your feelings about your father. I think that will be the key to supporting you and eventually freeing you up in your marriage.'

She avoided saying the word "impotence" again. It had been quite enough of a shock for Bruce to hear the word the first time, without her repeating it.

'Bruce, let's explore a little about what happened after your mother died, and the effect it had on you and the family. Are you happy to share your feelings about that?'

Bruce had already discovered that talking to Dr Hamilton about his father had helped him to shed a little of the stress of his childhood
memories.

'Yes of course,' he replied.

'What about Sadie, for example?'

'Sadie, my oldest sister, did not appear for my mother's funeral, I am sure that if she had heard my mother had died, she would have come. She and Mum loved each other very much, and there wasn't a day that passed without my mother wondering what had happened to her beloved eldest daughter. She had spent a lot of time trying to track Sadie down, pursuing various leads down various avenues of enquiry, only to draw a blank. Dad never bothered. He didn't seem to care.'

Bruce continued, finding that the words began to flow as if releasing him in some way.

'I lived with my father until I was sixteen. Poor Connie had five more years of him than I did. But I didn't worry much on the abuse front. My father withdrew more and more from us after my mother died, ignoring me and hardly looking at Connie apart from when she served him with a meal. Then he managed to murmur his thanks. But generally, he barely communicated. He didn't eat his meals with us but took them up to his workshop. He blamed me for Mum's death, saying if I hadn't interfered she would still be alive. He didn't acknowledge in any way that he was instrumental in it.'

'More than instrumental I would say,' said Dr Hamilton, sounding unusually accusatory.

'How did that make you feel, Bruce?'

'Wretched. Wretched and humiliated and desperate.'

'Desperate?'

'I thought seriously of doing what James had done, then I realised that Connie would be left all on her own with just my father. I just couldn't do it to her. Who knows what would have happened then?'

'How was Connie in all of this?'

'Connie.' Bruce's face crumpled and Dr Hamilton thought that he was about to break down. He thought of innocent, sweet-natured Connie, clutching her doll, confused and silent when the rest of the family returned from the funeral.

'I took Connie's mattress into my room and from then on she slept there where I could watch over her. My father didn't comment. I think he knew I had worked out what he did with Connie and was frightened I would make trouble for him — or maybe he just lost all his urges after Mum died. I don't know. Connie never cried over Mum, but every night, she would suck the material of my mother's winceyette nightdress and use it as a comforter — even into her teens.'

Bruce stopped and gulped before he could continue.

'She became very quiet and I noticed that she had deep pinch marks and scars up her arms that sometimes bled. She was doing it to herself. When I commented on them, she became angry and defensive, telling me to mind my own business. She seemed very depressed. She stopped eating and grew very thin. The school tried to contact my father about it but he never once responded. I think he had blotted her out of his existence, just like he had Sadie.'

Bruce stopped again, gulped down some water, then continued.

'I knew Connie was in a bad way. I felt instinctively she was ashamed of what had gone on, but whenever I hinted at it, she would become silent and the colour would drain from her face. She became wafer thin. I couldn't reach her at all in those days. I felt I had lost both my sisters as well as my mother, Dr Hamilton.'

Bruce paused.

'Connie had the sweetest temperament. Mum always said she came straight from heaven. She would have gone into Dad's when she was little because she thought she was being kind.'

Bruce rubbed his eyes furiously. Dr Hamilton refilled his glass of water, then waited.

'Connie left home at fifteen and she was employed straight away by a wealthy family and is now a nanny to four children. It's very sad, Dr Hamilton, because she was such a bright girl and she's a shadow now.'

'Children who are abused can appear to diminish,' said Dr Hamilton. 'We are just beginning to understand exactly what effect this all has on them — for life. It sounds as though your father has damaged your sister rather severely,' reflected Doctor Hamilton.

'Definitely,' replied Bruce. 'I see Connie quite often,' continued Bruce. 'She comes to our house. Clara is nice to her,' he said warmly. 'Clara doesn't want any children (thankfully, in view of my — er — problem), but she is maternal towards Connie. I'm so grateful to her.'

'It's lovely that she can regard you both as her friends,' said Dr Hamilton. 'A haven. And your father?'

'I've no idea,' replied Bruce. 'Great Aunt Edith provided a base for me in her home. She was crippled with arthritis and seemed glad to give me a bed in return for some help with things she couldn't do around the house. I heard my father sold our house but I really don't know any more than that. Nor I don't want to.'

The session ended with Dr Hamilton suggesting that at the following session they would talk about various practical strategies and exercises to help Bruce.

When Bruce had left, Sonia Hamilton lay her head on the desk, silently acknowledging the despair she felt when realising afresh that one man had very nearly destroyed the emotional well-being and happiness of his entire family.

She admired Bruce fulsomely for his honesty and the essential kindness she saw in the man. How he had managed to survive such a terrifying childhood was a miracle to her. She had never heard of a case quite like that of the Connors.

## *Chapter 12*

The show proceeded without its leading lady, who was pronounced "indisposed".

Oliver could not bear to go to a performance. He blamed himself and his lack of self-control for every single aspect of the current situation. It would be impossible for him to listen to a substitute Maria singing *There's a Place for Us*. For the first time in his adult life he lied, saying to Nick that the production was marvellous and that the understudy for Maria was remarkable, considering the shortness of notice for her. It seemed no one had noticed his absence, thankfully.

He could not stop thinking about Clara. She had looked so delicate, so wan, so beautiful on his sofa, even though she was poorly. He had wanted to take her in his arms, just him, Clara and their unborn child and tell her everything would be all right. The fact was that he loved her deeply, but the reality was that he had caused her to drop out of what in essence was her lifetime's ambition. In addition he had shaken hands with her husband, liking him instantly, which made his own betrayal even harder to live with and he had created a new life through an adulterous relationship, breaking every rule in the church's book, let alone in his own moral code.

Oliver tried to turn to prayer, to hand the situation over to God, and work out what to do from there on in, but prayer wouldn't come, nor was God going to give him easy answers, it seemed. What he did know was that he would have to resign as theatre Chaplain and ask the bishop to defrock him, or, put another way, to dismiss him "from his clerical state". He knew that in the days of the medieval church any defrocking took place publicly. Oliver felt he would have embraced that. He had broken the sixth commandment and he needed to be publicly admonished.

He also knew it was a case of "once a priest, always a priest". That had come through with great clarity at his ordination. So where did that leave him? He had an urgent, burning need to see Clara. The day after the last performance he phoned Bruce.

'How is she, Bruce?'

'It's strange,' said Bruce. 'This thing doesn't seem to be clearing up. I'm very worried about her. She's not eating and she's only drinking thimblefuls of fluid. I think part of it is her grief at not being able to do the show. She will be hospitalized if it goes on much longer.'

'Could I come and see her?'

'I'm sure she'd like that,' said Bruce. 'Just for a little while. She's very weak. She just can't stop throwing up.'

'I won't stay long. When would be convenient?'

'I must take my car to the garage tomorrow morning. I'm reluctant to leave her on her own for long, but if you were to come then, perhaps I could whizz out and get it sorted?'

'Perfect,' replied Oliver, and he meant it. He could not face the idea either of Bruce being in the room while he visited Clara, or, perhaps even worse, having furtive conversations with her when Bruce was downstairs.

'What time?' asked Oliver.

'Two o'clock?'

'I'll be there.'

'Lovely. Thanks.'

Bruce did not tell Clara that Oliver was coming. *That'll be a nice surprise for her,* he thought.

The next day, near noon, Clara got up, was sick, then had a long bath and washed her hair. Whenever she cleaned her teeth, she vomited. The sickness was making her feel unclean. She could hardly find the energy to massage the shampoo into her scalp, let alone take trouble to comb her hair into a decent shape, so she quickly scraped it up into a pony tail out of the way, as she had done as a child, tying it roughly with an elastic band.

'How come you look more beautiful than ever when you are ill?' commented Bruce. 'I love your hair up like that. You should tie it back more often. Shows off your high cheekbones — makes you look about fifteen!'

Clara dressed in casual clothes and went downstairs to eat some dry toast and curl up in front of the fire. She felt marginally better dressed than languishing in bed, although the sickness had not subsided. Midas was wild with joy. Clara had not been downstairs for two days and had not even wanted him on her bed. His tail wagged furiously.

'All right boy. I know. Bruce will take you out soon.' Clara stroked him and Midas put his front paws on her chest.

'Ow. No. That's sore. Down, Midas!' *Another reminder, as if she hadn't enough already,* she thought, as she felt her swelling breasts.

At two o'clock the doorbell rang.

'Whoever it is, I'm not around,' she said, scuttling back upstairs. 'I can't face anyone, Bruce. You must get rid of them'.

Oliver came into the hall. Bruce sshed him with a finger on his lips and went upstairs to Clara.

'Now Clara,' he said with a smile. 'I know you said no visitors, but I think you'll agree that this one is an exception.'

He beckoned to Oliver to come in.

'I'll be back in a bit,' said Bruce, kissing his wife as he went.

Clara immediately hid her face under the bedclothes.

'Clara, Clara, sweet one. I'm so, so sorry about everything.' He gently pulled the bedclothes off her face. 'What are we going to do?'

Clara pushed rogue strands of hair back from her face.

'I'll have to get rid of it.'

There was a long silence.

'Clara, please. There must be another way. We can't just destroy a life.'

'Can't we?' replied Clara. 'I just don't want it, and I will never be able to tell Bruce I'm pregnant, anyway. I'm amazed he hasn't guessed. It just shows the level of trust

145

he has in me that it obviously hasn't even crossed his mind.'

'It's a dreadful situation,' said Oliver. 'I feel so wretched — for you, for Bruce, for the — the baby — *our* baby.'

'Don't!' said Clara loudly. 'This is not a *baby.* This is a seed. No bigger than something you might plant. Some take root and some die.'

Oliver was reminded of the parable of the sower. "And some fall on stony ground, while some fall on good ground and they thrive and grow to full height". 'Clara, your baby will thrive and grow and be wonderful because it will have *you* as a mother.'

'I'm not cut out to be a mother,' replied Clara. 'I've never wanted children. And anyway, what about the *father?* This isn't fiction, Oliver. The fact is that I *will not* leave Bruce, not even — for — for you.' Suddenly she softened and whispered, 'Even though I love you.'

'And I love you. And the fruit of this illicit love is our baby.'

Suddenly, Clara rose and found her inner strength.

'Don't keep personalising this foetus, Oliver. It's ten weeks at the most. I can go to someone for an abortion.'

'It's not safe, Clara. It's not legal. At least, not yet.'

'It is in Iceland. A girl at school went over when she was fourteen. It was very hush-hush, but she had it done and when she came back everyone…'

'Clara, Clara. *Stop.*'

They sat in silence, both wrapped in their individual misery.

Finally, Oliver said, 'Clara, we must tell Bruce. He is the wronged party, and he should have a say. Should we tell him together when he gets home?'

'*No*' shouted Clara. 'I couldn't bear it. He will be crucified.'

Oliver had the common sense not to comment on her use of the word.

'I'll tell him when we are on our own and then I'll write to you about my decision. It is *my* decision, because it's *my* body, Oliver.'

She took his hand, seeing his broken face.

'There's no way we could keep this child. I can't leave Bruce, you are not able to be with me, and Oliver, I just don't want it. It's interrupted my career as it is. I am heartbroken about not playing Maria.'

'I know,' said Oliver sadly. He looked at her and sensed the thread of steel running through her. He knew that if she set her mind to it, she would find a way to terminate the pregnancy.

'How is the sickness, Clara? Any better at all?'

'No better. The doctor said I have a very bad form of it. It sometimes happens apparently. Hyperemesis it's called. This type can go on for months. Just my luck. Another reason not to delay.'

'I can see the decision is yours,' Oliver said reluctantly. 'I have no rights in all of this. I am totally the guilty party.'

'Not quite,' said Clara. 'Remember?'

How could he forget? The beautiful encounter, the body of this ravishing woman, the feeling of cherishing, and for a little while, being cherished, the utter sense of fulfilment, all too brief, but memorable for a lifetime.

He put his arms round her. 'You are exquisite, Clara. I don't know how to survive without you. These past few weeks have been terrible.' He paused. 'How can a love like ours be so wrong?'

'There's a song there,' said Clara, as she tucked herself more deeply into his arms. 'And you're going to say, "Also a big theological question".' They both laughed.

They heard Bruce's key in the door.

'Hi darling. I'm back. I've got you some Lucozade and some Turkish delight. Your favourites — just in case you feel like eating something.'

Oliver and Clara let go of each other and both felt each other's despair at the impossibility of the situation.

'Oh, hello Oliver. I saw your bike was outside. Glad you're still here and have kept Clara company. I knew she'd be pleased to see you.'

'Actually, I must go,' said Oliver quickly. 'There's a show post-mortem with the cast that I ought to be at. I'll give them all your love, shall I, Clara?'

'Yes please. Bye Oliver,' she said weakly.

He stood in the doorway and blew her the briefest of kisses.

With that he pounded down the stairs, two at a time, gave Midas a brief pat, opened the front door, and was gone.

# *Chapter 13*

The phone rang at eleven the next morning. Bruce had just taken Clara up some dry toast and tea and had picked a red rose from the garden to put on her tray.

He ran back downstairs to answer it.

'Hello, Bruce Connors here.'

'Bruce.' Silence. Then a woman's voice said rather coolly, 'I think I may have been working under false assumptions.'

Dr Hamilton.

'Sorry,' Bruce replied, 'I'm not quite sure I follow you.'

'No, on the contrary, I clearly wasn't following *you*,' she replied. 'But I hear congratulations are in order.'

'Congratulations?'

'Yes. I have heard your good news from a reliable source, Bruce. I'm glad you were able to — rectify the problem, although I would have appreciated your telling me face to face, Bruce. I feel I've been working under slightly false assumptions about your...'

Still Bruce did not understand.

'Anyway, well done on the pregnancy! That's very good news and I'm delighted for you.'

Bruce was silent, stunned to the core. Suddenly, the scales fell away from his eyes and in one fell swoop he realised the reason for Clara's sickness and her secretive attitude lately.

'Yes,' he replied in a muted whisper.

'Are you all right, Bruce? You don't sound very pleased. I don't know whether you want to continue our sessions. I'd say it was "mission accomplished" as far as the impotence is concerned, wouldn't you?'

'Er, yes, no, well…' Bruce could not think straight. 'Thank you, Dr Hamilton. You've been very helpful.'

'Good,' she replied. 'You may have achieved your objective, so to speak, but you still need to deal with the issues of your past, Bruce. One pregnancy doesn't wipe your history away, and you will want to be the best father you can be. I doubt very much you would follow your father's pattern of violence and abuse, in fact, I know you wouldn't, but you never know how your childhood experiences will inform your own ability to be a good father.'

'No, yes, no, I mean I'm sure you're right.' Bruce had no idea what he was saying. 'Thank you again.'

'Bruce, are you sure you are all right?'

'Yes, thanks.'

'My door is always open Bruce. Come back if you need to.'

He put the phone down. Dr Hamilton sat staring at receiver the other end. She was perplexed by Bruce's reaction and decided another call to Dr Spencer might be in order.

Bruce's head was in a whirl. He grabbed his coat from the hook, called Midas, put his lead on and slammed the door without saying goodbye to Clara. He and Midas headed for — Bruce knew not where — but the dog looked up delightedly, his tail wagging furiously. This was certainly an unscheduled walk!

They both walked and walked. Every so often Midas would look up at Bruce happily, blissfully unaware of the turmoil in his master's head. At first, Bruce could think of nothing. He felt stupid and a fool for not realising that Clara's sickness was due to early pregnancy. He knew it was impossible for the child to be his, telling himself angrily that he was impotent, impotent, *impotent*. He made the word sound like a punishment, self-flagellation. He hated himself.

When he eventually began to think more clearly, he acknowledged, as he had done throughout his marriage, that Clara had been seriously deprived of marital happiness in bed. Again and again she had eventually turned away in disappointment as he, Bruce, failed her. He realised that she must have felt desperate within herself for physical fulfilment. Decent man that he was, Bruce began to make excuses in his mind for her infidelity. All he knew was that despite everything, he did not want to lose her.

He wished it had been he who had fathered this child. He would have loved it dearly and he felt jealousy for whoever had had the luxury of planting his seed within Clara and making a baby. But who could it have been? Bruce would confront Clara, but first he needed a few clues. He decided that it must be someone she had been working with in the company. He knew theatre folk became very bonded together when focussed on rehearsals with a performance outcome. A member of the cast? The musical director? After all, Matt was personable, quite nice looking, and Clara spoke warmly of his skills in bringing a song to life. Perhaps closeness had tipped over into physical encounter?

And how many times had the two of them made love for a baby to be conceived? This new thought appalled Bruce as it struck him that Clara had clearly been living a double life for some time.

His mind continued whirling. He decided to go and see the chaplain, Oliver. He would share in confidence about Clara and see if Oliver could shed any light on it if he had observed anything. Bruce hailed a taxi, checked that Midas was allowed in, and asked for the theatre. Twenty minutes later he was tying up Midas outside when a couple of the students saw him.

'Oh he's *so* lovely,' said one, bending over and stroking the delighted dog. 'We'll look after him. Don't tie him up. What are they doing to you, darling?' she said to Midas in a baby voice.

'You're Clara's husband, aren't you? So sorry to hear how ill she is,' said another. 'We'll take the dog to the sitting room if that's OK with you and give him a drink. You'll find the Rev down the corridor and first left.'

'Thanks,' replied Bruce with a forced smile. 'That'll help. He hates being left on his own — barks the place down. Now Midas, be on your best behaviour.'

Midas trotted off, tail wagging furiously. Bruce made for the chaplain's room and knocked. Oliver opened the door and looked shocked, and then recovered himself.

'Cup of tea? Or coffee? How's Clara? How can I help, Bruce?'

'Clara's not well. Still very sick. That's what I wanted to talk to you about, in total confidence. It's — er — complicated. But I know I can trust you, Rev, because of everything you stand for.'

Oliver looked down.

Bruce slowly and bravely began to explain about his impotence, how he knew he had let Clara down in this area, how they had finally both settled for less and had found a kind of contentment latterly. He explained that Clara was pregnant, and then paused.

'You see, I have no idea who the father is. I need to know.'

Oliver avoided Bruce's blue, troubled, anxious eyes and looked down. There was a long silence.

'Can you shed any light on things at all? Do you know who she is particularly close to in the company? I *must* know,' appealed Bruce.

'Bruce,' replied Oliver eventually in a voice shot through with anguish. 'I am so sorry, so sorry.' Oliver's face crumpled in pain.

For a few seconds Bruce was perplexed and then suddenly stunned as the truth hit him.

'*What? You?*' The realization seared his heart.

Oliver nodded slowly, not looking up.

A fierce volcano erupted in Bruce. He suddenly grabbed Oliver round the throat and shook him violently. Oliver went puce in the face and started choking and gasping for breath. Still Bruce went on and on, his hands

153

growing tighter, with the shaking becoming increasingly violent. In that moment, he could have continued until he killed Oliver.

Quite suddenly he had the image of his father doing the same to his brother James. He had once witnessed an ugly scene between the two of them — the bullying, violent father and the cowering choking boy. Bruce released his grip immediately. Oliver bent over, coughing and spluttering, his neck bright red from Bruce's hands.

Bruce sat with his head in his hands, deeply shaken, and ashamed of the violent act that he had perpetrated and at the same time shocked to the core by the news. Finally, Oliver recovered enough to speak in a broken voice,

'What can I do to make amends? Is there anything at all?'

'You can tell me how many times, for a start,' replied Bruce, haunted by the thought that this might be a well-established affair and he would lose Clara forever.

'Once,' replied Oliver quietly. 'Just the once, I swear it. We both realised we had been very wrong and have kept out of each other's way ever since.'

'So this pregnancy is the result of one solitary time?'

'I swear it,' said Oliver, grabbing his Bible, 'I swear it on the Bible.'

'I came to you because I thought you were an honourable man,' said Bruce. 'I thought I could trust a clergyman, but now I see you're no better than anyone else,' he said bitterly.

'No, I'm worse than anyone else,' Oliver said quietly.

'I don't know what to do,' said Bruce, and quite suddenly started shaking violently and sobbing.

Oliver went up to Bruce and knelt in front of him.

'I am asking from my heart for you to forgive me, Bruce, and then maybe we might find a way ahead.'

'Do you love Clara?'

'She is an extraordinary human being.'

'That's not what I asked.'

'She's not hard to love, is she, Bruce?'

Bruce thought about Clara, her laugh, her vibrancy, her beauty, her teasing, her talent, her kindness towards his sister Connie, her — everything.

'She belongs to you, Bruce. She was forbidden fruit for me. I had no right. I know how much she loves you.'

'Does she?' Bruce wondered.

'Yes, she does. She has told me so. She never transferred her loyalty, Bruce. It just — happened. Neither of us planned it or expected it and both of us regretted it.'

'She needed release, I suppose. I can't blame her. But I *do* blame you.' The fire of anger was beginning to grow in his belly again.

'I suppose it was wonderful, was it? Something I have never been able to do for her.'

Now he spoke bitterly. Oliver said nothing. There was nothing to say. Yes, it had been wonderful, until the guilt set in. Finally, he said,

'Where do we go from here?'

'Clara wants to terminate the pregnancy,' said Bruce.

'Do you want her to?'

'It's not for me to say. I really don't come into it any more.'

'Don't you?' said Oliver.

Bruce turned to go, his hands on the door handle.

'Well, at least you have been honest with me,' he said. 'I suppose you could have denied any knowledge of it.' He looked at the marks, livid red, on Oliver's neck and felt ashamed.

'I shouldn't have been so violent.'

'I deserved it and more,' replied Oliver.

With that, Bruce left, collecting a delighted Midas on his way, and decided to walk home. He knew his thoughts needed processing and putting into order. Clara would be worried about him, but he couldn't help that, and for once he didn't care.

\*\*\*

Clara was indeed worried. Bruce had left without saying goodbye. She couldn't remember a time when he had not come up to her wherever she was in the house and given her a hug and a kiss as he was leaving. And the door slamming? What was that all about?

Panic began to take root as she wondered, with growing alarm if Bruce guessed about the pregnancy. *About time,* she thought, with the sickness and the tiredness that had incapacitated her for the last week. She intended to tell him very soon, but in an ordered way, at the right moment, (whenever that was).

She decided to go to the corner shop to buy food to make Bruce a decent supper for once. He had been so considerate all the time she had been ill. Nothing had been too much trouble, and she knew he had a backlog of work to catch up on as she had needed so much of his time. He was an unselfish man and she knew she didn't deserve him. Feeling incredibly weak as she walked the hundred yards or so, she scooped up some fresh food and limped back, staying near the wall. She had to rush to the sink immediately to be violently sick as soon as she was home, but at least she had made it to the shop and back. That was a result.

As the day progressed, Clara became increasingly anxious. Bruce had been out since breakfast time, and it was now five-thirty. He had taken the dog, so it couldn't have been a work issue. She started to prepare a shepherd's pie, eventually hearing Bruce's key in the lock. Midas came bounding in, practically throwing himself at Clara with joy, and then rushed to his water bowl. Bruce went straight to his workshop without acknowledging Clara, and there he sat in the darkening room.

Clara by this time was almost certain that somehow Bruce now knew about the pregnancy. Heart racing, she gently tapped on his workshop door, bracing herself for some sort of confrontation. Normally, she would have gone straight in and immediately launched into how her day had been. Bruce would stand there listening patiently, interjecting comments at the right moment. Only after she had blurted out everything would she remember to ask how his day had gone. It was always almost an afterthought. How selfish her behaviour was and how much she just did not deserve him began to dawn on her for the first time in their married life.

There was no answer from Bruce, so Clara pushed the door ajar.

'Bruce, Brucey, where have you been? I've been worried about you. It's late, and you didn't say goodbye this morning and now you've come straight in here. What's the matter?'

Bruce finally turned to look at Clara and she immediately saw that his face was contorted with pain and anger.

'How dare you ask what's the matter, Clara? You know very well,' he shouted, clenching his fists.

'I don't, Bruce. What is it?'

Something about her feigned innocence made him snap inside for the second time in the day. He looked as if he was going to hit her, but instead furiously picked up the violin bow he had been working on and smashed it in two over his knee and then pulled the horse's tail viciously from its hook, hurling it on the floor and stamping it furiously with his foot. He looked threateningly at Clara; his fists clenched.

'I *know,*' he said fiercely. 'I *know* and I have been speaking with the *father.*' He spat the last word out as if it was poisoning his mouth.

Clara sank to the floor. She was terrified of this sudden and rare display of violence and hid her face, cowering. Finally Bruce unclenched his fists and stood with arms akimbo, staring at Clara. Finally, she spoke.

'Bruce, I've been thinking how I could possibly tell you,' she said softly.

'I'm going to get rid of it, Brucey. I'm looking into it. I've found someone who will do it. I'm sorry, so, so sorry,' she said, sobbing. 'I swear before God it was only once,'

*This is the second time God has been called upon today as a witness,* thought Bruce wryly. Neither spoke. The only sound in the workshop was Clara's quiet sobbing and Midas' scratching at the door to be let in. Bruce looked at his wife. He was struck by what a waif-like figure she cut now; straggling matted hair, face deathly pale, with tears making liquid pools down her face. Even amid this desperation, Bruce's heart was stirred and he had an overwhelming urge to protect her and make her better. He suddenly had a vivid picture of how he had gone up to his weeping mother and taken her hand at the graveside when James was being buried. Clara was broken now and weeping and she needed his comfort.

He slowly went across to her, knelt and put his arms round her. He said nothing, but gently wiped her face with a precious piece of cloth that up to now was used solely to polish the costliest violins in his care. Clara sobbed deeply on his shoulder. They said nothing for several minutes. Midas, as if sensing the situation, stopped scratching the door and lay down on the rug outside quietly whimpering.

Finally, Bruce let her go.

'I've made you some supper,' Clara whispered.

'I'm not hungry,' replied Bruce. 'But thank you all the same. Save it for tomorrow.'

Clara went up to bed and lay there in the darkness, her head in turmoil and her stomach heaving with nausea. Bruce followed soon afterwards and they both fell asleep immediately, exhausted.

Neither had any idea how to shape the future.

# *Chapter 14*

The following morning, Bruce knew he urgently needed to talk to someone about the situation before Clara took the action she had outlined to him. He thought of Dr Hamilton, but after her cool tones on the telephone, he was disinclined to approach her. He hadn't liked Dr Spencer's innuendos either, even though at the time he had not appreciated their implication. He longed with a sudden deep pain for his mother's gentle touch and wisdom. She would have known what he should do.

Then he thought of Connie.

Connie lived a twenty-minute walk away. She was housekeeper to a large and noisy family with four children. Three of them would be at school. Connie looked after the baby throughout the day while his wealthy parents, the Rotherham's, were busy building their business empire, leaving most of the child care to Connie, who was overworked and underpaid.

Bruce decided he would confide in his younger sister. They had always been close, and Connie loved both Bruce and Clara, sometimes spending her days off in their house, taking delight in cleaning it from top to bottom. Bruce knew that Connie would find the news that Clara's baby was fathered by a priest very hard indeed to take. She had become a devout Catholic and held the priesthood in high esteem.

Bruce said goodbye to his wife, kissing her briefly this time and telling her he was going to see Connie. Clara knew Bruce would talk things over with her and was certain she could rely on Connie to take a loving approach to things, even though she would be appalled by the news and shocked by her adultery. Connie and she had a surprisingly close bond, considering they were opposites in personality. There was a kind of purity about Connie and Clara felt she was letting her down.

Bruce mounted the stone steps to the grand front door. The house was imposing and he suddenly felt nervous. This was going to be difficult. Connie opened the door and there she was, his little sister with a baby boy perched on her left hip, who was gurgling happily and waved his hands in the air excitedly at the visitor. Bruce noticed immediately that Connie's face, still pretty and young, was drawn and tired and very thin. Her sleeves were rolled up beyond her elbows and he saw the old scars from her self-harming all those years ago. Her fairish hair was parted in the centre, with a children's hair slide securing it on each side to keep it out of her eyes and stop Henry from pulling it. Dressed in a faded floral overall over a flimsy skirt, Connie looked a pathetic specimen of a young woman,

'Bruce!' Connie squealed delightedly. 'How lovely! This is a rare thing. Come in.'

She led him into a colourful nursery, the walls of which sported lively animal wallpaper. There was an orange carpet on the floor, which was littered with expensive toys, and an almost empty feeding bottle gently dripped the residue of its milk onto the carpet. A used nappy was in the corner and a half empty mug of tea perched precariously on the edge of the sideboard with a biscuit lying untouched by its side. Bruce had the distinct impression that Connie was only just coping.

Connie put the baby in his playpen, gave him a few toys and the biscuit saying, 'There you are, Henry, have my biscuit. Now let Uncle Bruce and I have a little time.' The obliging baby began crumbling the biscuit in his fingers before stuffing it in his mouth with the palms of his hands.

Connie looked hard at Bruce. She noticed how set his jaw was and his general demeanour of sadness. He was also looking unkempt and unshaven, which was not like him, but she did not comment.

'Cup of tea, Brucey?'

'Yes please Connie'.

Connie went to the kitchen so Bruce knelt and talked to Henry. The baby, who seemed permanently good-natured, smiled at him and offered him a small wedge of damp, half-chewed biscuit.

'Thank you Henry. What a kind boy you are!' said Bruce, breaking finally into a smile and pretending to eat the soggy biscuit noisily. Henry creased up his face and laughed with delight.

'You're a natural, Brucey' said Connie re-entering the room. 'Look at how Henry is responding to you!'

Plucking up her courage she asked the question she had been longing to ask for a long time now.

'Brucey, when are we going to see a little baby Connors then? I'm longing to be an Auntie.'

Bruce said nothing but looked down and picked up a non-existent crumb from the carpet. Connie quickly sensed his distress and changed the subject rapidly.

'Now Bruce, to what do I owe this pleasure?' she said handing him his tea and bobbing a playful curtsey.

'I need to talk to someone, Connie, and I thought of you. I know you'll listen sympathetically.'

Connie took his hand.

'Whatever it is, big bro, I'm yours.'

Bruce began his story. He decided to start from the beginning, rather than just blurting out that Clara was pregnant. He began with their childhood and related in halting terms how much he hated their father, and the main reason for the hatred.

'It was because of what he did to you, Connie. I heard him in Great Aunt Edith's room.'

There was compete silence in the room. Henry had quietly laid himself down and was curled up on a blanket fast asleep in the play pen. No one stirred. Eventually, Connie spoke in a whisper.

'I didn't know you knew, Brucey. I wish you'd told me before. I've been so ashamed all these years.'

'I didn't know how to,' Bruce replied. 'You wouldn't talk to me about it. I did try sometimes. Why did you let him do it, Connie? Why didn't you tell our mum?'

'I've gone over and over it. It haunts me. I supposed I thought it was Dad's right,' she said. 'He always said that. He used to say, "I made this body, kid" and then he would fondle my non-existent breasts and say, "I'm just seeing how you're shaping up, that's all — see how my little

164

chick is developing." He always said that. But I knew deep down that it was wrong.' She paused. 'Brucey, I was only six.'

What Connie did not tell Bruce was that one of the legacies her father's actions had left her with was an inability to sleep more than two hours at a time at night without waking up suddenly, in terror, often screaming, with nightmares. The nightmares were usually focused on her father coming into her room and heaving himself on top of her; or else some monstrous creature chasing her relentlessly and then devouring her. She slept with a pillow half covering her face to prevent her screams from waking the household.

'Brucey, carry on,' she said gently.

Bruce continued. He told Connie about his love for Clara, and coming to the most difficult part of all, shared with her that he had never been able to fulfil his lovemaking with his wife.

Again, the silence filled the room. Finally Connie, with a flash of insight, said very softly,

'I think that was Dad's doing. He put you off, Bruce, didn't he?'

'Yes. You're very wise, Connie. You've put in a nutshell what Dr Hamilton was trying to work out after three sessions.'

'I reckon no one else would believe how bad our dad was. I've worked it out because I know I will never get married because Dad has ruined it for me too.'

'Oh Connie,' said Bruce sadly. 'Oh my sweet Connie. That's terrible. In what way do you mean?'

'I can't say exactly. I just know.'

Bruce went over to her and held her.

'Have you heard from our dad?' enquired Bruce finally.

'No, and I don't want to. As far as I'm concerned, he's dead. I never want to see him again.'

'No information about Sadie, I suppose?'

'Of course not, Brucey. Don't you think I would have flown round to you if there had been? I've given up all hope of ever seeing her again.'

'Me too.' Sadness hung in the air.

There was a long pause, and Connie finally said,

'Go on, Bruce.'

He went on to explain how Clara and he had decided eventually to settle for less over that side of their marriage and how she would throw herself into her performing arts.

'But didn't the therapy work for you, Bruce?' asked Connie.

'It was stopped in its tracks.'

'Why? Were you ill?

Bruce then hesitatingly told Connie about Clara's pregnancy and how he had sought out the "culprit", wanting to beat him to a pulp.

'He was a — priest,' said Bruce slowly.

'A *priest!*' Connie crossed herself and reached quickly for her rosary which was on the sideboard.

'Holy mother of God! We must pray for forgiveness for him — for his trespasses, his sins.' Then she added, for once furiously angry.

'Such wickedness, such denial of his calling!'

Bruce thought of Oliver kneeling at his feet in penitence. Despite everything Bruce could no longer feel angry with him, could not even hate him. His own violence had shocked him to the core.

'I suppose according to your faith we should be praying for our father too, Connie. I feel the same as you, though. I never ever want to see him again.'

'So what will happen to the baby?' asked Connie, and quickly answered her own question. 'Bruce, you must keep it, bring it up as your own. Be a father to it. There's no doubt about it. This is an innocent new life and even though it will be born in original sin, it is not to blame for being conceived and shaped in its mother's womb. It is God's child.'

This was his sweet little sister, holding her devout Catholic beliefs, fingering her rosary rapidly, full of fury and righteous passion on his behalf, now telling him what to do. He smiled inwardly with a deep love for her.

Connie did not know it, but she had sown the first seeds of an idea in Bruce's head but could he find enough grace to think about it without the fierce anger rising in him? Anyway, there was Clara. It was, after all, Clara's child, and therefore her decision alone.

\*\*\*

Clara had made enquiries about having an abortion. She discovered that there were several back street operators who would have welcomed her and the fee she paid with open arms, but she winced at both the method she would have to endure and the money she would have to pay. Going to Iceland was out of the question. She had neither the fare nor the inclination to travel now. She doubted she would even make it to the airport in one piece.

Clara's sickness did not terminate at the usual twelve weeks. She was unfortunate to have a very serious form of it — which, she read, would carry on throughout her pregnancy unless she was very lucky — Hyperemesis Gravidarum — *my punishment,* she decided. She could feel herself becoming weaker and weaker from dehydration and her inability to keep anything more than dry toast down. She *had* to do something. She researched in the Encyclopaedia Britannica that was collecting dust on the bookshelves about various historical methods of self-abortion, but they would either involved poking ghastly instruments up herself or taking copious amounts of strange-sounding herbs mixed with large amounts of ginger.

Finally, she sat in an over-hot bath for half an hour, drinking copious amounts of gin. She neither liked alcohol nor the feeling it gave her afterwards, but she persevered. The heat of the bath made her drowsy and the alcohol overwhelmed her focus and reason. She drank over half a bottle and tipped the rest in the bath.

Somehow, after half an hour, she managed to clamber out and reach her purple towel from the rail. As she did so, her head swirled uncontrollably. She clutched the towel rail, and then fell. There she remained in a stupor.

Midas heard the thud and leapt up the stairs to find Clara sprawled on the bathroom floor. He whined and licked her face, trying to revive her, to no effect, and finally lay down beside her, head on his front paws, expression sad. There he stayed on guard by Clara until Bruce came home.

Connie, meanwhile, had given Bruce a sandwich for lunch and had insisted on praying with him. He found her voice and her words warm and comforting even though he did not share her faith. He had lost that years ago. Just as Bruce had said, 'Amen,' and was about to rise from his kneeling position, Connie continued her prayer:

'Father in Heaven, we pray for the life of this unborn child, your precious child. Please hold it in the palm of your hands and protect it until its time of birth. Keep it safe we pray. Amen.'

Bruce arrived home, less turbulent in his mind than when he had set off that morning. *It had been the right decision to talk to Connie,* he decided. He must see her more often. He put the key in the lock. No Midas bounding up to him? Unusual. As he entered the house his nostrils were hit by the distinctively sweet smell of gin coming from upstairs.

He raced up the stairs, two at a time, and found Clara on the floor, completely still, with Midas like an immovable rock beside her. Calling her name over and over, Bruce wrapped her gently in the purple towel, noticing her extreme thinness and floppy body with alarm, and carried her to the bed. She began to stir. He sat with her. Midas jumped on the bed, seemingly relieved that someone was sharing his watch.

Eventually, Clara opened her eyes.

'Bruce? You've come home,' she drawled blearily. 'Thank you for coming home.'

'Clara darling, what have you done?' he said, knowing perfectly well. 'Don't do it, Clara sweetheart. We will find a way.'

*He is lovely,* thought Clara. *I don't deserve him.* She stroked his face, turned over and fell asleep. Bruce and Midas stayed with her for several hours, until dusk fell and at last she awoke.

'Clara. Has the baby come away?' Bruce asked, realising with a shock that a voice that defied reason inside his head wanted her to say no.

'Not yet,' said Clara.

'It's a tough little thing. Like its mother.' He smiled.

'Don't, Bruce. Could I have some toast please? No butter.'

Bruce appeared with the toast and a cup of tea a few minutes later.

'Clara, we must talk.'

'Yes, but later,' she said. 'I've got a dreadful headache.'

'You drank *my* Christmas gin, that's why!' he said smiling.

'I'll get you another,' she replied. 'But it's useless stuff because nothing has shifted.'

'I told you, Clara, a baby of yours will be made of strong stuff.'

Clara turned and buried her face in the pillow. That was more than enough of that talk. When Bruce personalised the foetus inside her she felt panic-stricken.

# Chapter 15

Oliver felt unable to decide on a course of action, in fact he felt incapable of making any decisions whatsoever about anything at all. He thought constantly of Clara. The top priority in his mind, second only to her well-being, was to ascertain what Clara's intentions were regarding the unborn child. He knew that she must have the ultimate say in what was to happen, but he wanted at all costs to prevent her from having an illicit abortion. He knew that if he was successful in this then he was left with the dilemma of what was the honourable course of action for him to take.

Oliver's desk, normally tidy and organized, was chaotic today. Papers were strewn at random, books left half-open, paper clips scattered and several pens lay abandoned without their lids. He knew that the state of his desk today was an indication and outward sign of his state of mind. He went over and repeatedly in his head the various scenarios that might work with Clara, Bruce and himself in view of the expected baby — a triangle with a tiny beating heart at its centre. Every thought, every idea, seemed to be on a loop in his head like a recurring obsession or a hamster pacing on an inescapable wheel. Oliver was still shaken and shocked by the violence with which Bruce had nearly throttled him, leaving red wheels on his neck which he now had covered with a black polo neck sweater instead of the usual clerical collar.

'Get your thoughts organized!' he told himself. 'This isn't getting you anywhere, you idiot of a man.'

He remembered his father's political talks as a local MP and how he prepared in detail on paper what were the salient points of his talk. There were always four columns: the "fors and againsts", and the "what ifs" and "if not, what"? of the subject matter. He always backed up his political statements by researching sound facts and figures to support his arguments. In this way he was prepared for every question, however difficult and therefore was very rarely thrown off course. His forward planning self-discipline had been impeccable.

So Oliver, deciding to try and follow his father's example of orderliness, drew out a large, ruled notebook from his desk drawer and began to write down statements, scribbling his own thoughts underneath and backing them up with theological "evidence".

*Statement:*

1. *For Clara to divorce Bruce and for me to bring up the child with her*

    *Practical:* (a) *Would have to be unfrocked by the bishop.*

            (b) *Would have to find a new job and a home for us all.*

    *Objection.:(c) Bruce loves and cares for his wife.*

            (d) *Clara may not want this.*

*Theological: Divorce not an option in God's eyes: "Whoever divorces a wife and marries another commits adultery against her. And if a woman divorces her husband and marries another, she commits adultery",* (Mark 10, v.10).

*Hmm, well that's decisive,* thought Oliver.

*Statement:*

    *2. For me to support Clara and the baby under any circumstances.*

        *Practical: (a) Yes, do this whatever.*

                *(b) Must find a job that pays better than this.*

                *(c) What job?*

      *Objection (d) Got no money.*

                *(e) Would Clara and Bruce want this?*

*Theological: Once a priest, always a priest. Quintessence of my ordination service. Bishop's comment re priesthood: "You can't wipe it off, you can't shake it off, you can't rub it off". It wouldn't be fair on me either.*

*This is ironic,* mused Oliver. *I feel as though I have wiped out my priesthood vows in one fell swoop.*

*Statement*

    *3. To ask Bruce if he would bring the child up as his own.*

        *Practical:(a) Would child need to know that Bruce is not his real father?*

             *(b) Does this mean I would never see my own child?*

> (c) Would I have any part in its
> upbringing?

*Theological: "I would be to him a father and he shall be to me a son" (2 Samuel, v.12–15).*

Oliver wrote underneath the last theological statement, "But who does this apply to — Bruce or me"?

Suddenly, he threw the pen down in disgust at his ideas and angrily tossed the paper aside. It was a useless exercise. He wrung his hands despairingly and shouted:

'Lord, I need you. I'm sorry, I'm sorry, I'm sorry, but I love her so. Don't ask me to give her up! Please show me the path I must take.'

There was a knock at the door. Oliver hurriedly wiped his damp face on a tea towel that was hanging by the cooker, flicked his hair off his face, and ashamed of his messy desk covered it with the colourful throw from his sofa then opened the door.

Standing in the doorway was Bruce Connors.

Anyone passing the door at that moment would have seen two striking-looking men, both under thirty, standing stock still facing each other — the one outside the door tall, muscular and rugged-looking, with thick brown hair and strong features, the other with a mop of dark, straight hair, worn long, continually flopping into his eyes, olive-coloured skin, finely chiselled features and the strong look of an artist.

Clara certainly knew how to pick her men.

'Bruce,' said Oliver haltingly.

'Oliver,' Bruce replied.

'Come in. How's Clara?'

'Pretty bad, actually.'

'What can I do?' asked Oliver.

'Have you time to talk?'

'As long as it takes. I haven't known what to do, actually,' said Oliver. 'It's good you're here.'

'I've been thinking hard,' said Bruce.

Oliver indicated to Bruce to sit on the sofa.

Bruce slowly began to talk about Clara, giving an outline of her state of mind, her determination to be rid of the baby and his extreme anxiety about her, how he had spent hours and hours trying to imagine how the future might pan out, what it might hold. He told Oliver how his sister Connie had insisted on praying with him, even though he, Bruce, was more of an atheist than anything else. Certainly not a believer in answered prayer.

*Thank God for some more prayer support,* thought Oliver.

There was silence. The gas fire made gentle popping sounds intermittently. Bruce was finding it almost impossible to broach the next subject.

'Oliver. There is no reason why this child should be the innocent sufferer because of your liaison with Clara, is there?'

'No,' replied Oliver quietly.

*Well here goes,* thought Bruce. He faced Oliver squarely and spoke in a firm voice,

'I would like to try to persuade Clara to give this baby a chance. I believe I could find it in me to become a loving father in time — if I could persuade her of it.'

175

Oliver was silent. Everything inside him was twisting and screaming. He was being tortured and tormented by the words of an innocent man. Finally, without saying a word, Oliver reached for the piece of paper from his desk. In an expressionless monotone he read the list of statements. He came to the last one, folded the piece of paper and handed it to Bruce.

'I can't read this,' murmured Oliver. 'You read it to yourself.'

Bruce read,

*"To ask Bruce if he would bring the child up as his own".*

He said nothing.

Finally, Oliver spoke,

'It would take a huge amount of grace on your part.'

'And on yours,' Bruce replied.

Finally, Oliver said, 'Presumably Clara knows about this, Bruce?'

'Well, no. I thought there was no point in discussing it with her until I know your feelings on the matter.'

'Bruce, we shouldn't have had this discussion until you have broached the subject with Clara,' Oliver said, shocked. 'Will you allow me to talk to her?'

'Only after I have,' he replied. 'I'll phone you.'

With that he left and headed home to his wife.

\*\*\*

Since Bruce's visit Connie had spent many hours praying for Clara that she might make the right decision about the baby. Connie had a simple faith. She didn't ask herself questions such as what the right decision for Clara might be, how Bruce might feel being the father of someone else's child, or anything regarding the feelings of the natural father. For her it was a black and white issue: human life is sacred and that every human life has a right to be born. For Connie, there existed no extenuating circumstances. A baby was the precious gift of life in God's eyes from the moment it was conceived.

Whilst being shocked to the core by Clara's infidelity, and hurting mightily inside for Bruce and his dilemma, she nevertheless could not suppress a spark of joy inside when she thought about a new baby in the Connors' household. Bruce was cut out to be a father, she believed, and without realising it, Connie longed for a positive picture of fatherhood that would eradicate, or at the very least assist in healing the memory of her own father and his physical possession of her as a six-year-old.

Connie was more damaged from her childhood than she was prepared to acknowledge, even to herself. There were many incidents that stood out for her quite apart from the obvious one of her father's abuse. One of them which she had never been able to eliminate from her mind was the picture of James hanging from the rope in the bedroom, and the frantic efforts of her father and Bruce to cut him down. But most of all, the picture that made her bleed inside was her mummy wiping poor James' hair and sobbing her heart out.

Connie, nearly seven, had not been allowed to go to the funeral. Everyone agreed that she was too young to cope with it, so she was looked after by a neighbour. When she asked what would happen to James' body, everyone looked the other way, embarrassed, and avoided giving her any kind of satisfactory answer. She remembered feeling marginalised and jealous that every other member had been allowed to say goodbye to James, but not her.

But worst of all was the black hole in her heart that she knew was there from firstly the disappearance of her big sister Sadie, then the death of her brother, but most of all from the loss of her mother. She remembered the bang on the head, the stoical way in which her mother had served supper holding her head, and then the gut-wrenching grief of her death. Connie could never cry. The thoughts and the pain lay too deep for tears. They were locked at an unreachable place inside. She still had the old nightdress of her mother's that she secretly took to bed every night for comfort.

She had started self-harming about six months after her mother died. The physical hurt displaced some of the pain for her for a few seconds, bringing her a modicum of relief. A good session was when she dug deep and made herself bleed quite badly. That really did obliterate everything else for a few minutes.

Connie ruminated on this as she bathed the Rotherham's baby at six o'clock in the evening. She then lifted five-year-old Jemima into the bath, and more difficult, had to goad the two older children into action at about eight o'clock. Their parents had afternoon tea with them all (which Connie had prepared), then left the nursery for their early evening sherry. Connie preferred it when the parents were out of the way. The disciplining of the children by their parents was poor and ineffectual. Connie thought the children to be hugely overindulged for an hour or so a day and then when they were handed back, she invariably had to coax them to behave decently. Apart from that, she had few problems apart from the usual resistance to bedtime. They all loved her.

The family had a cook who always left a small plate of supper for Connie to heat up. Connie disliked eating, but by eight-thirty she was ravenous and managed to get some down. She never bothered to heat the supper. Food, to her, was a necessary evil and she had no delight in it. If she felt she had overeaten, then there was a course of action she sometimes took and that was to make herself vomit. Connie suffered from intermittent bulimia.

She loved babies, especially new born ones. She could sit and gaze at one for hours as its beautiful little hands and fingers moved. She thought them exquisite. She longed for a baby of her own more than anything in the world but knew it would never happen to her. She found the thought of a man touching her completely abhorrent, and furthermore, her "woman's monthly function" as she described it to the doctor, had stopped several years ago.

'It's all to do with your weight loss,' the doctor had said. 'Eat like a horse and you'll produce like a rabbit!'

The evening after Bruce had gone, Connie found her knitting needles and some cream wool that she had used to knit Henry a cardigan when he was first born. Yes. She would knit this new baby a matinee jacket. There was just enough wool. She then went to the family ragbag that was stuffed in a cupboard. It was full of cast-off dresses that Elizabeth, the eldest daughter, had worn and grown out of. They were never handed down to Jemima, and both girls in Connie's opinion, had a small fortune spent on their clothes. What they were short on in love was compensated by overindulgence of "pretty little girlie dresses", as their mother called them, together with matching shoes and hair slides that sparkled.

Connie pulled several dresses out of the ragbag. She knew that by giving them to the rag and bone man they would be sold to merchants for a pittance or regarded as disposable rubbish. Connie had a different idea for them. Carefully she unpicked the hems of the dresses and from two particularly dainty ones she painstakingly separated the bodices from the skirts. She then cut up the hems and bodices into exact squares, put them aside, rehemmed the skirts and replaced them in the ragbag in the hopes that someone might be grateful for them. With the squares she would make a patchwork quilt for the baby's cradle.

Maybe Clara and Bruce would let her look after the baby sometimes? It would give Clara a break. She could take it out in the pram, feed it and love it like only a devoted auntie could.

Connie had not spent such a happy evening in years.

\*\*\*

After Bruce had left, Oliver once again wanted to speak with bishop Timothy Hermes. This would be the last time. He telephoned his secretary, asking if there was any chance he could speak with him, or even come round at short notice, for instance *now.*

'It's his day off,' replied the secretary.

'Well, could you give him a message please? It's urgent. Just tell him that I want him to decommission me as soon as possible. I want to leave the ministry.'

There was a pause.

'Let me see if I can get hold of him. That sounds rather a dramatic step, I must say.'

Within a couple of minutes the bishop's voice spoke soothingly.

'Now Oliver. What is all this I hear? Is it about the young woman again?'

'Yes bishop. It is.'

He waved Mavis out of the room thinking how amazing it was that she somehow managed to find urgent work in his study just when there was a private phone call.

'Now. What is it, Oliver? Tell me what's the matter.'

The bishop held his breath. When Oliver had left the last time, it had crossed his mind that there might be the possibility of a pregnancy from their passionate encounter.

Oliver took a deep breath and then spoke rapidly, blurting out his position, hardly taking a breath.

'I have made Clara pregnant. It was just the one occasion I told you about but now she is three months gone. She wants a termination. My Lord Bishop, I am asking that you unfrock me, decommission me. I must leave the ministry. I couldn't live with the hypocrisy. Tell me what to do and I will do it. Presumably you need my clerical clothes back — Alb, stole, chasuble etcetera? I will return…'

'Now Oliver. Stop. Let's talk this through face to face. This is not a matter we can sort over the phone.'

No, Bishop. I've said all I need to say. I have broken the sacred trust of my ordination vows.'

'What about the child?'

'Clara is wanting to abort it. I've spoken to Bruce, her husband—'

'A very painful conversation I would imagine,' interjected the Bishop.

'—And we are trying to work something out. Please don't deter me. My mind is made up. Goodbye my Lord. I'll wait for you to contact me about the next official step I must take.'

Oliver terminated the conversation abruptly. He would not be dissuaded from this course of action.

The phone clicked off. The bishop stared at the receiver. His wife came into the room and saw a grim look on her husband's face.

'What is it, Tim?'

'Oliver Lockwood. A dilemma. I can't tell you, my love, until he gives me permission to do so. It really is very personal but knowing you you'll guess anyway. Now. I must phone the archbishop.'

'Oh dear,' replied Margaret. 'That serious?'

'Yes. I'm afraid so. I'll go and ask Mavis to get me the number for Lambeth Palace.'

'Tim, if it's anything to do with something of a sexual nature — an indiscretion perhaps — give the chap a chance,' she said persuasively. 'He's young and he's such a nice young fellow.'

'He is,' replied the bishop. 'One of the finest in the diocese, but niceness doesn't really come into it. does it? You know that.'

Margaret saw that her husband's face was full of distress. She knew not to comment further but gave her husband a brief kiss on his cheek and left him to his phone call.

'Good Afternoon. Archbishop's Palace.'

'Good afternoon. It's Bishop Timothy Hermes here. I need to speak urgently with the archbishop please.'

'One moment please. I will reach for the diary.'

'Yes,' she flicked the page. 'He has a half hour slot in ten days' time. Shall I book you in?.'

'No thank you', replied the bishop. 'I fear it will be too late by then. Thank you. Goodbye.'

'Shall I tell the archbishop you called in case he can move something in his diary?'

But Timothy Hermes had rung off. He was in no mood for delay.

## Chapter 16

'Sit down, please Clara.'

Something in Bruce's voice made Clara obey him immediately. She was not used to being spoken to so authoritatively by him. This was out of character.

'I don't want you to interrupt me until I have finished,' Bruce instructed sternly.

If he had not looked quite so serious, Clara would have been tempted to laugh at this change, or even mimic him. But not today.

Bruce spoke formally.

'I would like to offer to bring up your child with you, to be a father to it. We would have to come to some arrangement with its natural father, draw up guidelines for the future, but the offer is there, if you would entrust me to do it. This baby deserves a chance, Clara.'

Under normal circumstances, Clara would have said in a slightly mocking, slightly humorous tone, 'I can tell you've been talking to holy Connie,' but these were hardly normal circumstances.

Bruce was silent. Midas looked up inquisitively trying to work out what the strange atmosphere was all about. After a long time, Clara spoke.

'Bruce, could you really love a child you haven't fathered? Wouldn't you be thinking all the time about its real father? And what about Oliver? He deserves a say.'

'He's had a say,' said Bruce, knowing that quite possible his reply might cause an avalanche of anger and vitriol.

'*What?* So you and Oliver have been deciding on my future and my baby's future, have you?' she spat out.

She had called it a baby! Finally, she had acknowledged that this "thing" as she described it, this "foetus", was more than that. Even in her anger, Clara realised the significance of the moment.

Bruce heard it and his heart missed a beat. Despite her anger, he knew also that this was progress. He took her hand but Clara snatched it away.

'What gave you the right to talk to Oliver about it?' she said.

'And what gave you the right to commit adultery?' he replied, suddenly angry.

Both knew that the conversation was poised on a knife edge. Both found the wisdom to draw back. Finally, Clara spoke,

'This is a big shock. Let me think about it Bruce.'

She picked up her plate of dry toast and went upstairs.

*At least it's not an outright "no",* Bruce thought. *I'll take her a cup of tea.*

He went to the kitchen to make it but then had a change of mind, deciding to leave it until Clara was ready to talk again. As she had said, she needed thinking time. He went to his workshop and started varnishing a violin he had been repairing. After a few minutes, though, he reached for his clarinet. That always soothed him. He hadn't played for a long time, so started with a few scales to warm his fingers up. Then he began playing the musical flourish at the beginning of Clara's favourite piece: *Gershwin's Rhapsody in Blue*.

As always happened, he became wrapped up in the music, borne away by its beauty and at the same time concentrating hard on his rusty technique. *That was the amazing thing about music,* he thought. *It wasn't a case of learning the technique then superimposing the artistry. The two went hand in hand.* He was so absorbed he didn't hear Clara come in. She stood just inside the doorway. This was how she had met Bruce: him playing the clarinet and she playing her violin. Yes, she had acknowledged from the start, there was something calculated in the way she had wooed him. Her elderly parents were suffocating her and she saw a husband as a necessary part of her toolkit to escape them, but there was so much more to it than that.

Despite the lack of consummation in her marriage, Clara had come to love Bruce and had become emotionally dependant on him. She could always rely on his unconditional support when she was weepy, or angry or madly happy or grumbling furiously. Bruce had undoubtedly become the rock in her life.

As for Oliver. She had been wildly attracted to him, and passionate for him, had revelled in the wonderful encounter on the sofa she had with him, but despite all this, Bruce won the day hands down in her affections. She knew she needed him in her life.

She listened on, not disturbing him. She loved the musicality in him. Even now, in the confined space of the workshop, she saw how his body moved to the music, how he was entirely wrapped up in it and brought it to life in the most mesmerising way. Yes, she loved him all right. As she listened, the tears streamed down her face. It had been such a *hard* three months, and she was physically at her lowest ebb. But Bruce was still there, still loving her, despite everything.

He came to the end of the piece, put the clarinet back its box, and turned back to varnishing the violin. Then he saw Clara. She walked slowly up to him, put her arms around him and sobbed into his broad and comforting shoulders. He said nothing but rocked her gently as he held her. Finally she pulled away.

'Bruce, if you are willing to take on this child, I think we should go to Oliver and see what we can work out.' She paused. 'You'll make a wonderful father I know — and,' she smiled. 'You might even teach it to play the clarinet.'

He smiled.

'I think we may be able to work it out together.'

'Nothing in me wants this baby. This pregnancy has destroyed my career, and I know I'll be a ghastly mother. I have no maternal instinct at all, but I think I can just about contemplate going through with it if you are willing to take it on with me.' She paused. 'I love you, Bruce Connors.'

'And I you, Clara Connors,' he said softly. He held her for another minute.

'Now. Let me get you a cup of tea.'

'No Bruce. I'll get it and bring it in to you. You carry on with your varnishing.'

As she went downstairs, she patted her tummy.

'Well, you, whoever you are, it looks as though you've won the day.'

\*\*\*

Clara and Bruce agreed that they would ask Oliver to come to the house to work out if they could find a way forward, and what kind of shape the future might hold for all of them. Clara was nervously in agreement about the discussion, but with one proviso: that she could have half an hour on her own with Oliver first. She argued that this was the least she owed him, but in her heart, she knew that it might be her last chance to say goodbye.

Bruce found it a difficult suggestion to cope with, but being the man he was, with the welfare of Clara and her child at its heart, he agreed. He would work upstairs while Oliver was here, and then join them for discussion when Clara called him down.

The doorbell rang. While Bruce was answering the door, Clara quickly looked in the mirror once more, smoothed her hair down and decided that she really had lost her looks in this wearying first trimester of pregnancy. She had put on a loose dark green velvet top with a long sweeping black skirt. *Dull,* she thought, *but appropriate* and then she noticed with alarm there was the hint of a bump under her top.

188

Oliver came in and Clara noticed immediately that he had lost weight, that his face was drawn and the quiet joie de vivre he usually displayed was absent. *Not surprising,* thought Clara as she realised what an ordeal this must be for him as well as for her.

'I'll be upstairs,' said Bruce. 'Call me when you've finished.'

Clara nodded. Oliver drank in the sight of the green velvet top, the beautiful hair, longer now, the pale but beautiful face, the winsome half-smile, and most of all, the tiny bump that was almost hidden under her top. That was *his* child. No one else's, except his and Clara's.

*How can I possibly let another man bring up our child?* he thought. *I want them both to myself!.* But instead, he simply said,

'Hello Clara.'

'Hi Oliver.'

'How are you?'

'A bit better, thanks.'

The conversation stalled. On impulse, Oliver went over to the chair, knelt beside her and took her hand. He knew it was a risk.

'Clara, this is impossible.'

'I know. We must talk.'

He kissed her forehead, but she moved away slightly.

'Don't Oliver. It only makes things worse.'

Meanwhile, Bruce decided the only way to stop the demon jealousy from taking up residence in his brain during the half hour was to do something that required his total concentration, obliterating all other thoughts. He unlocked a glass cabinet in which he kept the more precious instruments for renovating and carefully brought out a brown violin case. Putting it down on his workbench, he unlocked the case and with the gentlest of hands, removed the gold silk in which the violin was wrapped. This was a Stradivarius, the most precious make of violin in the world, and he, Bruce Connors, had been entrusted with it to repair it.

When the owner, the leader of the national orchestra, had come to his workshop, he had asked Bruce if he could renovate it, mending the delicate crack that had appeared down the belly of the violin due to the age of the wood.

'The quality of sound has deteriorated, hmm, yes, deteriorated badly, and it simply won't do! Every note offends me! Listen. I'll play you a few bars and you will hear,' said the gifted little birdlike man.

He played. Bruce was immediately captivated by the intense sweetness of the sound. The tone was wonderful to his ears, light, bright, brilliant. He honestly could not fault it, although when he examined the violin, he could see the fine offending crack down its centre seam.

He now brought out from a drawer the clamps that would help to close the crack. His big hands became fine tools as he took the belly of the instrument off the back of the violin, putting a wedge of soft felt underneath before clamping one side and then the other. This was a delicate operation at the best of times, but if he felt so much as a slight tremor in his fingers then he would stop immediately. But there was no tremor. His craftsmanship was masterly and he knew that this kind of repair took courage as well as skill. The violin was worth in excess of six figures. Bruce handled it as if it were a baby, stopping occasionally to check that the maple wood stood the best chance of knitting together and that the clamps were exactly lined up to put maximum delicate pressure on the crack.

Meanwhile, downstairs, an intense and agonisingly painful conversation was taking place. Finally, Clara called up,

'Bruce. Can you come down now?'

When Bruce entered the room he saw two drawn, white-faced people. One of them, Oliver, had his head in his hands. Clara spoke without expression as if reading from a formal document. She knew it was the only way she could get through it. Oliver did not look up throughout its delivery.

'Bruce, if you are willing to father this child for Oliver, I will give birth to it and forget any thought from now on about aborting it. Oliver will keep a low profile for the rest of the pregnancy and for its childhood. The child will never know its true paternity, but Oliver will be allowed to see it immediately after birth and then once a year on its birthday. You, Bruce, will be registered as its father on the birth certificate and no one at all needs to know of this. Oliver has told no one except his bishop, who will know by the nature of his work how to keep a confidence. Presumably you haven't told anyone, Bruce, apart from Connie, and neither have I. Oliver has agreed to pay a monthly allowance to you to go towards the baby's keep and in acknowledgement of your role as...'

'*Stop!*' Bruce shouted, standing up. There was a long pause while he recovered himself and finally sat down again.

'There are two amendments here, for a start.' He managed to adopt the same formal tone as Clara had used.

'One: I will *not* take any money for this transaction if I am to be the legitimate father on the birth certificate. That is out of the question.

Two: Oliver must have nothing whatever to do with the child. He or she will become confused and begin to question things. We cannot have that.'

Bruce looked down and added almost to himself, 'It wouldn't be on me, either.'

Regaining his air of authority he continued,

Three:'Oliver will not be able to…'
Bruce broke off and looked across the room. Oliver had lifted his head and his eyes were streaming with tears. Clara was frantically wringing her hands. Bruce's voice softened.

'But Oliver must certainly see the baby soon after it is born. Yes, of course, of course he must.'

There was silence. Oliver wiped his face and blew his nose violently before speaking.

'Bruce, I will be honest with you. Nothing in me wants to let this child go. I long for nothing more than to be a father to it, and,' he hesitated. 'To have some contact still with Clara. But I am not prepared to break up your marriage, and anyway, I know that you are first in Clara's heart.'

Oliver stopped to gain control of himself.

'It's noble beyond words of you to take the child on and I will honour the agreement. I'm resigning my post as Theatre Chaplain and giving my ordination robes back. I'll move away.'

Clara was stunned. Oliver had given her no idea of this during their private half hour.

'But Oliver, you *can't*. You are so suited to the work and you are admired and respected. That is a very drastic step to take. I doubt I'll be coming back, more's the pity, so that wouldn't be an issue. Don't leave — for your own sake. Please,' she pleaded.

'Sorry, Clara, my mind's made up. It's really the only way ahead for me, for you, for Bruce, for the child — and I believe it is what God requires of me.'

Clara said nothing, but inside she was shocked to the core at this drastic step. She looked at Oliver who was now dry-eyed, resolute and stony-faced.

'I'll write out a contract,' said Bruce gently. 'We need an agreement in writing, don't we?'

'There's no need,' replied Oliver. 'I am a man of my word, whatever else I am not.'

He got up and shook hands firmly with Bruce.

'I swear before Almighty God I will stick to this agreement.'

Bruce went up to him and gave him a warm hug. Oliver then gave Clara a peck on the cheek.

'Goodbye Clara. Let me know when the baby is born—' Oliver allowed himself the briefest of pats on her abdomen, 'And I will pay it one visit,' he said, adopting the only tone he knew to keep himself from taking her in his arms and kissing her wildly in his grief.

With that, he was gone. Bruce hugged Clara.

'Now we can be a family, darling — you, me and the baby.'

Clara broke free. She rushed out of the room and was violently sick.

\*\*\*

Oliver went back to the theatre, packed his alb and stole in brown paper, wrote a brief note and left package and note on the doorstep of the bishop's house. He then carefully penned a letter of resignation to the theatre management with the briefest of explanations, dropped a short line to Nick the director and went back to his flat. The kittens were long gone and he was just left with Cat.

He dared not examine his feelings so he scooped up Cat, stroked her, picked up the phone and rang the church army hostel.

Bruce went to his workshop, put the Stradivarius back on the shelf in order that the crack might seal, and sorted out his most beautiful pieces of wood to make the baby a cradle. Clara sunk into a deep depression, where she stayed throughout her pregnancy.

Connie, meanwhile, having finished the patchwork quilt, was busy making a mountain of baby clothes, praying over each garment as she went.

## END OF PART ONE

# PART TWO

# Chapter 17

On a beautiful day in June, with the sky a periwinkle blue and the summer flowers perfect in colour and vibrancy, Clara went into labour. Her pregnancy had been uneventful apart from the ongoing sickness. She had taken no joy in the burgeoning of her belly, nor the insistent kicking of the baby tucked neatly inside. She would discuss no names for the child with either Bruce nor Connie. To her, at best, this child was an interruption to her career, and at worst, the cause of intense heartache for herself and Oliver. She had lost all contact with him since he walked out on that fateful day when the verbal contract was agreed. Furthermore, Clara had no idea how to reach him. She had phoned the theatre company, but no one there had any idea of his whereabouts. They had clearly been both annoyed and perplexed by his sudden departure, as had been the landlady of his flat.

She had heard Oliver tell Bruce that the bishop of the diocese knew of Oliver's fall from grace and predicament concerning the fathering of a child with a married woman. Perhaps the bishop could help her now.

Clara needed to be able to contact Oliver when the child was born. Bruce and she had agreed that they must honour their promise. In her head, Clara did not wish to resume any kind of a relationship with Oliver, her heart, however, was lagging behind in that thinking.

Clara had looked up the telephone number of the bishop in the directory. Finding it, she telephoned, but a recorded voice cut in straight away telling her that the number was ex-directory. There was only one thing to do — land up on the doorstep and ask to see the bishop. She was eight months pregnant, so she guessed that no one would turn her away. She knew she looked impossibly thin and waif-like despite her neat bump. The sickness had continued throughout her pregnancy. The midwife had pronounced that the baby seemed small, and that if she did not put on more weight, they would have to induce it early.

'Your placenta may be packing up,' said one nurse cheerfully. 'Your baby runs the risk of being undernourished. Are you eating enough?'

'Yes, yes I am,' Clara had replied, which was a lie as she could still barely keep down much food at all but she had been able to drink copious amounts of ice-cold milk.

Clara rang the bishop's doorbell, expecting a secretary to open it. A smiling woman with a blue Burmese cat draped round her shoulders came to the door. She took in the downbeat look of the pregnant woman in front of her.

'Come in, come in, my love. We mustn't keep you standing. Was it the bishop you wanted to see? Did you phone for an appointment?'

Clara explained that she had tried.

'Oh yes of course. The secretary is ill so the phone is diverted. Apologies for that but it's the only way we can have any personal space.'

'Oh I'm so sorry. I'll come back another time.'

'No, no, I didn't mean *you,'* she said, wishing she could have taken her words back. The woman looked thin and pale, although, Margaret Hermes thought to herself, *very beautiful in an Ophelia kind of way.*

'What a handsome cat!' said Clara, stroking it under its chin.

'Yes, this is Boy Blue, and she's just produced *another* six kittens! That's her fourth litter. We'll find out what's causing it one of these days!'

They both laughed.

'I've given up thinking of names for them all. I just call them Kitty One, Kitty Two, Kitty Three and so on.'

*Kitty. Yes, that's nice,* mused Clara. It was the first time she had ever thought about a name for the baby.

'I'll see if my husband is in, Mrs — er?'

'Clara. Clara Connors.'

Clara sat in the great hallway looking at the pictures of past bishops and thinking what a grim-faced lot they were. She hoped this current bishop looked a bit more approachable.

He turned out not to be the typical ecclesiastical stereotype that Clara had envisaged. He was pleasant looking and had a warm face, she decided. Once in his light and airy study, she introduced herself as simply Clara and told him she was trying to locate the whereabouts of Oliver Lockwood. The bishop's mind whirled. Here was a very pregnant woman asking for Oliver Lockwood. He guessed that this might be the woman who had caused him to break his self-imposed vow of celibacy. She had a winsome smile and a rare beauty about her.

'Mrs — er — Clara — I'm afraid I can't help you. He left suddenly without warning. We were all very sad. He left no forwarding address and no one can trace him. We have tried.'

'Oh,' replied Clara, disappointed. 'Oh well, never mind. I'll leave you in peace.'

'Can I ask you, would you like to tell me, if I can help you at all?' he said.

'I was at a theatre company with him when he was the Chaplain. I last saw him about…'

She stalled suddenly. The bishop had given her a quizzical look. Had he guessed the situation?

'If you hear from him, please could you let me know? I'll give you my address.'

'Yes of course, Clara. I'd like to help you if I can. When is your baby due?'

'In a month's time,' Clara replied.

Very quickly, the bishop did a mental calculation, counting on his fingers behind his back from when Oliver had come to see him to tell him about the pregnancy. Yes, the dates fitted.

He could see why Oliver had found this woman irresistible. There was both a vulnerability and a strength about her, as well as the rare beauty he had already noted.

'I'll give you my card. May I come and visit you in hospital when you have the baby, Clara? It's my pastoral duty, you know,' he said with a warm humorous smile. 'By then I may have an address for you for Oliver Lockwood. I'll get my diocesan spies on the job.'

'Thank you,' said Clara. 'I'd appreciate that.'

As she was walking up the path the bishop called her back.

'Clara. What are you going to call your baby?'

Without having to think, Clara replied,

'If it is a girl, I will call her Kitty. I nearly had one of Oliver Lockwood's you know.'

'Yes, and it looks as though you're about to have another,' the bishop said to himself wryly as he watched Clara continue down the path.

He vowed to himself to pray every day for her. She looked as though she needed it. He went inside and put her straight on his prayer list.

\*\*\*

Bruce had worked hard to create the baby's cradle. He built it from the finest ebony wood which he usually reserved for carving the fingerboards for his violin repairs. Connie suggested that she made some white drapes to fall softly from the sides of the cradle. At her further request Bruce fixed a tall stand to the back of the cradle so that she could hang fine cream parachute silk from it, forming a canopy 'to protect precious newborn eyes from the light,' she said.

Her mother had managed to hoard away considerable stocks of the silk, which in the immediate post-war years was going for a song, and Connie had retrieved it from its hiding place in the family home when she left.

She then painstakingly embroidered tiny rabbits on the inside of the fabric so that "the baby will have something to look at". The fabric was delicate and kept slipping away from her, but she persevered. She was just as excited as if it were her own baby. She forgot that Bruce was not actually its father. A baby was a baby to her — a precious miracle of life, even if she was not related to it by blood.

Connie's absorption in the task gave rise to the gift of self-forgetfulness, which in turn brought the beginnings of its own gentle healing to her. The violent nightmares she had been plagued with had finally begun to lessen.

Clara, meanwhile, showed no interest in the creation of the cradle and avoided going up to Bruce's workshop, not bearing to discuss anything connected with the child. Bruce saw that Clara was becoming more and more withdrawn and ill with depression.

Making the cradle had given him thinking time. He realised that initially after the agreement, he had been elated and relieved. He hadn't wanted Clara to go through an illicit abortion and he certainly could not bear the thought of her leaving him for Oliver. Now that the agreement had been settled, he had time to examine his own feelings in some depth. His main concern was that of being a good father to the child. He had no positive pattern or example of fatherhood to guide him and shuddered when he thought of his own father's aggression and bullying. He blamed him for James' death and his mother's, but he knew that he had his mother's deep maternal love as a pattern to guide him.

He rather hoped the baby would be a girl. A boy might look too much like Oliver, and this child must be seen by all as Bruce's child — for everyone's sake. *A girl baby stood more of a chance of looking like Clara,* he reasoned. He had no belief in prayer or God, but as he chiselled and planed the cradle he asked the great unknown someone or something to guide him and help him be the very best father he could be.

Now, finally, the baby was on its way. Clara's waters had broken as she bent down to refill Midas' water bowl. It was nine-thirty in the morning. She told Bruce calmly, and he rapidly rounded up her overnight bag, which he had packed for her two weeks ago as she had called out the list of contents for him to check that she would need. He then grabbed the small bag of going-home clothes for the baby that Connie had made and packaged up in readiness. Connie had also sewn and stuffed a small soft white toy bear which she had packed into the top of the bag. Clara calmly took it out and left it behind, saying, 'This is superfluous to requirements. No newborn needs a bear.'

There was an eerie calm and detachment about her as she put on a loose white summer jacket and walked slowly to the car holding a towel. Bruce noted it all and was suddenly gripped by a clutch of fear as he wondered if Clara would bond with the baby.

The labour was extremely long. By nine o'clock in the evening Clara was nowhere near stage two in labour. A brusque nurse bustled in.

'I'm going to turn your light off. This is taking far too long. Get some sleep, Mrs Connors. Most people drift off through the first stage of labour.'

Clara found out much later that this apparent fact that the nurse had tossed out to her was very far from the truth. Clara found the labour pains almost impossible to bear, but she had vowed she would *not* make an exhibition of herself by crying out or screaming as some other women were. She would suffer in silence if it killed her. She lay in the darkened room and refused to call anyone for help. Eventually, at four a.m. when the pains were virtually unbearable, Clara admitted she was beaten and pressed the buzzer for help. The night nurse came to examine her.

'My goodness, you're seven centimetres dilated. You *have* done well. No gas and air either! Clever girl. There you are. It wasn't that bad, was it? I think you're ready to walk to the delivery room. Your baby will be here very soon.'

To Clara it seemed like the longest walk in the world. As she staggered down the corridor holding her abdomen and stopping as another contraction swept over her, she kept singing obsessively in her head the song her father used to sing, "Keep right on to the end of the road; keep right on round the bend".

Clara continued to keep right on and after another hour she finally, with one last marathon effort, pushed the baby out. There it was, a writhing, crying tiny scrap of humanity. The baby was quickly scooped up and put on the scales: six pounds exactly.

'You have a beautiful daughter, Mrs Connors. I'll just clean her up and then you can hold her. Do you have a name for her yet?'

'Kitty,' said Clara weakly.

'Hmm. That's unusual. I don't think we've had a Kitty before. Presumably she's a Katharine really?'

'No, she's just Kitty.'

'Middle name?'

'No, she's just Kitty,' Clara replied through gritted teeth. She was exhausted. Who was this idiot of a woman that she couldn't understand when a name is a name?

The nurse kept quiet, sensing that she was a source of great irritation to her patient, who seemed to her to be behaving in a rather unusual way. She cleaned the baby up, wrapped her in a green rubber sheet supplied by the delivery suite and handed her to Clara.

'There. She's a sweet little thing. Very pretty for a newborn.'

Clara took a long look at her. Yes, she had ten of everything on her toes and on her hands. She had a nice cap of rich brown hair, and Clara noted, a sweet-shaped mouth. Her eyes, although screwed up, promised to be large. She was a good pink colour and cried healthily. As Connie remarked later the baby was "adorable and perfect in every way".

Clara was relieved with what she saw. 'Very sweet,' she said to herself, but realised she felt absolutely nothing at all for her.

Kitty was taken away and put in an adjoining nursery with several other new-borns, who were all wrapped in white cellular cotton blankets in their own individual plastic cradles and all joining in the crying and making a cacophony of sound. Clara asked to be moved to a ward further away where she couldn't hear them. Every cry reminded her of how inadequate she felt for the task, and how she regarded it with loathing.

When Bruce came in to see the baby, the tiny bundle was held up at the nursery window for one minute by a nurse. Even in that short space of time Bruce could see that she had the sweet looks of her mother.

'Congratulations, father. A daughter.'

'Perfect,' He said out loud. 'Isn't she exquisitely perfect?'

He had loved the way the nurse had called him "father". No one in the world apart from the chosen few — Clara, Connie and the bishop, would ever know that Kitty was not his own. That made him feel more of a man somehow. He had never really felt that in the marriage because his impotence had stripped him of every ounce of confidence he had as a husband

Clara desperately wanted to contact Oliver but had no address. The Bishop had not turned up with any news of his whereabouts, so there was no way he would know about his daughter's birth. However, two days after Kitty was born, the receptionist discovered a huge bouquet of pink roses, freshly delivered, lying at the foot of the steps outside. On the label attached to the flowers were the words,

'Clara. Thinking of you.'

That was all. There was no address anywhere attached to the card or the wrapping on the flowers. Clara asked the nurse if she would find who had delivered them and was informed that they had been left on the nursing home steps presumably in the middle of the night. No one had seen anyone.

Clara vowed to investigate further when she was up and around.

Meanwhile, Bishop Hermes had dropped into the maternity department and had peeped in the ward, intending to visit Clara. From the doorway he saw Bruce holding the baby lovingly with Clara looking on and decided not to intrude. Maybe things would work out well after all. He left quietly, vowing to hold them all in his prayers.

Bruce took his wife home nine days later. She cared for the baby dutifully — bathed her, changed her nappy, dressed her and fed her, but she never once spoke to her, called her name or cooed softly to her. That was left to Bruce, who was only too delighted when Kitty was handed over to him. Those early days, when he talked to her, comforted her and sang to her were to establish a deep love and affection between the two of them which lasted their entire lives.

Clara did not want to breast-feed her baby. She said she could not abide her breasts to become sagging as a result of it. She held Kitty close when she bottle-fed her, as Dr Spock advised in his book. Dr. Spock's mantra had always been, "You know more than you think you do", but Clara felt she knew absolutely nothing and was only too

207

happy to hand Kitty over to Bruce or into the competent, loving hands of Connie when she visited. Connie seemed a "natural," but Clara felt the whole motherhood scenario was, abnormal, aberrant to her.

Somehow Kitty would grow and thrive, but it would be more due to the love of those around her than to her own mother, whose emotional coldness towards her daughter was becoming increasingly evident, much to Bruce's concern.

# Chapter 18

Having written his letter of resignation, Oliver left the Theatre Company in Richmond upon Thames. He had loved the work, the company of actors and the lively atmosphere of the town, it had all suited him well, until he messed everything up, he reflected, by falling in love with Clara, who had been forbidden fruit.

He had no plans at all for the future except to gain employment somewhere, be it as a night porter or a car park attendant, but it had to pay him a decent enough wage. He had very few savings. The college had been generous enough to pay half the rent for his flat as part of his salary, but the actual amount of cash in hand that he earned was not exactly lavish. He had never minded. It went with the calling. He was used to the rather modest pay of a clergyman and up until now his needs had been minimal.

He decided to drive to Edinburgh to see his sister again. Her door was always open. He had his washing to do, having left in a hurry, and the residue of pastoral reports to write for the students. Also, he needed serious thinking time. It was quiet and peaceful at Morag's. He might even confide in his sister. Their parents had both died in a head-on road accident some years ago, His father seemed to have lost concentration, swerving across the central reservation and into an articulated lorry. It had left indelible scars on all their hearts. His sister was the only living relative to whom Oliver was close.

Oliver found himself grappling with an unfamiliar emotion. He had never really known what jealousy was. His parents had been fair and loving, and his sister of a kindly disposition. He had never had a girlfriend, so was unfamiliar with issues either of unrequited love or male rivalry involved in the "love game" as he used to call it — that is, until the "love game" drew him in and enticed him to become a prime player.

When he thought of Bruce being with Clara day and night, his stomach churned and he felt anguished. When he thought of Bruce with *his* baby, he felt positively thunderous. He had relinquished them both. He knew Clara would never have left Bruce for him, but now he pondered on whether he should have demanded more of a stake in the child's future. He saw his own future as one of endless wondering and wishing. Not to see the child once a year even now at this early stage felt like a slow form of torture.

He had ripped off his dog collar and put it in the package with his clerical garments to be returned. He always had mixed feelings about wearing it anyway. He disliked the way it singled him out, the way people changed when they saw it, the caricatures of vicars that appeared in *Punch* and suchlike. But he had felt proud and blessed to be an ordained minister and had always loved sharing his faith with others. When his parents were killed, rather than throwing him into complete disarray, he found that his faith held him steady through the tragedy. He had an unswerving belief that the God he put his faith in both identified with him and sustained him in the depths.

Until now, that is. God seemed remote, unreachable, silent, and in his darkest moments, irrelevant.

He had telephoned his sister before arriving this time, so it was with relief that she saw him walking slowly, head down, up to her cottage front door. He had made the journey then. That was reassuring. After hearing him on the phone she had braced herself for anything. Morag had coped — just — with her parents' untimely death, but the legacy she had been left with was a deep agitation when she knew her brother, or anyone else she cared for, was on the road. Time and again she had silently played out the memory of the police knocking on her door. But here now was Oliver looking grim, but down the years she had learnt how to soothe him, although from the look on his face this time it might be quite a challenge,

'Oli, Oli, you need a cup of tea, or something stronger?' she said, giving him a kiss and a hug.

Oliver drank two double whiskeys straight down, which was unheard of for him. Morag eyed him nervously. He really was in trouble.

The cottage was cosy, Morag's presence was comforting and the whiskey warming. Oliver slowly told Morag the whole story. She did not interrupt, knowing how difficult her brother was finding it.

In the end, after a long silence, she reached out her hand to him.

'Oli, you're the first one to say we all have feet of clay. You're a good and faithful man who has slipped.

Clara sounds quite a temptress actually. She was part of it. Don't chastise yourself quite so harshly and you mustn't blame yourself alone.' She paused. 'It took two, you know. Do you really have to give up your ministry? Couldn't you go back to parish life, or find something else as an ordained minister?'

'You don't understand, Morag. I have broken the sixth commandment by committing adultery and I've fathered a child, I've therefore been disobedient to my calling and that's all there is to it.'

Morag took some convincing, but she could see her brother's faith disallowed any compromise in this instance. They talked into the evening and Oliver gradually became clearer in his mind of a way ahead. Morag was worried that he would be worn down in the future by not seeing his child. But that was to worry about later. For now, she had allowed him to talk and she knew that he found it cathartic. His face looked more peaceful as he said goodnight.

Morag scooped up his big bag of washing and put it by the twin-tub washing machine. It could wait. That was quite enough for today.

The following morning, Oliver had made some decisions. He knew that whilst he could not stay in the ministry in the strictest sense — no robes, no dog collar, no services, no taking of holy communion and so on — he also bore in mind his ordination's mantra: *"Once a Priest, Always a Priest"*. He could serve as a priest in an entirely secular context. He telephoned several church army contacts in the London area. He'd at least start searching there.

He was grateful to his sister for scooping him up in his hour of need. She was not a "card-carrying Christian" but she had wonderful qualities of kindness, generosity and grace and he knew without a doubt that they weren't the exclusive prerogative of the Christian faith. She was a perfect example of a life full of goodness, walking in the light, without realising it. He was eternally grateful for her kindly, pragmatic approach to this situation.

Oliver was snapped up by the church army. He was taken on as a project worker for the homeless in the Wandsworth area. The pay was very basic, as was the room he was provided with, but it suited him. It was at the end of a dark corridor on the ground floor and it was appropriate, he mused, *to have a sort of sackcloth and ashes experience in a small and dimly lit room.* It suited his mood.

***

When Oliver knew it was time for his child to be born, he rang the maternity hospital, saying that he was a priest and had been caring for Clara Connors. She had been in his pastoral care. Hmm.

At the time of phoning, Clara apparently was not in the hospital, but was down on the list for admittance when she went into labour. Oliver interrupted the secretary, who was in full flight regarding what constituted the first signs of labour, by asking in his most authoritative voice if she would be sure to telephone him the moment the baby was born.

'There are issues of confidentiality, Rev — um — who was it? Your name is?'

'There's an issue of confidentiality there too,' Oliver replied slickly. 'I am Clara's pastor and she has requested I remain anonymous.'

A big fat lie, but it did the trick. Oliver couldn't help an inward smile.

*I'm really on a slippery slope to damnation here,* he thought. *How easily that lie came!*

Three days later the secretary phoned Oliver telling him that Clara Conners had given birth to a daughter and both were doing well.

'Can I pass on a message for you?' she enquired.

'No thank you,' replied Oliver.

The secretary put the telephone back on the receiver. What an odd phone call. She hoped she wouldn't get into trouble for giving out the news. Perhaps best not to tell a soul.

When Oliver heard the news, his heart sang. Everything leapt for joy inside him that Clara was safe, and that he had a daughter and he thanked God for a safe delivery for Clara and the baby.

He had already made the difficult decision not to see his daughter at all. He knew he would find it unbearable to walk out of the ward and know, according to the arrangement, that he would never see either the baby or Clara again. *Better to keep control and act with dignity from the outset,* he decided. Bruce didn't deserve any less.

Oliver went to a local florist and bought two dozen pink roses. Perhaps he could do that for his daughter's birthday every year. He realised he didn't even know her name, and probably never would if he honoured the promise to himself never to see her.

He went back to the church army hostel with a spring in his step. He was a father — if not in the conventional sense, then at least he could pray for his daughter, and her mother, of course, Clara Connors, the love of his life.

## Chapter 19
## *TWO YEARS LATER*

The church army hostel Oliver had been employed by was near Wandsworth Prison. He knew that originally the church army was set up to minister to "outcasts and criminals". The slums in the neighbourhood were nothing like they had been in 1882, when the hostel was set up, but they were certainly bad enough. Oliver often thought it seemed more like an overnight shelter for rough sleepers than anything else. He found it hard to believe the number of homeless, often inebriated or high on drugs, who knocked on the door at all hours of the day and night.

The church army disallowed any alcohol on its premises, which meant that many of the people that Oliver was able to persuade to come to the hostel left within a day or two to resume begging. A few coins would go towards a bottle of the hard stuff, or sometimes they might steal it from the local shop.

Some of them had simply fallen on hard times. Perfectly decent, law-abiding citizens had been unlucky — couldn't pay the rent, lost their jobs and therefore their livelihood, been booted out by their families and so on. Oliver found these people particularly heart-breaking. They were not used to sleeping rough and were humiliated and perplexed to find themselves in this position. *There but for the grace of God,* he often thought.

Sometimes, Oliver would tour the surrounding streets on foot, talking to the homeless who might be huddled in doorways, under bridges or inside shop fronts. He found that a surprising number had dogs with them, who would sit passively by their side and hope that a morsel or two would come their way. Often their dogs were fed before they were. Oliver did not find it hard to show compassion to them, but he knew that the most convincing way to help was to give them shelter, a bed and a decent meal. Actions, not words, spoke to them more clearly.

He often thought about the contrast between his work at the theatre and his work now. The theatre work had been fulfilling, exciting even, and he grew to love the actors there who were a colourful lot generally, and not without their emotional needs. But this work on the streets was strangely more rewarding. When he was able to persuade a rough sleeper to come inside, or managed to scoop up a bewildered ex-prisoner, he felt he was very close to ministering not only to them but to God — "Whatever you do to these my brethren" etcetera. Somehow his acts of self-sacrifice — Oliver was hard up himself, and often cold — were identifying in a real way with the homeless and the pitiful. This gave Oliver some peace of mind. He had a hopeful belief that he was somehow working his passage to forgiveness, even though his theology told him that there was a small matter — he smiled wryly — of the grace of God involved.

His little daughter would be nearly three years old now. On her first and second birthday he had delivered pink roses and went to great lengths to disguise from where they had been bought, always delivering them at the dead of night. He moved very quickly up to the front porch and back, as Midas always barked, but no one came to the window or the door, so he assumed he was unseen. The pain of it all had lessened considerably and he was now able to think of Clara more objectively, without his stomach turning a somersault every time.

\*\*\*

Some months later, on a cold winter's morning when the temperature was well below zero and ice was beginning to form on the edges of the river, Oliver went for a quick run before the day began. He would be back at the hostel in time to help serve the breakfast porridge. He was fitter than he used to be, eating just enough food to keep him healthy and no more. He had taken to having an early morning run in order to clear his head and refresh himself for the many demands his job put upon him.

He approached Wandsworth Bridge and began to run on the tow path underneath it. When he reached the middle, he almost skidded to a halt. He saw a big bundle of torn blankets roughly rolled into a shape. In the middle of the bundle what he thought was a dead body. On closer inspection he realised that the body was breathing — just. The hairs on a grey beard barely visible were frozen. Oliver gingerly pulled back the freezing blanket to reveal the bearded face of a man of indeterminate age. He was breathing irregularly and seemed hardly alive — virtually frozen to death, observed Oliver sadly. Oliver took off his own jacket, pulled back the blanket further and laid the jacket on the chest and neck of the man, tucking it in at the sides. This left Oliver with just his shirt on his upper body. He was about to set off to the nearest telephone box, when the man stirred and spoke in a cracked, breathy whisper,

'You. Leave — me — *alone.*'

Oliver knelt.

'You need help, Sir. You are freezing here.'

'I want to — die,' said the man weakly.

He then turned his head away and sank again into oblivion.

Oliver was not sure what his next course of action should be. Ambulance? Police? Or let the man have his way and be left to die?

Decision made. Oliver left the man and ran all the way back in his shirt. When he reached the church army, he was freezing cold himself despite the run, but went quickly inside to grab his car keys and a rough grey blanket from his bed. He ran into the breakfast room and asked Robbie, a rather truculent-looking lad who was already lining up for breakfast, to come and help him. Robbie was recently out of prison, and Oliver had gone to meet him at the gates of Wandsworth Prison on his release. Putting the blanket round his shoulders now, Oliver pulled him from the queue and out to Oliver's broken-down car and turned the key in the ignition. No response.

Oliver had not prayed in any formal sense for a long time he was ashamed to say, but here, at the steering wheel, he bent his head and prayed out loud that God would help him to rescue this man and that his car would start. Robbie witnessed this with a look of incredulity. Praying that a *car* would start? Oliver turned the ignition again several times. The car finally spluttered then sprang into life and he drove along the icy roads, skidding perilously at times, and parked at the top of the bridge under which the man lay. Both men raced down to the tow path. Between them they managed to carry the man up to the car. There was no sound from him. His body had become very floppy inside his frozen blankets. Oliver knew he was near death.

'He's not going to make it, Oli Locki.'

'We mustn't give up on him yet.'

Robbie shrugged.

'P'raps we'd better say a prayer for him to spring into life like your car did!' the lad said in a mocking tone.

'That's not a bad idea, Robbie. But for now let's concentrate on getting him back.'

'Afraid your miracle won't work a second time?' Robbie replied.

Inside himself, Robbie was not sure whether what he had said to Oliver was that funny. There was something about this Oli Locki that suddenly made him stop his cynical tone.

With great difficulty — the ground was slippery and the man a dead weight — they managed to heave him onto the back seat of the car. He smelt dreadfully of stale urine and filth. He was covered in his own detritus.

'Now Robbie, sit on the back seat with him and support his head. There's just about enough room.'

'You asking me to sit next to this filthy turd?'

'No, I'm not asking you, I'm telling you,' replied Oliver.

The tone of voice of "Oli Locki" meant that Robbie no longer questioned or contradicted him. Oliver, normally mild-mannered, was speaking with authority.

When they reached the church army hostel, they carried the dying man to Oliver's room along the corridor. Once inside, they lay him on the bed. Robbie noted that Oli Locki didn't seem worried by the fact that his sheets would be made filthy and smell of everything bad under the sun. Oliver put his head on the man's chest to see if he could hear breathing.

'He's alive,' he said to Robbie. 'Right. We must warm him up.'

'Let's take the bugger down to the bath,' suggested Robbie.

'No, no. He must be warmed up very gradually. That would be far too much of a shock for him.'

'OK. What shall I do?' said Robbie, embarrassed by his own sudden show of good will.

'Right. Help me take his coat off, then we'll wrap him in my bed cover,' said Oliver. 'But we have to be very gentle, otherwise it will be too much for him.'

"Gentle" was not a word Robbie was either used to hearing or acting out. He had been in prison for grievous bodily harm, having broken the cheekbone of a police officer amongst other things during a street brawl. He had never received gentleness from anyone very much at all, having been brought up in a run-down state orphanage from birth. Both parents had been heavily involved with a life of crime, locked up more times than they had been free, and Robbie certainly didn't intend to weaken himself by being "gentle" now.

*"The fathers have eaten sour grapes and the children's teeth have been set on edge".*

*How true,* Oliver had thought when Robbie had started to share his story with him one evening. Oliver decided that there was a great deal of unravelling of twisted threads to do in Robbie before he would begin to mend.

Robbie started tugging roughly at the sleeves.

'I said *gently,*' Oliver ordered. 'Either do as I say or get out, Robbie. Now.'

Robbie nodded, surprised by Oli-Lock's tone.

'OK Guv. I 'eard you.'

Together they worked on the frozen coat and eventually got it off.

'Thank you, Robbie. That was great.'

Robbie looked down. He wasn't used to anyone saying he had done anything of any worth.

'Now, let's wrap him in this.'

Robbie took the cotton bedspread from Oliver and the pair gently wrapped the man in it. 'Keep it loose, Robbie. We mustn't restrict his movements.'

Together they tended the man. They avoided warming his hands and feet — too much of a shock to the system, Oliver said for the second time. Then Oliver put the kettle on and made a cup of lukewarm, sweet tea in the hopes that the man might revive enough to have a few sips.

Very gradually he did begin to show signs of life. It was a heart-stopping moment for Oliver. He had feared there was no hope for the man.

'You did it, Guv,' Robbie whispered.

'No Robbie. *We* did it. You've been a tremendous help. Now, offer him the tea. Take it right up to his lips and be patient.'

Robbie did as Oliver said, and he dimly began to realise that he was being taught how to be gentle. The man did not respond.

'Robbie, take this piece of clean lint, dunk it in the tea and then moisten his lips,' Oliver said.

Robbie did as he said. The man revived a little more, and Robbie instinctively offered the cup of tea again to him. The man took a tiny sip and then spoke to Robbie.

'Thank you, boy.'

Robbie continued to hold the cup and offer sips. Oliver looked across at him and realised he had tears in his eyes. *Maybe there have been more miracles than one today,* he thought. The car was just the start of it.

\*\*\*

Robbie had fetched the one and only bedpan from the store cupboard, left it with Oliver and then went to his own quarters. Seeing to the man's toilet affairs was a step too far for him. Oliver managed it somehow and then the man slept in his bed all night. Oliver kipped down on the floor

223

in his clothes and covered himself with his one remaining thin grey blanket. It seemed like he was listening for the entire night to the man's intermittent breathing. He was certainly a very sick gentleman of the road.

In the morning, Oliver fetched a small bowl of porridge and left it to cool on his bedside cabinet. The man was still sleeping so he quickly went to the washroom, did his morning ablutions then, shivering with the cold, came back and dressed by the one-bar electric fire. Still the man slept. Oliver worried that he was slipping back into his comatose state, but within a few minutes the man began to stir, lifted his head and slowly gazed around.

'Good Morning, Sir. It's all right. You're safe. You're in a church army hostel. We brought you out of the cold. You were freezing.'

'I — didn't — want — that,' said the man gruffly, struggling for breath.

'I couldn't just leave you to die. You were only a step away from being swept up by the Grim Reaper, you know. My name's Oliver. What's your name, Sir?'

'It doesn't — matter,' wheezed the man.

'It would be nice to call you by it,' replied Oliver.

The man somehow eased himself up on his elbows and looked darkly at Oliver,

'I said — it doesn't — matter.'

'Would you like a little porridge,' said Oliver, ignoring the swipe of verbal anger. 'Try some.'

The man gingerly took a few mouthfuls then sank back onto his bed. This was going to be an uphill struggle. Just then, there was a knock at the door. It was Robbie.

'Just come to see how the old bugger is,' he said. 'Or if he popped his clogs in the night?'

'He's alive enough to put me in my place,' laughed Oliver. 'You have a go.'

Robbie bent over the man.

'Watcha mate. You nearly copped it yesterday. It if wasn't for 'im here you'd have been a goner. You should be bloody grateful.'

The man looked at Robbie.

'How — old are — you?' he whispered.

'Nineteen. Want to make something of it?'

The man sank back on the pillow, exhausted. He slept again, and when he finally woke, Oliver said,

'We must get you out of these clothes. I'll give you a blanket bath if you're agreeable.'

The man said nothing. Secretly, he was longing for dry clothes.

'Robbie will help me, I'm sure, won't you, Robbie?'

'Only if he tells me his name,' replied Robbie.

The man said nothing but turned his head away and shut his eyes.

'All right then, I'm just going to call you "Fred". OK Fred?'

No response.

'Come on, Fred, buck up. Let's get these disgusting trousers off. How long have you been in these, mate? They stink rotten.'

Oliver watched as Robbie took the trousers off. Robbie was learning to be gentle, Oliver noted, as he was stopping himself from pulling the trousers hard and hurting Fred. He seemed to be getting through to Fred in a way that he hadn't. While Robbie was struggling to take Fred's rancid socks off, Oliver went through the pockets of a long threadbare brownish cardigan Fred had on, looking for any signs of identification. All he could find was a piece of paper, brown with age, folded into an inside pocket. There was an address on it — soggy, but not obliterated. He just about deciphered it: a W5 address. *Hmm. A posh part of Ealing,* Oliver remembered. *Surely Fred couldn't have lived there? If so,* Oliver wondered, *exactly what was his story to have brought him so low?*

He thought it not a good idea to ask Fred about the address, but that once he was sure he was recovering reasonably well, Oliver would take a trip to Ealing W5 and see if he could find anyone who knew anything about him.

Slowly and steadily Fred began to recover. After two weeks he was able to move into another room, finally allowing Oliver to have a proper night's sleep in his own bed. On the first morning, Robbie knocked on Fred's door.

'Coming to breakfast, mate?'

Fred tried to walk with Robbie, but his legs simply would not work. He sank back down on the side of the bed.

'Don't worry, Fred. I'll fetch it for you again. No hurry, is there mate?'

By the end of the week, Oliver felt that Fred was safe enough in Robbie's care for the morning, so he set off for Ealing W5. He had no idea whether this was where Fred had lived, whether there might be a long-lost wife, or even ancient mother living there. He walked up the steps of the rather grand house, rang the door and waited. He could hear a child crying inside.

Eventually, a young woman, pretty, but looking harassed and flustered, opened the door.

'Sorry to keep you waiting. He's been having a temper tantrum, throwing himself on the ground. Terrible Twos,' she said grimacing. 'They all seem to have to go through them. I heard the bell but I couldn't come. Are you delivering something? Or are you a Jehovah's Witness?'

'No, I'm not, actually, on either counts,' said Oliver, looking down at his clothes. He wondered what kind of a sight he must be, with many nights of little sleep, overlong hair flopping in his eyes and rather jaded clothes.

'I've come to see if you might be able to help me — shed any light on something.'

The woman shrugged. 'I doubt I can, but I'll try.' The child was now pulling her hair in frustration. 'He used to be an angel but now he's the worst of the four,' she said, laughing. 'He's a little love really but more work than the others put together.'

The tiny boy suddenly pulled the woman's hair violently, making her cry out,

'Hey, you! That's *not kind!*'

The boy went into shrieks of laughter. Oliver suddenly thought of his own daughter. He wondered if she enjoyed pulling Clara's chestnut locks, but then he quickly banished the thought, and concentrated on the task in hand. He explained that he had found this address in a vagrant's pocket and went on to say how he had been freezing to death on the towpath under Wandsworth Bridge. The woman shook her head.

'Poor chap. Not the weather to be out. I don't think I can help you,' she said. 'No one like that lives around here — not in W5!' she said, and a smile suddenly lit up her face. 'They're all too well heeled here!'

'That must include you, then,' said Oliver, also smiling. 'I'm Oliver Lockwood,' he said, holding out his hand.

The toddler started crying again and interrupting what the young woman was going to say. She picked up the child.

'Pleased to meet you. I work here. I'm Connie.'

# Chapter 20

Over a cup of tea Oliver began to explain more about the man he had saved.

'He's rather aggressive and obviously bears a huge grudge against life in general. I don't know if he has any family. He won't say. He refuses even to tell me his name.'

He glanced down to put sugar in his tea and stir it.

When he looked up, he saw that the woman was examining the writing on the piece of paper closely and had turned a deathly pale.

'Are you all right, Mrs, Miss — er — Connie?'

'I'm thinking I might be recognizing the writing on this piece of paper,' she said almost to herself.

She put the child down, kept staring in disbelief at the piece of paper in her hand and fetched her rosary from the sideboard. She looked hard at the man opposite her. Oliver Lockwood somehow seemed to invite confidences. A man to be trusted.

'Can you tell me exactly how you found this man, would you, Mr Lockwood?'

Oliver explained to Connie the story of where he had found the man, how he had enlisted Robbie's help, Robbie's reaction to his prayer over the car, and how the old man seemed to respond to the lad.

As she listened, Connie sensed that there was something very special about this man. He was shot through with gentleness, and moreover, he was a man of faith. That resonated with Connie. When Oliver had come to the end, she found she wanted to share with him her story.

'My brother and I have become estranged to my father. I was — abused by him as a child — did all sorts of things he shouldn't have — so did I — but I didn't know at the time it was wrong. My brother could never forgive him.'

She moved along the beads of the rosary quickly with her fingers.

'It's a long story,' she continued. 'My mother died and I left home as soon as I could and I've worked here ever since. My father forced me to give him my new address. I didn't want to, but it was hard to disobey him.'

She paused, unsure of whether she should be telling Oliver all of this.

'Only tell me if you want to,' he said gently.

*He would make a good priest,* she thought. He was warm and patient with a loving manner. Connie began again hesitantly but gathered pace as she spoke.

'After I left, he sold our semi-detached family home. I don't think it would have fetched much. I've no idea what became of him. I assume he found himself another woman. I just hope he didn't marry again and put another woman what my mother had to go through.'

Oliver said nothing. She rapidly fingered round the rosary, and he realised that during her pauses she was praying under her breath.

'Oh dear, that sounds awful, doesn't it? But he was a terrible bully. I want to tell you something awful now.' Connie paused, her face twitching with pain.

'My brother hanged himself because—' She stopped suddenly 'Oh, it doesn't matter, you don't want to hear all this.'

Connie couldn't believe she was telling these things to a stranger. By this time, Oliver's stomach was starting to flip.

'What did you say your surname was?' he asked politely.

'Connors. I'm Constance Connors.'

It was Oliver's turn to blanch. He suddenly felt as though he was going to pass out, but instead gulped his tea and held his nerve.

'Are you thinking that this man might be your father?' She looked down.

'I'm thinking that God moves in a mysterious way,' she said softly.

'I second that,' replied Oliver.

Suddenly, Connie straightened herself and spoke in a voice that defied opposition,

'If it *is* him, I never want to see him or have anything to do with him, I'm afraid.'

'I understand that,' said Oliver. 'But could you bring yourself to stand in the doorway and tell me whether you think it is him? He doesn't need to see you. If not, I'll have to start all over again.'

'No. I'm sorry. There are too many painful memories.'

She looked down, a picture of sorrow and hurt. Quite suddenly, her face softened and she smiled.

'But God is good. The nightmares have got a much better since I've been looking after my little niece sometimes. She's coming up to three. A gorgeous little thing if ever I saw one.'

So this was Bruce's little sister whom he had spoken of sometimes. The next question felt as though it would burn his lips.

'Oh how lovely. What's your little niece's name?
'Kitty.'

Kitty. So now he finally knew the name of his child.
'That's unusual.'

'My sister-in-law is an unusual person'.

A pause.

'So how are your brother and his wife?'.

She looked at him quizzically.

'You don't know them, do you?'

Oliver quickly shook his head ambiguously, rapidly changing the subject.

'Connie, it's important that we identify this man. His family deserves to know what's happened to him.'

'His family may not care, Mr Lockwood. Look, I'd help if I could, but please don't ask me again.'

Desperate, Oliver played what he knew might seem a shabby card to Connie.

'Connie, I see you have a rosary. Could this be God calling you to meet your father?'

He didn't think much of himself for using what could be interpreted as spiritual blackmail. Clearly Connie didn't either.

'I really don't think that is a helpful thing to say. You don't know anything about me or how much I have prayed that I would find it in my heart to forgive my father for — for wrecking all our lives in some way or another.'

Suddenly she burst into tears. The little boy was frightened and started crying at the sight of her. Oliver bent down to him.

'Oh I'm sorry little one. We didn't mean to frighten you.' He gently put his hands on Connie's shoulders. 'Please forgive me, Connie, Miss Connors. I've trespassed on your feelings and I had no right to do that. I won't bother you again.'

With that, he made a quick exit. What a disaster! He had caused nothing but pain to the Connors family one way and another.

## Chapter 21

Oliver returned to the hostel deflated and feeling he had handled things badly. He knew there was no chance of Connie coming to see if Fred was indeed her father. Robbie ran up to him as he was parking the car.

'Oli Locki. Fred has taken a downward turn. He can't breathe very well.'

'Right. Has he got up at all today?'

'No. He seems very weak.'

Oliver went to see Fred. He was lying in a pool of sweat, with an obviously high temperature. His breathing was erratic and Oliver was sure he had pneumonia. It was even more imperative now that there was confirmation over his relations. Oliver called the hostel doctor to come.

'He's pretty ill,' the doctor told Oliver. 'Pneumonia on both lungs. Has he been sleeping rough?'

Oliver filled the doctor in with the story of the frozen man, the rescue, and his progress since then. This was certainly a swift relapse.

'You'd better inform his next of kin. We're looking at a dying man here. I won't hospitalize him. He's too ill to be moved. I'll prescribe some antibiotics, but we're probably too late. The infection has really got a grip on him.'

Oliver didn't want to leave him alone overnight, so he went back to his room, fetched the blankets from his bed, took them back to Fred's tiny room and once more spent a fitful night on the floor listening to the laboured, rasping breathing of his room companion. The next morning, Fred was worse. Oliver wondered if this was leading up to his final curtain. *Interesting,* he thought, *a theatrical metaphor from my past life.*

Since he had met Connie, Oliver found himself thinking more about Clara and Kitty. He was glad to know the name of his little girl. She felt more real, less anonymous. He realised that he was not really yearning for Clara much nowadays but he had a deep longing to see his daughter. Seeing the little lad at Connie's had unwittingly tapped into this desire.

Oliver thought about Connie as he sat by Fred's bed on watch. He knew he had mishandled the situation but had no idea if he should try to rectify it in any way or let sleeping dogs lie. He realised he had interrupted Connie when she was sharing something at the deepest level about her dead brother. Oliver knew he had selfishly pursued his own line of thinking and interrupted, asking what her surname was. *"Once a priest, always a priest".* Well, a good priest certainly wouldn't have done that, and it must have cost Connie a lot to even begin that conversation.

Oliver was full of remorse, but felt he could not, should not, take any further action. Robbie came to relieve him of his watch, so that he could get something to eat. Robbie was proving to be a marvellous support. Oliver was beginning to love the lad. *He has an element of the*

*happy-go-lucky about him — a bit like the Artful Dodger,*
Oliver mused, but also Robbie was learning to find within
himself a real gentleness, compassion even. In between the
feelings of remorse over Connie, Oliver allowed himself a
small pat on the back for having been instrumental in
teaching Robbie how vital it was to cultivate a spirit of
kindness towards Fred.

The doctor came again the next morning after another
bad night for Fred and thought that he would not last the
day. He instructed Oliver simply to try and keep him
comfortable.

Oliver was anguished that Fred would die without
seeing any of his family or having a chance to make peace
with them. He told Robbie how he was feeling but Robbie
just shrugged his shoulders.

'We're his family now, aren't we mate?' he said,
going close to Fred's face. 'You can go now, mate, cos
neither Oli-Locki or me are gonna leave your side, are we
Guv?'

'Absolutely not,' replied Oliver, moved by Robbie
simple statements.

The two of them stayed one each side of Fred's bed as
he wheezed and heaved his way towards death.

At six o'clock in the evening, one of the wardens
knocked on Oliver's door.

'There's someone to see you, Mr Lockwood. Shall I
send them in?'

Oliver assumed it was the doctor, or even an
ambulance man come to take Fred off after all, or even,
sadly, the undertaker come to take a glimpse at his next

customer. Unfortunately that happened in the hostel sometimes. Macabre, but realistic.

There was a hesitant knock at the door. Oliver opened it.

There in front of him, like a miracle, was Connie.

'Connie,' said Oliver softly. 'I'm so glad to see you. Come in.'

She stood in the doorway.

'I don't know. I've been thinking hard ever since you left. It doesn't seem right somehow for me not to do as you asked and see if it might be my father.'

'Connie, if it is your father, I have to tell you he is dying.'

'Dying?'

'Yes. He became very ill suddenly. The doctor said he has pneumonia on both lungs. Come in and see.'

As she slowly entered, Oliver saw that she was delicate and finely made, with an aura of something special about her. *A bit of an angel coming at that minute,* he mused.

Connie went softly up to Fred and just stood. Finally, after scrutinizing him, she bent down and with a huge effort of will, spoke to him:

'Dad? It's me. Connie.'

Fred, who had not responded to anything in twenty-four hours slowly opened his eyes and murmured,

'Sadie?'

'No, Dad. Connie.'

Connie forgot all the hurt, all the damage, the bullying, the shouting, the guilt as she knelt beside him, smoothed down his beard and with an act of supreme grace and forgiveness, kissed him.

'I'm not leaving you now, Dad.'

Fred looked up and murmured breathily,

'My little Connie.'

Fred shut his eyes and Oliver and Robbie could see for the first time an expression of peace on his face.

'I'd like to stay with him tonight,' Connie said.

'It gets very cold here and I think he might die.'

'I want to,' said Connie.

Oliver didn't argue.

'I'll bring you some blankets.'

Robbie, who had been standing in the shadows by the door, came forward.

'I'll get mine too. But Miss, this is no place for a lady. I'll stay in here and you have my bed. I'll wake you if anything happens to Fred here.'

'Fred? His name's Bert. Albert, actually.'

'Oh, so now we know. He looks more like a Fred to me! Albert's a bit posh, like a King,' he said with a laugh.

'I'll stay here,' said Connie. 'He is my father, after all, but thank you all the same.'

Oliver and Robbie fetched a blanket each. When finally Oliver was tucked up under his thin blanket shivering with cold and reflecting on the curious happenings of the last few hours, he thanked God for the miracle that was Connie.

\*\*\*

Bert survived the night. Connie was up several times mopping his brow, giving him his bedpan and generally nursing him. When Oliver went in, she was asleep with her head resting on the bed. He was about to tiptoe out when Connie spoke.

'Oliver — is it all right to call you that? I will have to let my employers know where I am. Could I use your phone?'

She made the phone call and reported that the people she worked for were furious with her and told her that unless she was back by the end of the day, they would dismiss her. Connie, too, in turn, was angry.

'I have worked for that family for twelve years. I have practically brought up their four children. They are never there and the children rely on me to be a mother, father and nanny. I don't know why they ever have had any. They couldn't be less interested. I can't believe…'

Oliver put his hands on her shoulders.

'Hey, hey, you can stay here as long as you like. Don't worry too much about them. I will go and see them and explain properly. I could tell that you had given body and soul to that family.'

Connie suddenly caved in and leant on Oliver's chest and cried. It had all been so traumatic for her, and in the presence of this kind man she finally let go. Oliver held her and felt tender towards her. She was fragile and vulnerable, but with a strength and commitment to her father that moved him. It was good to have someone to hold for a brief minute. He had virtually no physical contact with anyone in the hostel apart from an occasional encouraging pat on the back or arm around someone in need.

'I'm sorry. I just felt overwhelmed for a second. I'm all right now. Do you think we should try to wash my father?'

'I think we should leave him for a little bit longer and see how things are going. Has he spoken any more?'

'He just says "Connie" repeatedly, but this morning he said, "Where's Sadie? Where's Brucey"?'

Oliver's heart stopped. Yes, Bruce should be informed. But he said nothing in response to Connie.

'I'll try him with a little porridge. Would it be all right if I went to the kitchens to ask them?' Connie asked.

Oliver kept watch over Bert while Connie went into the steaming kitchen where two women and a surly-looking man were busy preparing the breakfast. The women looked up and smiled at Connie. One of the women spoke,

'You're new here, aren't you? I hope we can provide a bit of a home for you for a little while.'

'Thank you. I've come to see my father. I think he's dying, but I'd like to try him on a little porridge please.'

'Here you are, darling. I'll put an extra bit of brown sugar in it to give his energy a boost. Hope he gets better soon.'

'Thanks,' said Connie. 'That's lovely. I'll make sure the bowl is returned to you.'

When she had gone, the man said,

'Now there's a lady if ever I saw one, but you shouldn't be giving away our sugar rations.'

The women looked at each other and raised their eyebrows. They were used to "Surly Stu", as everyone called him, and his negative comments. On her way out, Connie bumped into Robbie, who was beginning to queue for his porridge.

'Watcha Con. How's the old geyser this morning?'

Connie smiled. She couldn't take exception to the way Robbie spoke. He was friendly and kind and she warmed to his rough and ready ways.

'He's no worse,' said Connie. 'I'm going to try him on some porridge.'

'I'll be down soon. Just 'aving my breakfast first.' He smiled.

'Thank you,' said Connie, returning the smile. She reflected that she had been smiled at more times since arriving at the church army hostel than ever she had been at the Rotherham's household, apart from the children, of course.

Connie returned and swiftly took her seat by her father.

'Do you think you could just help me to prop him up?' she asked Oliver.

'Of course.'

Together they heaved the limp weight up and plumped up the pillow, putting another cushion behind it. Bert opened his eyes.

'What's this? What's going on?' he said, with a little roughness returning to his voice.

'It's all right, Dad. It's Connie. Have a little spoonful of porridge,' she said persuasively.

Oliver stood back and watched Connie. She was the personification of kindness. What a woman, to have forgiven her father so completely in such a short space of time! It was by God's grace, he knew. As he watched, something stirred in his heart. She was nothing like Clara. Clara was charismatic with a streak of wildness about her; fascinating, mercurial, beautiful, sensual. Connie was not any of those things, but she had a serenity and inner beauty about her that attracted him profoundly. Her simple spirit of goodness drew him.

Throughout the day, Bert remained stable, but Connie became agitated.

'I really ought to let Bruce know. Maybe he would like the opportunity to make his peace with Father, although somehow I doubt it.' She paused. 'I don't think it should be a phone call. It's not right to give him a shock like that.'

She paused again. Oliver held his breath. He had a feeling he knew what was coming next.

'I don't want to leave Dad. I promised him I would stay by his side,' she said. Another long pause.

Oliver felt he should volunteer to go to the house, but the ramifications of such a visit seemed endless. He remained silent.

'Oliver, you've been so kind. Could I ask you to do one more thing for me?' She was hesitant.

'Let me guess. You want me to go and tell Bruce face to face.'

'Yes please,' Connie said shyly. 'Would you?'

'Of course,' replied Oliver, but everything was screaming against it inside him.

He set off that afternoon, taking the train to give him more thinking time for the ordeal ahead. When he had first gone to the hostel in Wandsworth, he had been full of the pain of leaving Clara and had often gone through the stations he would have to travel through to reach her again. He knew this was obsessional thinking, but it soothed him somehow. It was a mental exercise that he did at night. He named the stations on the way and on the way back repeating them endlessly, but it did usually end up with his falling asleep. Putney, Barnes, Mortlake, North Sheen, Richmond upon Thames

He found himself doing it again now.

Oliver's great fear was that he might be rejected on the doorstep before he had time to get his message across. He realised with a jolt that his thinking was more about soothing Connie and fulfilling her request than anything else, although when he finally plucked up the courage to ring the doorbell, it was a young child's voice he heard. Kitty's.

Clara opened the door, with Kitty standing beside her. Clara looked thinner than ever and her hair was unkempt. Midas came bounding up, greeting Oliver like a long-lost friend.

'Oliver!' Clara almost shouted, stunned. 'Oliver! What are you doing here?'

Before he had time to answer, Kitty thrust a small soft, white bear into his hand.

'My bear,' she said sweetly. 'Dada's bear.'

'No, no, it's *Kitty's* bear,' said Clara, confused and embarrassed.

It was all that Oliver could do to remain composed. His little daughter, who had never seen her real father, was thrusting her toy into his hand. He took in that she was as pretty as a picture, with her mother's colour hair, curlier and a shade or two lighter, but veering towards chestnut.

'What do you want, Oliver?'

'I need to see Bruce, please. It's urgent. It's a message from Connie.'

'Connie? But we only saw her a fortnight ago. What's this all about?'

'Please Clara. Could you just get him for me?'

Clara could see from Oliver's demeanour that this was serious.

'You'd better come in then,' said Clara awkwardly.

'No, I'll stay here, thank you. I'd prefer to speak on the doorstep.'

Clara shrugged.

'OK. Keep an eye on Kitty while I fetch him. Watch her with the road. She's learnt to run and she's surprisingly fast when she puts her mind to it. Midas, *back!*' Clara shouted, pulling the insistent golden retriever dog by the collar.

Oliver bent down on his haunches. He played with the bear with Kitty, pretending to hide it and then making it pop up somewhere else. Kitty went into a joyous rapture of cascading laughter.

'More, more!' she said every time Oliver stopped. He played on then he heard Bruce's footsteps and stood up.

He pushed the bear into his pocket quickly so that Bruce couldn't see the bond forming between himself and Kitty.

'Oliver. What is it?'

There on the doorstep, Oliver explained the whole saga about Bert, Bruce's father. Clara removed herself and the child, moving swiftly back into the house. At the end, Oliver said simply,

'So please come back, for the sake of your father and for Connie.'

Bruce had listened intently to the story, not moving a muscle. He was shocked to the core and could feel an intense fire burning into life inside. When Oliver had finally finished, Bruce told him in no uncertain terms that nothing on this earth would make him meet his father again. He raged about Connie, saying how on earth could she do such a thing after such abuse? He declared several times that he could never, ever forgive his father, outlining the abuse of Connie, the hanging in the deepest despair of his brother James and the blow to the head that caused his mother's death.

'Are you really asking me to forgive all that?' asked Bruce, his eyes burning with anger.

'No. It's not my place to ask you, Bruce. The message comes from Connie.'

'I'm sorry, Oliver. Tell Connie I simply haven't got it in me. I do know how to forgive and move on — as you know only too well, Oliver...'

He paused before continuing, 'But this is beyond anything reasonable.'

'No, I agree. It's not reasonable. I don't think forgiveness is ever "reasonable",' replied Oliver ambiguously. He looked hard at Bruce but could see there was no way to reach him. He had built a protective ring of steel around himself.

'I'll be off then.'

'Tell Connie she's still welcome here, but I can't run to forgiveness, I'm afraid. Perhaps Connie's God is the only one who can dish out forgiveness and I think in this case even He will be hard-pressed. I hate my father too much for the damage he's done ever to be reconciled.'

'That's fair enough. I understand. I'll go. Goodbye Bruce.' He held out his hand.

'Goodbye Oliver.' He paused. 'I'm sorry to disappoint. This won't have been easy for you. Thank you.'

Bruce shut the door emphatically. Clara was waiting at the end of the hallway.

'What was that all about, Bruce?'

'I'll tell you later,' replied Bruce. 'It's weighing a bit heavy at the moment, Clara. It's what you might call a shock. It's about my father.'

'Oh *him!*' said Clara disdainfully. 'The cause of all the trouble. I hope Oliver came to tell you he's dead.'

There was a hardness in Clara's tone. He didn't blame her.

'As good as,' replied Bruce.

'Thank God for that,' she replied. 'Who knows, perhaps the damage he's done might finally die with him.'

*** 

Oliver made his way back to the station with a heavy heart. He knew why Bruce wouldn't forgive his father. It would have taken superhuman effort, and Oliver wasn't sure that the old man deserved it anyway. He had wreaked physical and emotional havoc on the entire family. How had Connie managed it — she who had been used so abusively in Bert's bed and so damaged? Oliver had seen the old scars of self-harm which extended up both arms. Even now they had not completely faded into her skin colour and he doubted they ever would. Visibly scarred for life. Oliver knew there must be many invisible scars too, but all he saw in her now was her forgiveness, her reconciliation to her father and her love in action.

He had searched her out, and in doing so he now realised he had entertained "an angel unawares".

He thought again about Clara. He was shocked to see her so changed, and there seemed a hardness about her that he hadn't seen before. Was it just that falling in love had so blown him off course that he had only noticed all the lovely things about her or had the hardness entered her since having a child? He didn't know.

He put his hand in his pocket to find money for his return ticket and drew out the soft little bear of Kitty's. He was less than fifteen minutes away from their house so decided on quickly running back and giving it back to his little girl. He remembered how attached he had been to a soft toy rabbit when he was a very small boy, and he did not want Kitty to be pining for her little bear the same way as he had.

He knocked at the door once more, panting a little from the run. Bruce opened it.

'I'm so sorry. I found Kitty's bear in my pocket. She may need it.'

Bruce took it questioningly and Clara immediately brushed past him.

'I'll come back with you, Oliver. Albert Connors needs to know what he's done. It's all very well for Connie to be all sweetness and light, but he should be answerable in some way to Bruce. If he shows signs of remorse, then Bruce will see him. I will talk to him. We've agreed.'

With that, she went quickly inside, reached for her coat, and said a brief goodbye to Kitty and Bruce.

'Trust me, Brucey' she said.

The two of them walked to the station in a constrained silence. Once on the train, Oliver, wanting to make conversation, said,

'How have things been with you, Clara?'

'Oh fine,' replied Clara. 'If you call an endless round of washing, shopping, mothering and cooking a fulfilled life.'

'Kitty is beautiful,' said Oliver, wondering if he was treading dangerously.

'Yes, she is,' replied Clara. 'But she's a wilful little thing. Always wants her own way.'

Oliver resisted saying anything but smiled a little. *Like mother, like daughter,* he thought.

Clara saw the smile and read his thoughts. A flash of the old Clara burst out laughing.

'Yes, I know just what you're thinking, Rev.'

Oliver recognised it, and laughed too, enjoying the fact that she called him "Rev" and realizing with relief that it was pleasant to be with Clara, but nothing more. He thought ruefully of the lines from Romeo and Juliet about love, *Too like the lightning which does cease to be 'ere one can say, "it lightens".*

He thought. His "lightning" had lasted over three years and his feelings had been overwhelming, but he could safely say that he felt he was more or less "over" Clara. What he did not acknowledge, perhaps sensed only dimly, was that someone else was taking up residence in his heart.

***

They arrived at the hostel. This might as well be a foreign land to Clara. She was suddenly nervous.

'Come on, Clara. Connie will be pleased to see you.'

They entered Bert's room. It was dark and dingy, with a slightly musty smell to it. Curtains hung from poles and some had come adrift from their hooks and drooped down forlornly. There in the middle of the room was Bert, now sitting up a little, with Connie one side and Robbie the other. Connie, dressed in a simple green uniform that the carers of the hostel wore, was combing his hair and Robbie was enticing him to drink from a cup with a plastic spout.

'Clara!' exclaimed Connie. 'It's nice to see you. I was expecting Bruce. Where is he? Is he coming?'

'He may come later. That depends on *him*,' said Clara, pointing her finger at Bert.

'He's definitely a little better,' said Connie.

'You two have done that,' said Oliver.

'Not me, Guv. She hasn't left his side. Reckon she's worn out.'

'Let me sit by him,' said Clara, oversweetly.

Both Connie and Robbie moved aside.

As soon as Clara sat by Bert, she started speaking slowly and clearly in his ear.

'I have a message from Bruce.'

'Bruce! Here?' said Bert distinctly.

'Not yet,' said Clara. 'But he sends a message. This is the message.' She spoke a little louder without hesitation:

'Bruce says that you are responsible for several things in his childhood:

*One:* you abused your youngest daughter Connie by using her, a six-year-old, for your own sexual gratification. This happened night after night because he heard you. You damaged Bruce's chances in marriage through your — sexual exploits.' She spat the last two words at him.

*Two:* You mauled his older sister Sadie's friends in a most dirty way. She left home early because of you and has not been seen since, depriving her mother of her eldest daughter. She was only fifteen.

*Three:* You bullied and ridiculed your eldest son James to such an extent that he *hanged himself, he took his own life because of you!*' she shouted.

Oliver moved quickly up to Clara.

'Clara, you cannot do this to a dying man. Hold your tongue for pity's sake.'

Clara shoved him away angrily.

'Don't tell me what to do. This is *my* business and Bruce's. Not yours.'

Bert was already cowering in the bed, pulling the covers up around himself. Robbie had left the room. Connie stood silently weeping in the corner.

'*Four:* It was *your* fault that Bruce's mother died. *your fault*! Bruce told me he had been trying to defend his mother and *you* made her bash her head against the wall, causing a brain haemorrhage.'

Clara was screaming now. It was as if all the failed attempts of Bruce to reach fulfilment in bed with Clara were tumbling out in a torrent of blame and loathing.

'Now. What have you got to say for yourself, Mr Albert Connors? Hmm?'

Her eyes were wild with fury. She was out of control. She started pummelling the bedclothes and punching his stomach.

'Well? Anything?'

This time Oliver restrained her forcibly and made her sit down.

'Leave me alone, *Rev* Lockwood. You're not so perfect. After all, I'm saddled with *your* child.'

There was a shocked silence. Connie took her hands away from her face and stared at Oliver in disbelief. Oliver looked down.

Bert had hidden himself completely under the bedclothes. Finally, Clara pulled the covers down and spoke clearly into his ear.

'So you have a lot to say sorry for. Are you going to or are you going to die unrepentant and leave your children bitter forever?'

Connie interjected in a whisper.

'No, Clara. I'm not bitter. You're wrong about that.'

'Well Bruce is that's for sure. He's not coming near the place unless his father shows some remorse and then he *might* consider it.'

Bert had turned his head away. Oliver remained looking down and Connie silently went up to the bed and took Bert's hand. Clara was finally quiet, burnt out.

'I must go. He's clearly not going to give any kind of an apology.' She turned to Oliver and took his hand.

'I'm sorry, Oliver, I shouldn't have said that about you. I went too far.'

With that she was gone. No one followed her or asked her to come back. Oliver never wanted to see her again. He turned back to Bert. Bert was whispering to Connie. Tears fell from his misty dark eyes and rolled down his cheek. He spoke hesitatingly but clearly.

'Connie. I'm — sorry — if — I hurt you.'

She put his head on her chest and rocked him.

'Don't fret, Daddy,' she said. 'It was a long time ago.'

Oliver saw in Connie the quintessential spirit of humanity and at that moment he wanted to preserve it and keep it with him for the rest of his life. The comparison with Clara was starkly clear.

During the night, Bert had a major relapse. Oliver knew it was almost certainly hastened by the shock of Clara's angry words. He didn't blame Clara. She clearly needed Bruce's father to know in no uncertain terms the woes he had inflicted on his family. Oliver was shocked and saddened, however, that the woman he had loved so deeply could show such transparent venom, and frankly, cruelty to a dying man. Connie too was deeply appalled, and little did she know that it was to change her relationship with Clara for ever.

Connie called Oliver to Bert's bedroom where she had been keeping watch. Bert's breathing was rapid and heaving. Oliver stood by his bed, and Connie and he stayed there for the rest of the night. With one marathon effort, Bert reached out for Oliver's hand, and with the strength that sometimes seems to come very near death, he spoke strongly and clearly.

'Sorry, Bruce. Sorry. Please forgive me.'

Oliver realised that he was mistaking him for Bruce in his last moments. He could not let this man go to his grave with his request unacknowledged.

'Yes. You're forgiven,' said Oliver softly, and added in a whisper, 'Dad.'

As Bert drifted towards his final moments, Oliver crossed him on his forehead.

'Into thy hands O Lord we commend his spirit.'

Connie joined in with, 'Amen.'

Albert breathed his last without a struggle and died at 7.47 a.m.

They remained silent for some time. Finally, Connie whispered to Oliver,

'Don't call anyone yet. I just want to stay with him for a bit.'

Oliver sensed that Connie wanted to be on her own, so he left her and went to find Robbie, who was in the breakfast queue.

'Robbie, Bert's gone,' he said quietly. 'He died peacefully.'

'Blimey and I thought he was getting better,' said Robbie, who had turned pale.

'I know what it was,' he added angrily. 'It was that witch of a woman giving him what for on his deathbed. I hope she rots in hell.'

Oliver touched his arm, saying, 'Everyone's in pain, Robbie. This isn't a time for anger.'

Robbie gave him a disparaging look and carried on queuing for his porridge.

# Chapter 22

When Clara had returned home from her momentous visit, she related to Bruce what had happened and what she had said.

'When I saw your father lying there, I was so angry that I probably said too much, but I don't regret it. I hate him for all the devastation he has caused Bruce.'

Bruce said nothing. He knew what Clara was like when she was fired up. He had been on the receiving end on several occasions. He also knew that at grass roots Clara was not a vindictive person and that sooner or later she would regret having spoken so ferociously to him. That was the usual pattern after an outburst. He also admired his wife for her courage.

'How did you leave it then, Clara?'

'I told him that unless he was prepared to say sorry, you wouldn't come to see him. Then I just left.'

Bruce made his decision, and the next day he set off for the church army hostel.

'I don't want to do this, but I think I must go, not for him, for Connie.'

'Yes,' said Clara 'I knew you'd say that. She deserves you but he certainly doesn't.'

She looked at Kitty. Kitty didn't deserve the harsh words Clara had said to Oliver about her either and Clara had a pang of shame. She wanted to put it right.

'Kitty, would you like a treat today as Daddy's going out?'

Kitty reached for her bear and kissed it joyfully. Clara knelt.

'Shall we go to the cafe and have a beef burger, Kitty?'

'Ooh yes, yes!' said Kitty, jumping up and down and at her most winsome asked, with a coquettish smile,

'And Bear?' She thrust Bear into Clara's face.

'Yes, and for Bear too,' Clara smiled. 'And we may even have an ice cream and a milkshake!'

'Nice Muma, nice Muma,' said Kitty, kissing her bear.

Bruce was always pleased when he saw a glimmer of real warmth coming from Clara to her child. It was in rather short supply and Kitty was delighted. Clara must be feeling bad.

\*\*\*

It was nearly half-past-nine when Bruce arrived at the hostel door. He had been delayed by the morning rush hour on the train and was later than he intended to be.

Clara had described where his father's room was. Bruce was let in by a kindly young girl who was helping at the hostel. He made his way to the room and knocked. No answer. Tentatively opening the door and looking inside he saw that on a bed in the middle of the room was a large white sheet which was clearly covering a body. Bruce tiptoed up and slowly lifted the top end of the sheet. The body underneath was already beginning to show signs of rigor mortis.

Bruce scrutinized the face closely. Despite the beard, the grey-white hair and the alabaster pallor, Bruce could see that it was his father, older, but recognizable. He immediately remembered his father's loud, domineering voice, and shuddered. No one had shut his father's eyes in death, so they now stared out, unseeing, glazed and grey as granite, powerless to hurt. Bruce remembered them flashing and bloodshot as his father shouted drunkenly at his mother and she cowered into a corner and shielded her face from the blows which were bound to come. Bruce remembered all these things and felt afresh how much he hated his father. He felt nothing but loathing as he stared at the dead body. He towered over his father and said out loud,

'Thank God we're all finally rid of you, Albert Connors. May you rot in hell,'

With more force than was needed, he closed his father's eyelids, saying,

'Now you can't look your evil out to the world, you wicked old man.'

He stared for a final time then replaced the sheet, moved back and drawing out a piece of paper and a pen from his pocket, scribbled a note:

"Dear Connie. I came to see our father, but I'm too late. Thank you for dealing with all this. Hope you're OK. I'll be in touch very soon. Love Bruce xx."

He couldn't face anyone now so he went for a long walk around Wandsworth. It was a misty morning, which lent a subtle charm to the place. The sound of traffic was muted and a kind of peace had descended on buildings and streets that were normally buzzing. Bruce headed for Wandsworth bridge where Oliver had told him he had found his father almost frozen to death. The mist hung over the water so that the other side of the bank was invisible, as if wrapped in a shroud. He shivered. Standing under the bridge he waited for shock, or even sadness to take hold of him, but all he could feel was utter, utter relief as the chill of the mist swirled around him. He had no belief in God, but he thanked Him for his father's death.

He suddenly felt an urgent desire to get back to Clara. He needed her arms around him. Clara could be cold and dismissive, mocking even, but he knew that in his hour of need, whatever it was, she was always there, and he for her. There was a deep love between them even though Clara's tongue could have an abrasive edge that was often directed at him.

Clara had returned from an early lunch with Kitty, who was now having her customary sleep after lunch. She looked at Bruce's face but could not quite read his expression.

'Bruce, how was it? Did you speak to him?'

'He's dead, Clara. Dead as a doornail. He will never ever be a force to reckon with again.'

'Thank God,' said Clara and meant it.

She made him a sandwich — his favourite — stilton cheese and pickle on thick farmhouse bread, and they sat quietly mulling things over. After lunch, Bruce sat on the sofa with his wife and he felt a depth of peace he could never remember feeling before. Eventually, he said,

'Clara, darling, will you come upstairs with me?'

Clara for once did not resist. She could see that something had changed in Bruce. Wanting to respond, she put her arms around him.

'Come on then,' she said gently, leading him by the hand.

There followed the most tender, generous, leisurely lovemaking between the two of them. Afterwards they lay in each other's arms, both fulfilled and moved by the momentousness of what had just happened. Bruce realised that it was his father's power alone now that was impotent. He himself was released. He and Clara lay there in peace holding each other until finally Kitty tottered in.

'You bed? Not night time yet. Silly Mummy, silly Daddy!'

They both laughed and Clara opened her arms to welcome her daughter in to lie between them in the warmth.

'Bear too?'

'Bear too,' they both said in unison.

Kitty snuggled down with an ecstatic smile on her face. This was very nice!

\*\*\*

There were many things that Connie wanted to ask Oliver about as a result of Clara's outburst. She knew full well that Kitty was not Bruce's child, although it no longer felt relevant. He had shared that with her some time ago. In her mind she began to piece together the jigsaw puzzle. Bruce had said that it was a priest who had fathered Clara's child, and Connie remembered being appalled. Now, faced with the possibility that kind and decent Oliver might be the father, Connie was forced to revise her opinion. Oliver, a priest? It had a ring of truth about it. How many times had she thought he bore the hallmark of a man of God? Singled out — special somehow.

Connie decided not to ask Oliver about it for a while. There were urgent practicalities to be put in place.

The body of Albert Connors was removed without fuss. Connie decided that he should have the simplest of funerals, with just a short service at the crematorium, but conducted by a Roman Catholic priest. She found the undertaker's questions quaint almost. What kind of coffin would she like for him? What should her father be dressed in? Would she like the coffin left unsealed? In answer to the type of coffin, she simply replied, 'The cheapest,' and was informed that it would be plywood. No thank you, no fancy dress. So just the white Alb that was included in the price of the funeral? Yes please, and yes, leave the coffin unsealed in case her sister Sadie might by some miracle come and want to see him.

Connie had very little money and the cost of the funeral was way beyond her means. She decided she would have to ask Bruce if he could manage to pay. She telephoned him to tell him the date of the funeral and he straight away said he would pay outright to have his father buried (adding ambiguously 'It'll be a pleasure'), so that was one problem crossed off the list. No, he would rather not see their father. It certainly wasn't the usual case of wanting to remember him as he was. Bruce did not want to remember him at all, ever.

Connie decided to have one last try to get a message to Sadie, wherever she was and whoever she was with. She had heard the SOS messages that went out on the BBC Home Service just before the main six o'clock news. She had always thought how chilling it must be to receive a message about a loved one in trouble in that way. The BBC agreed to broadcast it:

*This is an SOS message from her brother and sister for Miss Sadie Connors no fixed address: please could she come to the church army hostel in Wandsworth where her father has sadly died. For more details contact…*

(Then the BBC telephone number followed).

Connie also asked Robbie if he would come to the funeral.

'Yep. I'll be there to see the old geyser off. Never been to a funeral. It'll be a novelty. Anyway, I liked the old boy. 'Him and me, we was like this.' He crossed his index and middle fingers indicating closeness.

Connie was gratified to hear that someone spoke well of him. Having forgiven him herself she found it difficult that her siblings could not at least make some attempt to manage their feelings of bitterness. It looked, therefore, as though there would be just three mourners attending: Oliver, Robbie and herself. She wondered if Bruce might come to support her, but she couldn't bank on that.

The day before the funeral Connie decided that she was going down by the river bank to pick wild flowers from the long grasses that lined the path to put on her father's coffin. Oliver asked if she would like company, and replying in the affirmative, the two set off together. Along the river bank were a few early spring flowers beginning to shoot – celandines, one or two primroses, plenty of snowdrops and here and there a few tiny wild orchids. Oliver and Connie spent an absorbed half-hour picking them. They came to the bridge under which Albert Connors had almost frozen to death. Connie shuddered.

'Connie, walk under the bridge with me. You need to do it otherwise you'll never set foot on this part of the towpath again and it's a lovely walk that leads eventually to Greenwich.'

Still she hesitated, so Oliver gently took her hand and guided her through the dark passage and out the other side. He didn't let go of her hand. Once, when they had to walk single file to let a cyclist go by, and Oliver reluctantly had to let her hand go, it was Connie who then reached out for his when it was safe again. They only dropped hands when they were within a few yards of the church army hostel.

She smiled up at him.

'Thanks so, Oliver. The path to Greenwich next time!'

'Absolutely,' he replied and raised her hand and kissed it.

***

That evening Robbie, Connie and Oliver sat by the same table as each other for supper. There were several new folks in, some, as usual, much the worse for wear and drink. Oliver mentally made a list of them and decided that he would catch them all at breakfast the following day and make a point of welcoming them. *Sufficient unto the day,* he thought, as for now the three of them needed to remain close to each other to provide mutual support in preparation for the following day. That was what he told himself, anyway, as he slid himself down the bench as far as he could towards Connie.

'Coffee in my room afterwards?' said Oliver.

'I'm on the washing up rota. Tough, innit?' said Robbie with a smile. 'Thanks though, Oli-Locki.'

Just then the senior cook, round and red-faced — the one who had put the extra sugar in Bert's tea — came out of the kitchen.

'We've got a job going in the kitchen, Connie. Mary's left to look after her mother. Can you take it up? We're very short-staffed.'

Connie looked at Oliver.

'Go on, Connie. We'd all love you to stay, wouldn't we, Robbie?'

'You bet,' replied Robbie. 'I need someone to throw plates to when I'm on drying-up. It'll be boring without Mary. She was good fun. Anyway,' he added with a knowing smile 'I think our Oli-Locki might miss you just a bit if you went.'

Oliver swiped him over the head with a newspaper. Embarrassed, he realised that their closeness had not gone unnoticed. Connie blushed.

'Thank you,' replied Connie with very little hesitation. 'I'd love to,' and meant it.

'Drop into the office after breakfast tomorrow and we'll sort you out. Mind you, we don't pay a king's ransom, but you get all your food and keep.'

That evening, Connie went back to Oliver's room for the coffee she had been promised. It was time for some answers before anything further developed.

***

Connie didn't know how to start, so she fingered her rosary in her tunic pocket. 'Help me say it right,' she silently prayed.

'Oliver, I need to talk to you about what happened the other day with Clara.'

'I thought you might,' sighed Oliver, thinking this was *the* make-or-break conversation.

'I want to tell you that I have always known that Kitty is not Bruce's child, although God knows he is a really wonderful father and Kitty loves him to pieces,' she said.

Oliver went to interrupt her, but she held up a hand.

'Please let me finish,' said Connie. 'I'm not as good with words as you are and I need to keep going.'

Oliver nodded.

'When Clara said about being saddled with the child…' She suddenly broke away from her measured tones and went over to Oliver and kneeled impulsively at his feet, looking up and blurting out the urgent question that she had been wanting to ask for three weeks.

'Oh Oliver, is it true? *Are* you Kitty's father?'

Oliver said nothing. He took her face in his hands and said with a whisper,

'I am, Connie. Yes. I'm so sorry.'

Quite suddenly, it was as though a river of tears opened in Oliver. All the conflict, the guilt, the anguish of his relationship with Clara and the sorrow over his daughter broke through the dam that had been shoring up the vast reservoir of pain inside him.

Connie laid her head on his knees. He kissed her head, and said,

'Walk away, Connie. Walk away now. I have failed God and my calling. I've given my priestly robes back and my dog collar. I knew I was no longer fit to minister or call myself a priest.'

Connie looked up at him with a steady gaze.

'Oliver — Once a priest, always a priest.'

Oliver could hardly believe what he heard. These words were spoken to him at his ordination and had reassured him in his darkest hours of self-loathing that he might still have something to offer. Now they were being spoken to him by the most truly holy person he thought he had ever met, who had been abused and bullied and who knew a depth of suffering that most had never experienced, who also knew what it was to forgive her abuser. There was a beauty about Connie, inside and out, a beauty that Oliver knew would never fade with the passing of time.

'Connie. What do you want to do? I've wronged your brother and I know how you love him. He didn't deserve it. There hasn't been a day when I haven't got down on my knees and prayed to be forgiven for the wrong I've done and how I have abused the privilege of serving God. I swear it, I swear it.' He wrung his hands.

Connie thought hard before she spoke.

'My brother's happy, Oliver. He can be a father to Kitty in a lovely way. He would not have…' She hesitated. 'He might never have been a father, Oliver.' She hesitated again. 'Please, though, lock that piece of knowledge away and never speak of it, promise me? It's personal to Bruce.'

'Connie, I know. Clara told me.'

'She told you?'

'Yes. She came one day to talk to me. She was very distressed.'

For the first time, Connie's face clouded over.

'And you took advantage of her then?'

'No, no, Connie. I swear it wasn't like that. I fell in love with Clara. I'd never known anything like it. Clara was an equal part in what happened, but the greater responsibility was mine, of course.'

'I suppose she was desperate,' said Connie quietly.

Even in this dark moment, Oliver allowed himself a small inward smile. In another circumstance he might have agreed that Clara was indeed rather scraping the bottom of the barrel in her choice…

There was silence. Oliver had wiped his face and sat with a resigned expression waiting for the rejection. Connie said nothing.

Eventually, he said,

'Connie, I have grown to love you even in this short space of time. I need to walk away now if there is no future for us. I won't hurt anyone else ever again.'

Connie was still silent. Finally she spoke.

'What are your feelings for Clara now? Tell me the truth, please Oliver.'

Oliver could reply immediately,

'I have no feelings of the kind of love I had before. They have evaporated, Connie. It was a sort of aberration in a way. It was violent and passionate, but circumstances quenched it almost as soon as it had begun. I don't think for Clara it meant as much. I swear to you I have no residual feelings for her apart from the usual sort of mild affection.'

Connie looked at him hard. She believed him. She spoke quietly.

'As soon as I met you, I knew you were special. You know, as a Catholic, I've always believed that priests are infallible. You may laugh at that, but I have put them up on a pedestal. It's something to do with wanting to believe that people *can* be completely good. My faith says that only the Pope is infallible, but I've wanted to believe that priests are perfect too. Now, meeting you, I see that is not true.'

If it had not been for the deadly seriousness of the situation, Oliver might have needed to suppress another smile. But there was no smile in his reply.

'We all have feet of clay, Connie, and most particularly, priests, I dare say, and most especially *me.*'

'No Oliver. I know you're a good man. I knew it from the start. And,' she paused, 'I love you for your struggles and for your honesty. Well, to be honest if you really want to know the truth, I just *love* you.'

She leant up and Oliver kissed her gently and with his whole heart. He would never abuse the beautiful spirit in Connie. They would take whatever the future held at her pace and he would thank God every day for her understanding and for sending him this lovely woman. Oliver's spirit was singing.

Eventually, Connie said,

'Oliver, let's go for a long walk tomorrow after the funeral shall we — go down to the river, and through that awful passageway under the bridge again where my dad was found. It'll prove I can do it a second time.'

'Yes,' said Oliver with a smile. 'And you know what? We might even find a light at the end of the tunnel!'.

## Chapter 23

The following morning was suitably rainy for a funeral. Oliver had always found it easier in his parish days to take a funeral when it was bleak or rainy. He felt somehow that sunshine was an insult to the level of grief and mourning that usually enveloped those left behind. He told Connie his thoughts, but she wagged her finger at him.

'Now Oliver Lockwood, what about the resurrection? Sunshine, light, hope?'

'That's true, but I thought Catholics believed that unrepentant sinners went straight to hell?'

'Ah yes, but my father said sorry in the end, didn't he? We believe in purgatory. Dad will be judged and cleansed and then go to heaven.'

Oliver simply smiled, but inwardly he thought it must be lovely to have an uncomplicated faith like Connie's. He had much to learn from her. He kissed her lightly on the cheek before going to collect Robbie from the hallway. Robbie had clearly made a huge effort with his clothes and had borrowed a reasonably smart jacket from the stack of charity garments that were hanging in the store room and found a suitably sombre tie. Connie and Oliver both complimented him on his appearance and he positively glowed with pleasure.

The hearse arrived outside the hostel and Connie gave her posy of wild flowers to the funeral director to place on her father's coffin. *It looked surprisingly pretty,* Connie thought, *considering it was early in the season for spring flowers and there wasn't exactly an abundance of them.* The sight of them made her both smile and shed a tear in equal measure. Her heart was full of the wonderful memory of the words of love exchanged between Oliver and herself by the river, but it was heavy with sadness that she had received no word from either of her living siblings, Bruce nor Sadie. She held out no hope of seeing Sadie ever again, but she had prayed that Bruce would soften the hard, unforgiving line he had taken over their father.

They followed the hearse to the crematorium slowly, slowly, the three miles or so journey to Streatham taking about fifty minutes. All of them were silent in Oliver's car, each absorbed in their own thoughts. They followed the coffin into the chapel to the strains of Handel's Largo. Had Bruce wanted to be involved in drawing up the service, Connie knew that he would have strong ideas about the music, but Connie, who was not musical, simply asked the funeral director for whatever was usually played.

The service proceeded with words that were familiar to Oliver. During the singing of *The Lord is my Shepherd*, there was a sound of the great door creaking open at the back of the chapel. No one turned round, but the three of them were aware of it. Slowly, slowly a woman enshrouded in a black cloak and pushing a small wheelchair with a sleeping child in it walked up the empty chapel towards the coffin. She put the brakes on the chair,

270

walked up to the coffin and stood there. Everyone stopped singing, aghast, except the minister, who staggered through with a dry mouth to the end.

*And in God's house for ever more*
*My dwelling place shall be*

As the last chord finished (*why do organists always hang it out for so long*, the minister thought) he went to the young woman and whispered in her ear.

'What are you doing? I'm sorry, but you can't just walk up and stand here. I'm afraid this is a private service.'

'I know,' she said clearly. 'But I'd like to say a few words please about Albert Connors. He was my father.'

Connie let out a gasp.

'Sadie!'

The minister looked perplexed. Sadie took no notice of either him or the three shocked people comprising the congregation. She drew the piece of lined paper out of her pocket, then spoke clearly and authoritatively.

'In this coffin lies my father and in this wheelchair lies his son.'

Connie gasped and put her hand up to her mouth.

'He is also *my* son. His name is Jack. My father raped me several times when I was fifteen. Jack is the product of those rapes. I am glad my son is asleep. You may stare at him. You can see that Jack will never be able to walk or live a normal life. My son bears the lifelong punishment of my father's incest. *You* may wish my father God's speed into the afterlife, but *I* wish him nothing but the flames of hell.'

Quietly she took the brakes off the wheelchair and without a word or a smile to Connie walked out of the crematorium.

Connie had a moment of searing indecision. Everything in her wanted to rush out and find Sadie, but the minister had not yet spoken the words of committal and drawn the curtains around the coffin.

Oliver, sensing it, touched her arm. 'Stay, Connie. We'll find her immediately afterwards.'

Finally the familiar words were spoken:

*'To everything there is a season and a time to every purpose on earth; a time to be born and a time to die. Here in this last act, in sorrow but without fear, in love and appreciation, we commit the body of Albert Connors to its natural end.'*

'What's he drawing the curtain for, Oli-Locki?'

Oliver remembered that Robbie had never been to a funeral or cremation service, having no relatives to grieve over. Oliver gave himself a silent reprimand for not having talked the service through with Robbie beforehand.

'Tell you when we're outside, Robbie.'

Connie did not wait for the dirge of the voluntary on the organ. She dashed out of the door into the pouring rain. She ran around like a headless chicken looking for Sadie, her hair and clothes getting soaked. After ten minutes she decided with a heart as heavy as lead that Sadie must have driven out of their lives once more at top speed.

She decided to have one more look around the back of the chapel in the garden of remembrance. There in the far corner, sheltering under a large tree with low hanging

272

branches and practically hidden under her cloak's black hood was Sadie. Connie stopped in her tracks and then very slowly walked up to her. When she recalled the scene in her mind's eye, she saw herself walking up as if drifting in a dream, or as part of some slowed up film sequence. It seemed to take her forever to reach Sadie.

'Sadie!'

Slowly Sadie looked up.

'Connie!'

The two young women said nothing but remained intertwined in a long embrace for what seemed like several minutes. Finally, Connie broke away and looked at Jack, who was beginning to wake.

'Tell me about my little nephew, Sadie.'

They were the most beautiful words that Connie could possibly have spoken. It was as though the warmth of them and the sweet claiming of her sister's twisted, broken boy as part of the family, unlocked Sadie's heart.

'He'll never walk, Connie and both his kidneys are defective. He'll always be an invalid. But he's bright. Talk to him.'

'Jack,' said Connie. 'You look a very nice boy and I do like your silver chair! What have you got there?'

'It's a space robot,' said Jack in a strange and strangulated-sounding voice. He thrust it towards Connie.

Connie had always had the knack of talking to children in an adult way, avoiding the overused patronising tones of some adults.

'It's very nice, Jack. Are there any more in this series?'

273

'Yes,' said Jack. 'There's the Electronic B9 robot. Mummy's saving up for it.'

'Lovely!' said Connie. 'Jack, did you know I'm your auntie?'

'Auntie what?'

'Auntie Connie.'

Quick as a flash, Jack made up a rhyme and related it in a singsong voice:

*'Auntie Connie,*

*Auntie Connie,*

*Auntie Connie sat on a dolly,*

*Auntie Connie bought me a lolly,*

*Auntie Connie may be soppy,*

*Auntie Connie may be jolly!'*

They all laughed. 'He's only five,' said Sadie, suddenly proud of her little boy.

'Very bright, I'd say,' replied Connie.

Connie sat down on the seat next to Sadie.

'Sadie, how've you managed for nearly six years?'

'I hid myself away because I've been so ashamed. I've been ashamed of being raped, ashamed of being pregnant, and,' she paused, and Connie noticed her eyes shining with tears. 'Guilty and ashamed of having such a deformed son. I know that's a terrible thing to say, but people are so cruel. In the end it was easier just to hide us both away from the world.'

'Oh Sadie. You poor thing. I'm so glad you've come back.'

'I heard your radio message.' Sadie's face suddenly hardened.

'I'm going back to Scotland but I wanted to put the record straight in case anyone eulogized about our father at the funeral without knowing the facts.'

'Bruce and I know the facts. Not about you, but about everything else. Bruce won't forgive him.'

'Good!' said Sadie emphatically. 'And you, Connie? You know, our father would have done the same to you when you got a bit older.'

'I know' Connie whispered, 'and he tried to, but it hurt and I was only six and I made noises so he — he didn't quite ...' Her voice trailed off. 'It wasn't because he minded about me. He was just frightened that it might wake our mother.'

Sadie gulped hard.

'The *monster*,' she said. 'I hope you haven't forgiven him, Connie?'

Connie said nothing.

'I heard our Mum died. I wanted to get back, but it was exactly the time when I was due to give birth. I cried myself silly. I dreamt of Mum being with me and forgiving me.'

'Forgiving *you?*' said Connie.

'I always felt that somehow I deserved to be raped — that it was my fault — that I should have been able to stop him.'

Connie thought. *Yes, she recognised those feelings.*

'How did you find out about Mum?'

'Great Aunt Edith. I went to her.'

Connie thought of Great Aunt Edith. In her eyes, the old lady had indeed been *very* old. In fact she was only nearing seventy and had all her faculties about her. She had been a ward sister, and stood no nonsense, but had a very big heart under her fierce exterior. But she had the white curly hair of a tight perm and to six-year-old Connie that made her old.

'Are you still there with her?'

'No. Great Aunt Edith died, but she gave me money to buy a caravan. It's up in the highlands of Scotland, as far away as I could get. Just Jack and me.'

Just then, Oliver and Robbie appeared, soaked to the skin. They stopped, suddenly seeing Sadie, Jack and Connie in the far corner of the garden.

'Who are they?' asked Sadie.

Connie gave Sadie a sketchy outline, then beckoning them over. Immediately Robbie was on his haunches talking to Jack.

'Hey, you! Nice chariot!'

'I want a wee wee,' said Jack suddenly.

'Oh dear,' said Sadie. 'I knew this would happen. He can't hold it at all. We went just before we arrived. It's his poorly kidneys.'

'Don't worry,' said Robbie promptly. 'There's a Gents by the Chapel. Had to go myself before the service. Phew! One hundred percent fallout! Nerves — much better than castor oil! Tell you what, I'll take the little lad.'

Sadie looked dubious.

'It's quite a palaver. You must unharness him, lift him out of his chair, sit on the seat with him, undo his trousers, fish Percy out and then poke him at the porcelain!'

'Come on Jack. You'll have to teach me,' said Robbie, laughing.

'What a lovely young man,' said Sadie as she watched Robbie sprint down the path in a zigzag with the chair, with Jack giggling incessantly.

'He *is* lovely,' said Connie.

'He's got quite a story,' said Oliver, speaking for the first time, 'But then it seems we all have.'

'Come and see Brucey with me, Sadie. He'll be so pleased to see you. He's got a little girl — Kitty. She's nearly three.'

'So Jack has a cousin!' said Sadie, smiling. 'Yes, I'll come, but I'll have to get going after that. I came by train. It's one hell of a trek.'

'Sadie, why don't you stay the night at the hostel? You can set off in the morning when you're fresh. That would be all right, wouldn't it, Oliver? They can sleep in my room.'

'Of course,' replied Oliver. 'I could drive you up to King's Cross Station in the morning to get the main line train to Edinburgh. It would save you a bit of time and I can help you on the train with the chair.'

Sadie was just about to speak when they saw Robbie returning with Jack, who was grinning from ear to ear.

'He not clever,' said Jack. 'He got wee down my trousers.'

'Never mind, Jack, I've got another pair in my bag,' said Sadie, laughing at her son.

Jack suddenly looked tired again.

'Mummy I got a pain.'

'Where, Jack?'

'In my head,' he said, pointing to his stomach.

'You're hungry,' said Sadie. 'Never mind, I'm sure Uncle Bruce will give us something to eat.'

'Uncle *Bruce?*' retorted Jack.

'Yes and you've got a little cousin called Kitty,' said Connie.

'Kitty!' laughed Jack.

*'Kitty, Kitty Catkins*
*She sat on a matkins*
*She…'*

'OK. Jack, that's enough,' said Sadie, afraid he was going to launch into one of his genitals rhymes that always sent him off into gales of laughter and might set the pattern for the visit.

'He rhymes everything,' she said. 'I don't know whether he's going to be a poet or a prat!'

'Let's go for poet!' laughed Connie.

Oliver suddenly felt he was a bystander, an outsider, standing on the fringe of things and watching an unfolding game of Happy Families. He felt a pang of pain — was it jealousy? For once he longed to claim Kitty as his own daughter. Maybe, just maybe, if things worked out with Connie, he might eventually have a child who wasn't a secret, who he could love openly, and without fear. Meanwhile, he had feelings he hardly recognised to contend with. He was thoroughly glad Connie was reunited with Sadie but could not help the feeling of being marginalised somehow. He had his sister Morag, who he loved very much, but she had no children and his mother

278

and father had died in the most, untimely manner, so he could hardly claim he had a family. Suddenly Oliver felt alone.

Connie got Oliver aside and asked if he might drive them to Bruce and Clara's house. Oliver replied that of course he would, but inwardly his spirits sank even lower as he thought of the tension that was involved in the meeting regarding Bruce, Clara and himself. He decided that he would park outside the house, drop them off, then he and Robbie would go for a coffee somewhere to fill in the time.

Sadie and Connie chatted animatedly all the way to Richmond.. They had several years of news and experiences to mull over and the delight of each seeing the other again was palpable. Robbie played games with Jack, who was jammed in between Sadie and himself. Just as Oliver had decided that he was dealing with a most uncomfortable set of feelings, Connie, in the passenger seat, silently slid her hand onto Oliver's knee and left it there for a minute. The surge of electricity he had once felt when Clara had put her hand on his chest surged through him again. Yes, there was a chemistry between Connie and himself all right! He took her hand and squeezed it. She smiled at him and he felt reassured for the rest of the journey.

Connie had phoned a delighted Bruce beforehand to ask if she could drop in, but she had not told him about the presence of either Oliver or Robbie. When they drew up at the house, Connie jumped out of the car and went to ring the front doorbell while Oliver helped Sadie out with the wheelchair. Suddenly, as the front door opened, Kitty rushed out and ran down the road. In a flash, Oliver chased after the little girl, who was surprisingly fast, and scooped her up. Kitty was laughing and kicking her legs in the air in Oliver's arms.

Bruce, panic-stricken, was shouting outside as the two walked back.

'Kitty! Kitty! You naughty girl! How many times have I told you?'

He was pale with anxiety, and with huge relief took Kitty out of Oliver's arms, hugging her and reprimanding her at the same time in equal measure.

'Thank you so much, Oliver. You must come in.'

'No, no, I'm just the chauffeur,' Oliver replied, smiling.

'And the child rescuer! Please come in. At least have a cup of tea?' Bruce peered inside the passenger seat of the car.

'Who's the lad? He can come in too.'

Clara welcomed Oliver with a light kiss on his cheek and led him into the living room. Once the vast surprise of seeing Sadie and her son in the flesh had sunk in, Bruce sat opposite her and scrutinized his eldest sister. Before she left home, she had been slim despite her stocky frame, and in Bruce's young eyes, unprepossessing. Now, she had filled out, was a shapely woman who had dark-brown hair that nearly reached her waist and a lovely smile that he had never noticed before. She had borne a lot of pain and sorrow in her young life, although her looks belied that fact, and Bruce hurt for her as he saw the crooked little boy, twisted and shrivelled in his wheelchair.

Clara made tea for everyone and laid out a selection of biscuits. She made the children some toast and chocolate spread. Oliver thought Clara looked distinctly better than last time he saw her and wondered what had changed. She seemed both more peaceful, and conversely, more animated than before.

Kitty was excited to see Connie and pulled at her, saying,

'Play with me, play with me, Auntie Connie!'

Connie took her over to Jack who was in his chair and had just woken.

'Say hello to your cousin, Kitty. His name is Jack.'

Kitty went close to him and stared.

'You got a funny face. You're ugly.'

Quick as a flash, Jack replied,

'And your bear is dirty. I'm ugly because my bones are wrong.'

'My bear is dirty 'cos Mummy never washes it.'

They both laughed as though they had cracked the funniest joke in the world. All the adults laughed too, loving the children's instant rapport with each other.

'It looks as though they're going to be friends,' said Connie, relieved.

'Yes, I expect they recognise the blood tie,' replied Sadie, pleased.

A momentary silence fell as Oliver, Clara, Bruce and Connie, fellow conspirators at that moment, took in the irony of the situation. Each knew that Sadie must be protected from the truth for now. There was time enough. Let her enjoy this moment.

Robbie spoke.

'Sadie, can I get Jack out of his wheelchair in the garden and sit him on the grass? Reckon you'd love that, wouldn't you Jack?'

Jack laughed.

*'Sitting on the grass*
*Sitting on the grass,*
*Sitting on the grass*
*On my great fat...'*

'*Jack*!' *No*!' Sadie shouted.

Jack and Robbie both creased up with laughter.

'I can see they are going to be partners in crime,' laughed Oliver.

Jack was duly taken out of his wheelchair by Robbie, watched carefully by Sadie. Clara provided a bright blanket for the grass and Kitty danced around in delight. Oliver tried not to watch Kitty too much but he could see that already she was a carbon copy of her mother — pretty, lithe, a little dancer already and very determined.

While Robbie, Jack and Kitty played in the garden, the adults talked. Sadie filled Bruce in with her father's rape and her subsequent fleeing from the home when she realised she was pregnant. She related how Aunt Edith supported her and the birth of her "imperfect miracle" as she called Jack. Bruce listened with a breaking heart and his hatred for his father grew until it threatened to consume him. Sadie tuned in with Bruce's feelings exactly.

'Why don't you move down here, Sade?' Bruce asked. 'We could help you with Jack?'

'I've got a life up there now, Brucey. It suits me.'

'But you'll need support with Jack.'

'I haven't so far.'

'Think about it, Sadie.'

Clara joined in.

'It must be awful having such a badly disfigured child. I don't think I could bear it. Let us help you.'

Sadie winced inwardly. She had not met Clara before, and she wasn't sure that they would hit it off for any length of time.

'I've had great joy from my Jack. It's just other people's attitudes that hurt,' she said.

Clara was quiet. She sensed there was a rebuke in Sadie's reply, so had the wisdom not to pursue the subject. Bruce knew that Clara was right in her self-assessment, though. She would not have coped with an "imperfect" child, as she later described Jack. Clara loved beauty of all kinds and to have a physically unlovely child would have been a challenge to which he knew Clara could not rise. She had found it hard enough to love bright, winsome, beautiful little Kitty as it was.

After lengthy discussions, and some sharing of mutual tears, Bruce realised that Robbie had been entertaining the children for far too long. He went to his workshop and brought down his clarinet. He had begun playing it again after his wonderful "release" with Clara, as he called it.

'Daddy, Daddy, play, play!' shouted Kitty jumping up and down excitedly.

Bruce began to play his clarinet, wandering into the garden, and Kitty, as if following the Pied Piper, danced merrily after him. Clara quickly picked up her violin from the top of the piano, tuned it, and began to play together with the clarinet. Bruce went through the nursery rhyme repertoire (again) that Kitty loved so much, with Clara joining in. Robbie began to dance and then zigzagged the wheelchair after Bruce. Connie went into the garden, took Kitty's hand and began to twirl her around in time with the music. It was a moment of pure magic for Sadie: two children integrating, her beloved brother and her little sister, for a little while all completely happy. Her father had done nothing but cause them horrendous pain and a damaging unravelling of their lives as adults. It appeared though, that thanks to their mother's kind and loving guidance, together with the positive strength running through the Connors' genes, the twisted threads of their childhood seemed at last to be untangling.

They all arrived back at the hostel in the early evening after the happiest day that Sadie could remember for a very long time. Robbie had been wonderful with Jack and they all commented on it. Robbie glowed with pride at the unexpected praise. Jack announced that he was still hungry so Robbie suggested he took him down to the kitchens before they shut up for the night.

He trundled the wheelchair down the corridor with Jack whooping with delight. They entered the kitchen. It wasn't the usual cook on duty but "Surly Stuart" as everyone called him, and he was just about to lock up.

Surly Stu was full of muscle and brawn and known for his bullying tactics. He stared hard at Jack then pointed at him.

'Blimey, what do call that? I call it a fucking freak! If you put him in a cage you could charge money for people to gawp at him. Animals and geeks belong in a circus. What you doing with it?'

A terrifying change took place in Robbie. It was as if a fire had ignited inside him, erupting and lighting a hundred flames then burning to a mighty peak and bursting into furious incandescence.

Acting instinctively, Robbie grabbed a large kitchen knife from the knife block on the side and held it threateningly at Surly Stu's neck.

'He's not a fucking freak, he's a living—'

It was too late. Surly Stuart was much bigger than Robbie and he grabbed the knife from him and wrestled Robbie to the ground. Robbie head-butted him and somehow managed to twist and prize the knife out of Surly Stu's hand and began slashing at his face. Blood poured from deep cuts. Robbie didn't stop. While Surly Stuart was holding his face in agony, Robbie stabbed the knife into his abdomen and Surly Stuart collapsed in a heap. Robbie withdrew the bloodstained knife and stared in disbelief at what he had done. Surly Stu was groaning and writhing. Jack started crying.

'Stay there, Jack. I'm coming back!' shouted Robbie and he ran to fetch Oliver, charging into his room. Oliver took one glance at his bloodstained face and the bloody knife and picked up the phone.

'Ambulance, now, please. Wandsworth Church Army Hostel.'

Meanwhile Sadie had run down to the kitchen for Jack, having heard his screams. There was no movement from Surly Stu and he was lying in a huge pool of bright blood. Sadie's only thought was for her son. She flew to his side and rocked his head in her arms.

'There, there Jack, there, there. Let's get you out of here.'

She turned the wheelchair round and as fast as she could go left the kitchen and bumped into Oliver and Connie.

'He's in there. I think he's dead.'

She went back to the room to find Robbie sitting on the bed, his head in his hands and rocking violently. He was in shock and couldn't speak. Jack sat in silence. After a minute or two he began to chant in a low, menacing strangulated voice:

*'Nasty man, nasty man,*
*Robbie got cross with*
*The nasty man.*
*Robbie was sad*
*And Robbie was mad,*
*Grabbed a knife*
*And had a fight.'*

Jack kept obsessionally chanting his rhyme over and repeatedly in the same dark voice, while Sadie rocked him, weeping silently.

In the kitchen, Connie had quickly grabbed two tea towels, poured some disinfectant in a bowl, soaked the tea towels, given one to Oliver, kept the other and soothed his facial wounds while Oliver tried to stem the flow of blood which was pumping forcibly out of Surly Stuart's abdomen.

The ambulance arrived very soon, quickly followed by the police. The paramedics dealt with Surly Stuart. They found a pulse but looked pessimistic. A police officer asked Oliver who had done the stabbing. Oliver hedged for a minute. The police turned round in the kitchen and came face to face with an ashen Robbie.

'I did it,' he said in a broken voice. 'He was taunting a crippled boy.'

'That's no excuse for stabbing someone,' the policeman replied brusquely and he and his companion snapped the handcuffs on Robbie's wrists and locked them. *'You do not have to say anything, but anything you do say will be taken down and may be given in evidence.'*

Robbie murmured under his breath, 'Yep, heard it all before,', and with head bowed, walked slowly out into the waiting police car, flanked by two police officers.

Connie and Oliver stared after Robbie. The afternoon had been full of joy but the promise of better times had been swept away in an instant.

\*\*\*

Sadie was already in Connie's bed, asleep, or at least, thought Connie, giving the impression of sleep. Her head was turned to the wall and clearly she had no intention of talking. Jack's chair had been slung back into a lying-down position which formed a makeshift bed and he was fast asleep.

Connie and Oliver talked in low voices well into the early hours of the morning. They did not know what the future would hold, but one thing was for certain, they would stand by Robbie whatever. Oliver finally made it back to his room by two-thirty a.m.

Sadie was awake much earlier than Connie and Jack. She washed quickly — what her mother would have called "a lick and a promise". Jack woke and she took him down to the bathroom. When he came back, he started his obsessional chanting once more, waking Connie.

*'Nasty man, nasty man,*
*Robbie got cross with*
*The nasty man.*
*So Robbie was sad*
*And Robbie was mad.*
*Grabbed a knife*
*And had a fight.'*

Connie rubbed her eyes and was immediately wide awake. The memories of the stabbing flooded back instantly like a terrible dream.

'Is that what happened, Jack?' asked Connie. 'What made Robbie pick up the knife, Jack?'

Jack answered in an instant. What his five-year-old body lacked in strength was more than made up for by his intellectual capacity.

'The nasty man said horrid things.'

'What horrid things, Jack? You can tell me.'

'He said I was a fucking freak.'

288

'Oh my goodness, that was *not* very nice, wasn't it?'

'No it was *not*,' shouted Jack. 'And he said another bad thing.'

Connie knelt by Jack's chair.

'Can you remember what it was, Jack?'

''Course I can. He said, "put me in a cage".'

'What a terrible thing to say, Jack. Are you sure?'

'*'Course I'm sure*! *I'm clever!'*

*'Jack isn't nimble, Jack isn't, quick,*
*But Jack doesn't miss a single trick.'*

And he looked up with a mischievous grin at his mother and added,

*'And Jack has got an enormous dick!'*

'*Jack!*' reprimanded Sadie half-heartedly but to no avail as Jack was dissolving into peals of laughter. The joke didn't matter one little bit, did it? Sadie was just glad to see her son was recovering from the trauma he had witnessed and to hear what she called his "bottom" humour again.

Oliver heard them as he came down the corridor towards Connie's room and wondered if Jack might be shedding some light on the stabbing.

'I heard you, Jack. What's your rhyme this time?'

He started on, *'Jack isn't nimble,'* but Connie stopped him.

'Jack, tell Oliver the one about the nasty man.'

Jack repeated the rhyme and Oliver and Connie looked at each other. Obviously Robbie had been grievously provoked and rose to defend the boy.

'And tell Oliver what the nasty man said about you.'

289

Jack repeated what he had said.

'That might hold up in court,' said Oliver, and Jack said it slowly so that Oliver could scribble the rhyme down, followed by "fucking freak" and "put in cage".

Sadie, suddenly looking determined and efficient, harnessed Jack into his pushchair and took the brake off.

'I must go and get my train,' said Sadie. 'You see why I live in the Highlands of Scotland? It's damage limitation, Oliver. We've only been down here one night and look what's happened? Everything's unravelled. A man has probably been murdered.'.

'Mummy, *not* Robbie's fault. Robbie is good.'

'He was certainly kind to you, Jack, wasn't he?'

'Jack loved him,' said Jack simply.

The four of them set off for King's Cross Station. Oliver parked and they trundled up the platform for Sadie and Jack to board their train. Oliver helped with the wheelchair and once they were settled in the carriage in the stationary train, Sadie wound down her window and said, 'Sorry. I'm so, so sorry.'

'Keep in touch, Sadie,' begged Connie.

As they waved the train off, Connie realised that it was the second time they had said a sorrowful goodbye — once to Robbie and once to Sadie and Jack. The fact that Connie had also waved her father's coffin off into the flames of cremation the day before didn't even figure. It paled into insignificance beside the huge trauma that had befallen them all, and most particularly Robbie.

## Chapter 24

Things were relatively peaceful in Bruce Connors' household. Clara was distinctly more biddable and less on edge lately. She was slowly becoming more affectionate to her daughter, although could only tolerate a certain amount of noise and mess. She read Kitty stories under sufferance, feeling very bored most of the time. Now and again she commented on Kitty's progress, and she had been moved to see how Kitty was so unafraid and unaffected by her cousin Jack's appearance.

'That's the gift kids give each other,' replied Bruce. 'Total acceptance.'

'Yes, but you must admit, Bruce, that he's pretty grotesque.'

'Clara, don't,' said Bruce.

'Well you know it's true.'

'Yes, but I saw a wonderful spark of humour in the lad, and his rhymes are incredible for a five-year-old.'

'They are, but they're also rather freaky,' Clara replied. 'He'll get terribly bullied, won't he?'

'Did you see how amazing that lad Robbie was? He seemed to have a bit of magic about him. Jack had obviously built up a lovely relationship with him.'

'He had, but Jack will have to take a lot of teasing and worse from other kids, won't he? And some adults, I shouldn't wonder.'

'Yes, those ignorant peasants who know no better. Shame on them. He'll need a lot of Robbies in his life to protect him.'

Bruce looked across at Kitty, who was painting a rainbow with all the precision her nearly-three-year-old fingers could muster. He often thought how irresistible she was. He realised that he had quite miraculously regarded her as his own daughter from the day of her birth. It never crossed his mind to think otherwise, apart from when he occasionally saw Oliver. It was rather a complex set of emotions when that happened, as he liked what he saw of Oliver, almost despite himself. Kitty, Bruce observed, had many of her mother's characteristics. She was winsome, pretty, determined, articulate and charming and she could dance well even at this early age. Clara could be kind and loving, and sometimes her heart was quickened by certain poignant situations, but she also had what Bruce called "her tough streak".

Kitty had a softness and a kindness shot through her personality and Bruce wondered if it had come from Oliver's genes. He hoped it had more to do with his own handling of her from the start, but it was always the nature versus nurture question in his mind. Bruce adored his daughter. He was turning out to be a lovely father despite the dubious model his own father set. Bruce thought back to the time he spent with Bert his dad in the workshop, and how, from the moment he entered, he could hardly wait to be "released" from this upstairs prison. He was grateful to his father for one thing, though. His father was a fine craftsman in wood, and he taught Bruce some of the basic skills. Bruce had to endure the put-downs and frequent humiliations of not reaching his father's exacting standards, but nevertheless the sparks of his interest were fanned into flames by his father's skills.

Bruce spent vast swathes of time with Kitty and sometimes took her up into his workshop where he would let her try one of the quarter-size Suzuki violins he might be repairing. Kitty's behaviour had been the opposite of how Bruce had been with his own father. Kitty danced and pestered and persuaded her father to take her up with him. She loved nothing more. Dolls were shunned in favour of wood so Bruce helped her execute a simple jigsaw puzzle. He had carved out a little chair just the right height for her and painted it purple at her request so that she could perch up and work with Bruce. He sat gazing at her concentrated efforts sometimes, thinking what a little miracle she was. Perhaps, now it was physically possible, he could persuade Clara to have another baby sometime soon to complete their family, or maybe she had already conceived. After all, it took just once for Kitty to be created.

Clara had tiptoed back into a little work. She now read dialogue to action films, usually voicing the character of the seductive temptress or the wronged princess of the dramatis personae. For her it was a marking time exercise before she could go back to the theatre. In two years Kitty would be five and going to school. For Clara, another child simply did not enter the equation. It had been bad enough being stuck at home with Kitty. A second baby would delay her freedom by several years.

There was no doubt that Bruce's long-awaited success in the marital bed had given them both a great deal of pleasure and reassurance. For Bruce, it felt like the making of him and the healing of some of the damage of his upbringing. For Clara it was gratifying and comforting that she was loved so fulsomely finally. However, never once did it enter her mind, now that it was possible, how lovely it might be for Bruce to recreate his own flesh and blood in the form of another child. Clara was innately selfish and spoilt.

Coincidentally, a day after the funeral there was a knock on their front door. Opening it, Clara saw a youngish woman on the step holding a small battered, dusty brown attaché case.

'Sorry to bother you. Are you Mrs Connors?

Clara nodded.

'Well, my husband and I have just bought this house, which we heard had been sold two or three times in the last ten years. I said to my husband that we mustn't buy it 'cos it might have a curse on it, so he said, "don't be silly," so we went ahead. We decided to knock the wall down between the living room and the sitting room. They are not big rooms, you know, and we have two boys. Oh my goodness, they need such a lot of space. It's a small garden and they race around as it is. They are well made boys you know and they...'

Clara saw that the woman would be a compulsive chatterbox given half the chance, so she tried to steer her to the point of her visit.

'Yes, yes, I have a live wire daughter too. Were you bringing the case round by any chance?'

'Yes. We started knocking through the fireplace — the walls are so, so thick — my husband says that's all to the good for warmth and all that. Well, we found there were two alcoves either side of it that had been bricked up. When we started removing those bricks, we found this case. Now. Mr Connors is going to provide our Jimmy with a first size violin for him to learn on — he seems to be musical. We first noticed it when—'

'What makes you think this case has anything to do with us?' said Clara gently, not wanting to offend the woman, but desperate to move on.

'Well,' she replied 'It's got *Albert Edwin Connors* embossed on it, so we were just wondering — after all, it's a small world, isn't it? — if he—'

'Yes, he was my husband's father.'

'Oh, so he's your father-in-law then?'

Clara was beginning to lose the will to live, but desperate not to show it.

'I'll give it to him. Thanks so much for bringing it round.'

'Now if it turns out not to be your husband's, please return it and I'll take it to the police. Well, well, fancy your Mr Connors being this Mr Connors' son! It's a small world, isn't it?' she repeated.

'It is,' said Clara, gently prising the case out of the woman's hands.

'So we've been sitting on a secret, you could say,' said the woman conspiratorially.

'I expect it's just old papers but thank you very much again. Goodbye.'

Clara was just about to close the door emphatically when the woman put her foot in it.

'So will you ask your husband when my Tommy's fiddle will be ready? He's ever so keen. It's a small world, isn't it, Mrs Connors? Fancy that, us finding your father-in-law's case and you not knowing anything about it!'

'It is indeed a small world,' said Clara, dying inside.

'Let's have a coffee together some time, shall we? We can put the world to rights. After all there's a lot wrong, isn't there, what with…'

'Yes. Many thanks for bringing it here. I agree, it's a small world, isn't it? Goodbye.'

Clara pushed the door gently to move the woman's foot and then finally slammed it shut. She shouted upstairs.

'Bruce! Brucey! Can you come down a minute?'

'Why you want Daddy, Muma?'

'I want to show him this box, Kitty.'

'It's dirty,' said Kitty, wrinkling up her nose.

Bruce appeared, looking mildly irritated at being disturbed.

'I was just sticking the bridge back on Professor Eliot's double bass. Hope it's important, Clara.'

'It might be,' replied Clara.

She told Bruce about the case that had been found in between the fire bricks. Bruce examined it and confirmed that it was his father's name on the case.

'I'll finish doing the bridge then I'll be down,' said Bruce, putting the case to one side.

Kitty and Clara exclaimed at the identical moment,

'*Bruce/Daddy*!'

'*Secret* box, Daddy!'

'Open it now,' pleaded Clara.

Bruce sighed. Anything of his father's held no interest for him, in fact he found the slightest conversation or reference to his father abhorrent. Because he liked to please Clara and Kitty, however, he blew the dust off the case and coaxed the rusty hinges into life. Gingerly he opened the case. Inside were some papers, yellow with age. Bruce flicked through them.

'They are records of my father.'

Clara picked out a birth certificate. 'Look at this, Bruce.'

*Birth Certificate*

| *Where and When:* | Lambeth    Workhouse, Princes Road, London 10th September 1885. |
| --- | --- |
| *Name:* | Albert Edgar Connors |
| *Sex:* | Male |
| *Father's full name:* | — |
| *Father's date of birth:* | — |
| *Mother's full name:* | Alice Sadie Connors |
| *Mother's date of birth:* | 24th April 1870 |

Bruce stared. He had never seen or heard anything about his father's birth. Fastened onto the back of the birth certificate was another: a death certificate.

*Death Certificate*

| | |
|---|---|
| *Name:* | Alice Sadie Connors |
| *Date of birth:* | 24th April 1870 |
| *Age:* | Fifteen |
| *Date of death:* | 25th April 1885 |
| *Cause of death:* | Puerperal Pyrexia |
| *Place of death:* | Lambeth Workhouse Princes Road London |
| *Buried at:* | Common Grave, Lambeth |

Neither Bruce nor Clara spoke. Kitty, sensing the significant change of atmosphere, was silent. Bruce slowly reread the two certificates out loud, one after the other, then turned to Clara, who spoke first.

'Your father's mother was only fifteen, and the father is unknown. That means your father was illegitimate.'

'Yes. And it means that my father was only held in his mother's arms for one day before she died.'

'If he was born in a workhouse, she may not even have got to hold him,' added Clara. 'They would probably have taken him away at birth for adoption.'

'She died one day after giving birth to him. Just fifteen.'

298

Together they continued searching through the papers. By this time, Kitty had returned to her painting, bored by her mother and father's conversation.

Bruce found a notebook, curled at the edges. Inside, there were address entries, written in his father's distinctive hand,

| | |
|---|---|
| Lambeth Workhouse | 1885 |
| Lambeth Orphanage | 1886 – 1890 |
| Church of England Home | |
| for Waifs and Strays | 1890 – 1892 |
| Ragged School Southwark | 1892 – 1894 |
| Truant School, Highbury Grove | 1894 – 1895 |
| Lambeth Workhouse | 1895 – 1900 |

'This was my father's childhood,' said Bruce quietly. 'So many changes in such a short time. Shipped from pillar to post.'

'Poor little boy,' replied Clara softly. For once, her heart was genuinely moved. 'He didn't stand a chance, did he?'

'And a fifteen-year-old mother! I wonder what her story was.'

They were both quiet, each touched by the tragedy embedded in the paperwork. After a minute, Clara spoke.

'1900. What happened then I wonder? He would have left school, I guess.'

'Perhaps he got an apprenticeship. He must have learned his carpentry from somewhere. He was more than just a self-taught amateur, wasn't he? He was a fine craftsman.'

Clara pulled out a further piece of paper, again dog-eared and yellow with age, but otherwise intact.

*Albert Edgar Connors*          *Pauper apprenticeship to Edward and Sons (Carpenters and Joiners) Acton, West London.*

That answered the question.

The only other paper was the marriage certificate of Albert Edgar Connors, bachelor of the parish of St Mary's Acton to Rosa Emily Taylor, spinster of the parish of St Mary's Acton in 1920, soon after the end of the First World War. Strangely, there was no record of Albert's activities between 1898 and 1920, but Bruce picked up a brown and white photograph of what must have been his father in a soldier's uniform, holding to attention a rifle with a bayonet fixed on the end.

'He was a handsome man,' said Clara, looking carefully at the photograph.

'Yes. I recognise the gun. My father never talked about his past,' said Bruce. A new thought occurred to him as if scales were slowly falling from his eyes.

'He must have been very damaged by his childhood — learnt to fend for himself and just — survive. I wish now I'd known more about him.'

'Can you imagine Kitty without a home or a mother or a father. She'd turn feral in no time,' said Clara with a grim smile. 'Any child would with his history.'

Kitty looked up.

'What's feral, Muma?'

'It means *wild,*' replied Clara, mimicking a cat clawing in the air and hissing.

Kitty laughed.

'Again, Muma!'

'No Kitty, but why don't you draw a feral cat?'

Kitty trotted off and Clara turned back to Bruce.

'My mother must have rescued him, Clara. Perhaps she turned a blind eye to so many of his ways because she knew what a terrible childhood he'd had.'

'Yes, but it doesn't excuse him for his sexual behaviour one little bit,' said Clara, eyes flashing. 'Maybe the bullying, but not the paedophilia.'

Bruce always winced whenever Clara called his father that.

'No, I totally agree, but Dr Hamilton who I saw over my "trouble" would start from early childhood to pick up clues about his adult behaviour,' said Bruce soberly. Suddenly, he found himself wanting to defend his father for the first time in his life.

Kitty was becoming bored. She danced back over to the case, peered inside and quick as a flash said,

'Daddy, Daddy, secret! Look!'

She put her small hand down the faded yellow silk side pockets and drew out two envelopes from one side and two from the other.

'Muma. More secrets! Open, Daddy.'

Bruce examined the envelopes. Each one had a name written on, barely decipherable, in faded grey pencil,

*Sadie, James, Bruce, Constance.*

Bruce opened his envelope and looked inside. A faded white paper money note to the value of £100.00 lay neatly folded in half. He realised that his father must have put aside the money for his children well before James took his own life. Bruce sat down, stunned. His father not only had never talked about his past, but in addition he certainly had never told any of the four, and probably not their mother either, that he had secretly been saving to put aside money for his children. £100.00 each would have been a great deal for him.

'Open James' envelope, Bruce. I would imagine it's the same.'

And it was — a £100.00 note folded neatly in half.

'Shall we put that away for Kitty?' asked Clara.

'We'll see. Maybe Jack? They won't be worth anything now. It'll be of historical value though. This actual find is priceless, isn't it?'

Clara shrugged.

'It is, but it's a pity the money's not worth anything — for the old boy's sake,' she added quickly.

Bruce carefully put the envelopes back in the side pocket of the case, found a strong brown envelope and put the loose certificates and information inside the envelope and wrote on it: "My Father's History".

'Kitty, please can I have one of your long hair ribbons? Could you fetch it for me?'

Kitty came back dancing a purple ribbon back as though it was a streamer.

Bruce put the ribbon around the case for added security and tied it in a double bow. He didn't trust the rusty hinges on the case.

'There we are. That's your grandad all tied up!' remarked Clara.

'All that's left of his life is a handful of faded papers in an envelope,' said Bruce.

Kitty looked at Bruce and climbed onto his lap. She turned his face with her hands so that they were looking closely at each other.

'He's all right now, Daddy. Grandad's got my purple ribbon.'

Bruce looked into her clear, innocent eyes and thanked God for the precious gift of a daughter.

## Chapter 25

The following day Bruce drove to Wandsworth Church Army Hostel. He had phoned beforehand to tell Connie he was coming and arrived in the hall of the building within half an hour.

Oliver was talking to a police officer in the porch. Bruce was about to squeeze past him when Oliver put out his arm to stop him.

'Officer, I'll get back to you, but I'm afraid I have to go.'

'You've got my number, haven't you? As you know, it's urgent.'

'Sounds like trouble,' commented Bruce as Oliver ushered him in. He took Bruce to a trestle table and bench that were in the large hall inside the porch.

'I must tell you something, Bruce, before you see Connie if possible. It's not pleasant.'

Oliver began to relate the happenings of two days ago with Robbie, Jack and Surly Stuart. Bruce saw that at times Oliver could hardly speak, the pain was so great. Both men agreed that Robbie had something special about him and that he had shown a rare affection and affinity to Jack.

After hearing the story, Bruce immediately said,

'Oliver, if you need someone to speak about the young man's character in court, I'd be more than happy to do so, based on what I saw of him.'

'Thank you,' said Oliver. 'I'll bear that in mind.'

Two police officers arrived at that moment and drew Oliver away.

'Wait there?' asked Oliver of Bruce.

The officers and Oliver talked together in undertones. After a few minutes, Oliver returned, ashen faced.

'Surly Stuart has taken a turn for the worse. He's in intensive care and not expected to survive the night. That means Robbie will be tried for murder.'

Oliver lay his head in his hands for a minute, then blew his nose quickly.

'He was essentially kind. He has a good heart and this is a cruel twist of — no, not fate, but it *can't* be God's work either. I'll never forgive myself for letting him go down to the kitchen on his own with Jack.'

Bruce touched his arm lightly.

'He's Sadie's boy, Oliver. Her responsibility. You mustn't take the guilt on yourself. It's misplaced.'

Oliver wiped his eyes, apologised for the display of emotion, and looked up at Bruce.

'Robbie had a rotten childhood, you know. He was abandoned by his parents as a baby, brought up in numerous foster homes, returned finally and sent back into care. What chance had he? Yet he turned out with a heart of gold, but,' Oliver paused. 'his Achilles heel was his violent temper which he just could not control if provoked. Now it looks as though it will be the ruin of him.' He paused. 'Anyway, sorry Bruce, what was it you came for? Yes, you want to see Connie of course. I've kept you.'

Bruce was intending to save the news of the attaché case for Connie's ears only, but as a result of the turn the conversation had taken about Robbie's early years, he found himself explaining in broad brushstrokes the attaché case and its contents.

'You talked about feeling guilty, Oliver. See what you make of this, then. No one knows, but when my father had died, I came here to see him. I don't know whether I hoped to find him alive or dead. I saw him lying under the sheet and I pulled it back and — in effect — cursed him. Yes, I *cursed* him. I told him I was glad he was dead, and I meant it.'

Oliver had a sudden sharp intake of breath, then both men were quiet. Eventually, Oliver said, without an ounce of judgement in his voice,

'Bruce, you had good reason to be glad he was dead. He abused both your sisters mercilessly and Connie told me he bullied you and your brother James so much that James took his own life,' said Oliver solemnly. 'Who wouldn't wish him dead?'

'Connie,' said Bruce simply.

\*\*\*

Bruce opened the case for Connie and took out the brown envelope. She read the certificates in silence. After several minutes of turning them over, reading them and rereading them, she folded them up, and putting them back in the envelope, said quietly,

'Our poor father.'

'Yes,' replied Bruce.

Then Connie said fervently,

'Bruce I *so* wish he had known your forgiveness before he died. I pleaded with you to come.'

'I know,' replied Bruce. 'But to forgive someone you must open the chance of being reconciled, musn't you? I didn't want to be reconciled to him. He was responsible for so much damage.'

'Does this make any difference to how you feel?' said Connie, tapping the case.

Bruce didn't answer, but instead took out the four envelopes.

'Look at these, Connie.'

Connie opened her envelope and began to cry a little.

Bruce said softly,

'They're not worth anything now in terms of money but…'

'—They're worth everything in terms of *value,*' Connie finished his sentence for him.

'Yes,' replied Bruce. 'Exactly, Connie.'

'Oh Brucey,' said Connie. 'What a tragedy this is. If only father could have got help of some kind the whole future might have been different.'

'Our poor mother,' said Bruce. 'She was the saint in all this.'

Connie frowned.

'She was and she wasn't, Brucey. Saints aren't passive necessarily, are they? They're called upon to be active. Mum had more than an inkling of what was going on, but she chose to say nothing rather than confront Dad.'

'—Because she was terrified of his violence, Connie. She had good reason to be, didn't she? Look what happened in the end.'

There was a knock at the door. Connie let Oliver in and they kissed briefly. It was little more than a kiss of comfort but Bruce noticed. Oliver broke the news of Surly Stuart and when Connie cried softly Oliver took her in his arms.

'Oh Connie, Connie, it was all looking so hopeful over Robbie, wasn't it?' He smoothed back her hair from her face, then kissed her softly again. They stayed for a few seconds in an embrace, then Connie gently broke away from Oliver, looked him squarely in the face and said emphatically,

'Oliver, you know what we must do. We must *pray* Surly Stuart better, that's all there is to it, for the sake of Robbie if not for him.'

Bruce felt uneasy. He knew what periods of extemporary prayer could be like, very exposing, very lengthy. He knew Connie once she got going, too. Suddenly he felt naked, stripped, vulnerable. Nothing in him wanted to take part in this sudden prayer session.

Oliver, sensing this, said,

'Bruce, this won't take a minute. Please pray for Surly Stu with us if you can.' He and Connie, completely comfortable in each other's spiritual presence, bent their

308

heads a little and prayed out loud for Robbie and for Surly Stuart, asking God to heal him. Connie then prayed a simple prayer for Sadie and Jack, and finally, briefly, for Bruce. At the end, there was silence. Connie had been fingering her rosary quietly throughout and continued to do so after her words had ended. Bruce found himself speaking out loud to whoever would listen — hopefully it would be the God he was dimly beginning to perceive.

'Sorry God, Sorry Dad that I wasn't there at the end. I'm sorry I didn't forgive you. I should have. Amen.'

'Amen.'

Bruce hung his head, very embarrassed by his spontaneous prayer. His face was scarlet and burning. A few seconds passed, then Oliver spoke very quietly.

'Bruce, I want to confess something and I do not know whether you will be relieved or will want to kick me into the middle of next week! It's about your father.'

Oliver explained how he knew that Bert Connors, dipping in and out of consciousness on his death bed, thought that the figure leaning over him was his son Bruce, not recognizing it was Oliver. Oliver hesitatingly related how Bert Connors had, in his final moments, put out a hand, named his son, and asked for his forgiveness.

'Bruce, in that moment, with your father sliding from one world into the next, I had to make a split second decision. I could not see your father go to his death without receiving the forgiveness he was craving.'

Oliver did not move a muscle. He held his breath.

'I'm sorry Bruce, but I took your place. I said, "I forgive you, father," and then I silently said to God, "Father, forgive *me*." Bruce, he died seconds later.'

Bruce looked up, tears streaming down his face. He walked over and put his arms round Oliver.

'Thank you, Oliver. Thank you,' he said. 'I will be forever in your debt for that.'

# Chapter 26

Whether it was through the power of prayer, or the skills of the medics in the intensive care department, or, as Oliver believed, a combination of the two working together, Surly Stuart defied all the odds and pulled through. In five days' time he was back on a main ward, sitting half up and nursing his abdomen stitches.

Meanwhile, Oliver had arranged for a solicitor to take on Robbie's case. Robbie was taken into custody, refused bail due to his previous conviction and was consigned to solitary confinement until the court hearing.

Oliver intended visiting both Robbie and Surly Stuart. Thinking that he needed to reach Surly Stuart while he was still vulnerable and before the press could get at him, he asked Connie if she would be prepared to visit Robbie. Connie therefore set off in one direction and Oliver in the other.

When Oliver entered the hospital and identified Stuart's bed at the end of a long ward, he tentatively walked up to him, not knowing what kind of a reception he would receive from Stuart. Stuart, on seeing Oliver, weakly held out a hand towards him.

'Hello Stu. How are you feeling?'

'Pretty rotten, Oli-Locki.'

'Sorry to hear that. You've had a rough time.'

'Yes, thanks to that murdering bastard Robbie. I hope he is going down for a very long time. He tried to kill me, you know.'

'Yes. He lost his temper, Stu.'

'You can say that again.'

'That was a criminal act and he will pay for it, but he was provoked, wasn't he?'

'You weren't there, so how do you know?' Stuart suddenly flashed his eyes angrily.

'The boy was there witnessing everything,' replied Oliver.

'What that little twisted half-wit? Pull the other one!'

'That little "half-wit", Stuart, has a very smart brain which retains everything. He told us all about the "nasty man". That was you.'

'It's still no reason for stabbing me in the belly. If I'd have died, that Robbie monster would have hung.'

'Actually you're wrong. Hanging was abolished a couple of years ago, Stu. He would have served life imprisonment.'

'Well, there you go then.'

'Stu, do you take any of the blame at all?'

'Have you seen that kid? Looks like an animal. You know what I think? Kids like that should be smothered at birth. He's grotesque.'

'So you are not to be held responsible in any way at all for what happened?'

'Not bloody likely!'

'No remorse at all about what you said about the little boy?'

'I told you, he should have been done in at birth. He's a monster,' he repeated.

Oliver wasn't often defeated. He thought back to various situations in his parish ministry and latterly in the college. There had been some tough ones, but he had never met anyone quite as hardened at Stuart. He realised that at present there was no way in to have a meaningful conversation with him, so he decided to shake the dust off his feet and leave. But before he went, he spoke,

'Stuart, that boy has more inner beauty than you will have in a lifetime.'

He said a brief goodbye to Stuart, wished him well, and walked the length of the long ward to the exit.

'Oy, Oli-Locki! Come back here a minute!'

Oliver slowly returned, conscious of his rubber-soled shoes squeaking on the lino floor as he returned to the bed.

'Where's that lovely girl — Connie? Her that has started work in the kitchen. She's a cracker. I'd like to see her. Will you ask her to visit me?'

'Stuart, Connie won't take kindly to know that you have called her little nephew "grotesque" and a "monster".'

'What? Her *nephew?*'

'Yes. Some of her own flesh and blood. Her sister's child.'

Surly Stu was silenced. Eventually he said,

'I didn't know, Guv. Don't tell her will you? She's like a little angel in the kitchen. Everybody loves her. Do anything for anyone. Please, Oli-Locki, don't tell her?'

Oliver smiled very slightly and turned on his heels to the door. Perhaps there was a flicker of self-awareness there after all? As he walked out, he found the words of one of his favourite writings by Mary Baker Eddy running through his head:

*When angels visit, we do not hear the rustle of wings, nor feel the feathery touch of the breast of a dove, but we know their presence by the love they create.*

Maybe Connie was the way in here.

\*\*\*

Connie was first back and went straight to her room. She was very shaken by the conditions in which Robbie was being held. She had no previous experience of anything to do with prisons or, for that matter, the legal system. Heavily persuasive, she had been allowed to see him for ten minutes.

She waited now to hear Oliver's knock on the door and share her impressions. She had been realising how much she had begun to love him and how dear he was to her now. Their lives had become intertwined and she wondered if he felt as dependent on her as she on him. She longed it would be so.

Oliver knocked on the door and she opened it immediately. Without hesitation, Oliver took Connie in his arms and they stayed locked entwined for a minute. Finally, Oliver spoke.

'Oh Connie, I need you so. It's been awful today. How was it with Robbie?'

'Dreadful,' replied Connie. 'He's been charged with grievous bodily harm with intent and he pleaded guilty even before the solicitor arrived. He was shaking all the time I was with him and said he deserved everything that was coming to him. I said it was a noble thought to defend little Jack, but all he could focus on was the loss of his temper again. Oh, Oliver, it all seems so unfair. He thinks he has let us down.'

'I'll see if I can talk to the solicitor before he draws up the defence,' replied Oliver. 'We have got to put up all the extenuating circumstances we can.'

'But what if Surly Stu dies? Robbie will be charged with murder.'

'Yes he will, but Surly Stu isn't going to die, Connie. He's picking up, but "breathing threats and slaughters" against Robbie. He denies that he provoked him in any way.'

'Robbie really cared about Jack,' said Connie. 'It was amazing how quickly they bonded with each other, wasn't it?'

'I suppose in a way they both know what rejection is,' replied Oliver.

'Connie, Surly Stuart asked to see you.'

'Oh no, *no, no*! I couldn't bear to. Please don't ask me to.'

'Of course not,' said Oliver.

'I might be tempted into violence myself if I saw him,' said Connie, with a small smile.

She had lightened the atmosphere. Oliver pulled her over to him and kissed her.

'Don't disillusion me,' he said finally. 'or I might stop believing I've met an angel.'

'An angel?' Connie retorted. 'You must be joking! You haven't seen me angry yet. We Connors have all got tempers.'

'I want to see you in all your moods, Connie. I want to be with you forever.'

There was silence. Oliver realised that was just a step away from wanting to ask Connie to marry him.

'Oliver, I'm not good enough for you. You're a priest.'

'I'm a priest, yes, but it's with warts and all, Connie. I come with baggage.'

'What baggage?' asked Connie.

'Well, Kitty for a start.'

Connie pulled away, suddenly angry.

'*Don't* call my niece your "baggage". Don't dare, Oliver! She is a perfect little girl and Bruce loves her as his own. You forfeited all rights over her, from what you have told me. She belongs entirely to Bruce and Clara. *Never* call her "baggage" again.' Connie's eyes were flashing and her fists were clenched.

Oliver was quiet. Finally, he said,

'You're right, Connie, but I didn't mean it like that. I mean I don't come exactly whiter than white, do I?'

Connie calmed down.

'Who does?' she said. 'I come as damaged goods. My father saw to that.'

He tentatively took her in his arms, shocked by her sudden flare up.

316

'All right then. That makes us quits, Connie.'

He kissed her. 'Sorry, Connie, sorry,' and finally, looked at her with eyes full of merriment.

'Anyway, at least I've most definitely seen you angry, so now I know you're for sure you're no plaster angel!'

Connie broke free from his arms, purposefully walked over to the sink, poured herself a glass of cold water, returned to Oliver and calmly tipped it all over his head.

'Oy, what are you *doing*, Connie,' yelled Oliver, reeling from the cold.

'Call it your baptism of enlightenment,' she said, laughing jubilantly. 'With love from your fallen angel!'

## Chapter 27

Robbie remained in custody until his court appearance. A criminal defence lawyer was employed to draw up the defence, who advised Robbie to plead "not guilty" on grounds of diminished responsibility. Robbie took a while to agree to this advice, as he argued that he had indeed intended to stab Surly Stuart and he could not guarantee, given the same circumstances, that he would not do so again. The solicitor counteracted this by saying that Robbie's rational judgement and exercising of self-control were "substantially impaired".

Connie had let Sadie know about the trial but insisted there was no need for her to come. Sadie agreed, saying, to be honest, she did not feel up to it. Jack had apparently been traumatised by the stabbing and would only now talk in rhymes, obsessively and compulsively repeating them constantly. Connie herself did not visit Surly Stuart, despite his request. She didn't want to open her heart in any way or be influenced to feel compassion towards him but wanted to concentrate her focus entirely on Robbie.

She visited Robbie several times in custody and each time came away feeling deeply moved by his repentance and sorrow. There was no self-justification or anger in him, simply remorse, and he always repeated to Connie and Oliver that he had let down the only two people who have ever cared about him.

Oliver continued to see both Surly Stuart and Robbie, despite Connie's doubt about the wisdom of this. It was out of character with her usual loving and forgiving nature and she knew it, but the more she saw Robbie, the more her heart ached for him. Oliver was motivated by what he saw as his pastoral duty, believing that Surly Stuart had a soul to be ministered to just the same as Robbie.

There was no softening in Surly Stuart, but he was very keen to see Connie. Oliver could not fathom out whether it was because he wanted to say sorry for what he called Jack, or for some other reason. Whatever it was, Oliver did not pass his requests on to Connie, understanding that she did not want to relent in any way.

The day of the trial set by the crown prosecution service finally arrived, nearly ten weeks after Robbie had been taken into custody. Surly Stuart was out of hospital now and advised by his solicitor not to attend the trial as he was still in a lot of pain from stitches that were threatening to turn septic.

The public gallery of the courtroom was half full; a motley crew up there, Oliver decided, probably sightseeing rather than being interested in this actual case. Robbie was led, handcuffed, into court. He looked up, saw Oliver and Connie sitting together and gave them the flicker of a smile. He looked resigned and beaten rather than anxious.

The trial progressed through the usual stages: opening statements, witness examinations and cross-examinations.

When questioned, Robbie answered monosyllabically, his eyes never lifting beyond floor level. This added to the general sense of weariness in the courtroom. Robbie's was obviously one of hundreds of cases of stabbings in London. The judge was probably sick to death of hearing the catalogue of excuses and extenuating circumstances that led to this behaviour of violence. In the jurors' eyes, give or take a fact or two, Robbie's case seemed no different from the usual violent acts characterising many young men who came before him. He had even pleaded guilty to one of the charges. They would have been more engaged in the case had Surly Stuart died. Then, at least, they would have had a murder on their hands, but this case was run-of-the-mill GBH.

But how quickly things change.

No one except perhaps one or two members of the public gallery noticed a woman manoeuvring a child's disability wheelchair sidle in and sit at the end of the bench.

The judge was giving his final summing up. It looked as though Robbie would go down for a long time judging by the general tone of things. Oliver had put in a substantial character reference, relating how Robbie had shown compassion for Connie's father, not leaving his side, how Robbie had supported Jack and shown a distinct ability to communicate with him when others had failed, etcetera, etcetera, etcetera. Oliver knew he had to be succinct, but he felt passionate about the case and tried to communicate that to the judge and jury.

The prosecution was winding up his evidence.

'So, your honour, we conclude that this young man has violence running through his veins and we must take into consideration the fact that Stuart Stanley Walton very nearly died of his wounds and is not entirely out of the woods yet. This is the second act of violence Robbie Taylor has been involved in and the prosecution has no doubt there would be a third given the slightest provocation were he not to be locked up for the maximum sentence of life imprisonment.'

Suddenly there was a scream from the public gallery.

'*No your honour*! You cannot, in the name of all that is lawful, lock Robbie Taylor up for Life. You see here.' Sadie hauled Jack out of his chair and stood the twisted, contorted, strange little boy up on the ledge in front, holding him tightly.

'My son has had ridicule, mockery, name-calling, faeces put through the letter box, anonymous death threats and a whole lot more. Why? Because he had the misfortune to be born imperfect. Flawed. I challenge every one of you here.' She paused. 'Have you not got something in you that stops you from being the perfect creature God intended you to be? Maybe yours is not visible like Jack's but it will be there all right, buried somewhere that maybe only you know about.'

The judge rose to his feet. Addressing the Bailiff, he commanded,

'Please take this woman and her son from the court.'

'I will *not* go!' Sadie screamed. Do you want to hide us away and pretend we are invisible? That is the best the world does to my son. The worst is to want him locked up or put to sleep like an unwanted animal. Except for one man, Robbie Taylor. He showed my son more love, kindness, decency and respect than he has ever known. I tell you as God is my judge, you are locking the wrong person away. He has done nothing wrong except stand up for my boy.' She looked straight at the judge. 'If you lock him up, Your Honour, you will be insulting the whole of your precious, *sacred* criminal justice system.'

Sadie sat down. There was total silence in the court room. The judge sat down in shock. Into the silence came the sound of chanting, at first in a low menacing voice, and gradually growing in volume into a loud, shrill, strangulated sound for everyone to hear:

*'Jack isn't nimble,*
*Jack isn't quick,*
*But Jack doesn't miss*
*A single trick.*
*Nasty man, nasty man,*
*Robbie got cross with*
*The nasty man.*
*Called Jack a freak*
*Called Jack a geek*
*So Robbie was sad*
*And Robbie got mad*
*Robbie was kind*
*But the man turned him bad.'*

Suddenly Jack saw Robbie in the dock. Jack lifted his withered, deformed little arm and waved.

'Hi Robbie!'

Robbie made a small wave back and momentarily the two smiled at each other. Sadie and Jack left the court. There was a stunned silence. The judge, eventually rising slowly to his feet, using a minimum of words, told Robbie he would be locked away at Her Majesty's Pleasure for two years.'

Robbie's solicitor told him afterwards that with good behaviour and possibility of parole he might serve only one year inside. The judge had erred on the side of leniency, thanks in no small part to Sadie's passionate plea.

\*\*\*

Sadie had booked a taxi to wait outside the court. As soon as she heard the verdict, she hurriedly harnessed Jack into his chair, asked for help down the stairs, boarded the taxi and headed for King's Cross Station. Oliver went over to try to speak with Robbie, who was already being led out. He also wanted to thank the defence lawyer for his work, and perhaps just might be able to see the judge and speak with him in recognition of the leniency of the sentence for Robbie.

Connie watched with dismay as she saw Sadie leaving, not quite believing that her sister would go without a single word to her. She watched Oliver going over to the steps where Robbie would be taken down to an awaiting police van and back to his cell to begin his sentence.

She made her decision in a split second. Not having enough money with her to hail a taxi, she would take the underground to King's Cross Station and pray that the Edinburgh train would not have left. The underground might even be quicker than the taxi as the traffic was heavy. Heart pounding, she willed the train not to stop in between stations in the darkness, as it sometimes did. She had at least to talk to Sadie before she returned to her isolated life in the Highlands of Scotland.

Connie arrived at the station and looked on the board frantically to see from which platform the Edinburgh train was departing. Thankfully, it was not due to go for another twenty minutes. Connie ran to platform nine and was just about to cajole the ticket collector to let her through the barrier, when she saw Sadie queuing up at an ice cream kiosk and Jack waving his thin arms in excitement as he saw the cornet being prepared.

'Sadie,' shouted Connie as she approached. 'Sadie!'

Sadie turned round, looked shocked and then broke into a huge smile. She spoke rapidly.

'Connie! I wanted to speak to you but I knew Jack would become exhibit A after what happened. I had to get him away before the press got hold of him. Did you see how many there were? I don't want his photograph splashed all over the front pages of the newspaper. A couple of them took photos as I was manoeuvring down the steps with the wheelchair as it is.'

'Madam, are you going to take the ice cream or not?' said an impatient voice.

The cornet was paid for and handed to an ecstatic Jack.

'Sadie, you were brilliant in there, and so were you, Jack,' Connie said, ruffling his hair gently. 'It was very impressive when you shouted at the judge! I wouldn't have had the nerve.'

'Well, I can thank Father for that I suppose. He had a fiery temper, didn't he? The Connors temper.'

'But you put yours to very good use, Sadie. It was wonderful that you came all the way down for the hearing. You and Jack saved the day. Robbie was heading for a life sentence, you know.'

'Well, at least some good has come out of all this,' replied Sadie. 'I must go. It takes a while to unharness Jack and fold the chair up.'.

'I'll help you. They'll let me through the barrier.'

'It's OK Connie. I'm an old hand at this. There will be a porter waiting for me.'

'Sadie. Come back soon. I miss you so. And look how our Jack got on with his cousin Kitty!'

'I'll try to,' said Sadie. They kissed and hugged each other. Connie leant down to kiss Jack and he poked the cornet in her face, putting ice cream all over her nose. He went into gales of laughter.

'Connie, have some,' he said finally.

Connie took a small bite of cold ice cream and watched them go — her sister and her nephew, so precious to her, passed through the ticket barrier and linked up with the awaiting porter. As they walked up the platform to the middle carriages, Jack chanted back,

> *'Clever Jack he saved the day,*
> *But poor old Robbie's gone away.*
> *He did nothing wrong,*
> *I'm singing this song*
> *'Cos he will come back*
> *One sunny day.'*

Jack kept repeating it until as they climbed the steps of the train, all Connie could hear was his strange, strangulated voice.

> *'He will come back*
> *One sunny day.*
> *He will come back*
> *One sunny day.*
> *He will come back*
> *One sunny day.'*

The whistle blew, Sadie waved out of the open window, and once again Connie's sister was disappearing out of her life and into the distance.

\*\*\*

Oliver was beside himself with worry. He hadn't been aware of Connie slipping away from the courtroom. He had been allowed the briefest of words with Robbie, who was then handcuffed, hooded and hustled out, amidst a battery of flashing cameras, into the awaiting police van.

Robbie was expressionless still, resigned to his fate, which, although could have been much worse, still meant that he was behind bars for two years with his freedom gone. What Robbie minded about more than anything else was not being able to delight in his friendship with Oliver and Connie. It had been the first time in his life that he had received anything nearing love.

All Oliver managed to say to him was, 'We'll be waiting, Robbie,' and then he was gone.

Oliver had then found the defence lawyer, shaken his hand and congratulated him on the result. The defence lawyer was gracious enough to admit that the woman and the "strange little boy" had almost certainly been the deciding factor in the awarding of a lenient sentence. Oliver also then managed to catch the judge before he went into the changing room to take off his garb. Oliver sympathised. In his days as a priest, he couldn't reach the vestry quickly enough after a service to take off his cassock and surplus and return his appearance to something resembling normal. Oliver thanked the judge, whereupon the judge congratulated Oliver on his "heartfelt input".

'What I want to know is who that extraordinary woman was and her even more extraordinary boy. Never in the whole of my time as a judge have I had such an interruption. It was scandalous, but,' he paused and smiled slightly at Oliver. 'It was also magnificent.'

With that, he was gone, removing his wig as he went.

Oliver made his way back to where he had left Connie. She wasn't there. He went to wait for her outside the ladies' toilets, presuming she was inside. A few minutes passed. Oliver, who was not generally given to instant anxiety, began to feel his stomach churn. His recurring nightmare was that Connie would disappear from his life. After all, the Connors family had a history of it. Albert Connors had sunk without trace for many years, Sadie had bolted (with good reason) to the Highlands of Scotland, and James, poor troubled James, had taken his own life in the most dramatic of all exits.

Oliver knew his thinking was out of proportion to the situation, and probably an emotional reaction to the trauma of the day and the subsequent nervous fatigue he felt, but he simply could not banish the thoughts. Eventually, having searched for Connie in the building, he decided he had to drive home. He even wondered if Connie had, on an impulse, abandoned everything and gone back with Sadie.

It was during the journey back that he acknowledged to himself that he was deeply in love with Connie, that he could not live without her and he wanted her to be his wife.

'Steady on, steady on,' he told himself. 'You're out of control. Don't rush into anything. Nothing has happened to her. She'll be waiting back at the hostel for you.'

But Connie was not waiting, and Oliver was plunged into despair. Thoughts of abandonment raced round his brain. His parents had died suddenly in that massive car crash. That was the ultimate in abandonment in its way.

'Stop now!' Oliver commanded his thoughts. He wished he had Robbie a few rooms down to talk to and take his mind off things.

A few minutes later, there was a knock at his door. He raced to open it. There, stood Connie — his beautiful, fragile, strong, Anam Cara — his soulmate. The girl he loved.

'Oh Connie, I've been desperate about you. Where have you *been?*'

'I'm so sorry, Oliver. I had to move quickly.'

She explained briefly about catching up with Sadie and Jack before they left for Scotland.

Oliver kissed her passionately.

'Connie. Marry me! Please say yes. I adore you.'

Connie looked up at him.

'*What!*'

'Marry me.'

She paused for just a second.

'Yes, yes, Oliver. With all my heart yes!'

'My precious beloved girl. I will do everything in my power to make you happy.'

'I think this will be a marriage made in heaven, with not a plaster angel to be seen!'

'No, just a wife who is beautiful inside and out.'

A shadow suddenly cast over Connie's face and she hesitated.

'Oliver, you know I told you I was — damaged goods?'.

Oliver knew what she was talking about and thinking.

'We'll take everything at your pace, Connie. Nothing in the world will matter with you by my side.'

Connie snuggled into his shoulder. She never dreamt she would find such happiness. The threads of abuse and guilt from her childhood memories had finally become unravelled and were weaving themselves into a new pattern.

# Chapter 28

The church army at Wandsworth was delighted to provide Oliver and Connie with a small but adequate flat for when they were married. Connie was asked if she would take a pastoral interest alongside Oliver in the folk who came to the hostel as "guests". She could think of nothing better than to be his partner in work as well as his partner in life. Connie was not an academic young woman but what she lacked in terms of ability in the intellectual field she more than made up for in gifts of emotional intelligence — sensitivity, an empathetic sense and insight into people. Her "love in action" mantra stood her in good stead for the work. The team of people at the church army knew they were lucky to have her.

Bruce was not surprised when Oliver and Connie told him of their upcoming wedding. He had sensed a synergy between them which went far beyond physical attraction. When he had seen them together around the time of the events of his father's death, he observed that it was as if their souls met. He was delighted for Connie, and in a way that he could not quite comprehend, was pleased that Oliver would be part of the family. He would not have thought it possible two years ago, but he could see that Oliver had not been at all intrusive into his life with Clara and had made no demands about seeing Kitty. As Oliver had said of himself when he made the verbal contract with Bruce — "I am a man of my word". Ahead of all those important factors was the gratitude from Bruce that Oliver had taken his place beside his dying father and forgiven him on his, Bruce Connors, behalf.

Clara found it all rather difficult. Having Oliver as a more permanent part of their lives would mean there would be no forgetting that Kitty's blood father was not Bruce. She was feeling sudden twinges of jealousy at the thought of it, which surprised her as she thought she had doused any flames of love she had for Oliver a long time ago now. She was prepared to see how it all panned out in the future but secretly reserved the right to keep family interactions through visits to an absolute minimum as necessary.

The summer wedding of Oliver and Connie was a simple one. Connie wore a full length, unadorned white dress and carried a spray of hand-picked poppies gathered the morning of the wedding. Oliver was happy for Connie to be married in the local Roman Catholic church, and once the special dispensation had been granted by the Catholic bishop, the couple were pronounced man and wife.

Sadie did not come down for the wedding but sent a present of a beautiful tartan mohair blanket for the couple's bed. Connie need not have worried about being "damaged goods". Oliver's sensitivity reassured her and her deep love for him overcame all her fears.

She became pregnant very quickly and spent nine happy months doing exactly what she had done for Bruce's forthcoming child: hand knitting and sewing a mountain of exquisite baby clothes and praying over each garment as she went.

The entire community at the church army was full of excited anticipation about its "newest member", and in the fullness of time Connie gave birth to a beautiful baby boy, who had the dark hair from his father's genes. The baby was named James Bruce Oliver for obvious reasons and was adored by everyone.

Oliver was delighted with his new son. When little James was born, he wept over his baby boy, and in a secret place in his heart felt a shaft of pain for his little daughter who he had not been able to welcome into the world in the same way. Connie was quietly serene and totally overjoyed to be a mother. She had assumed a few years ago that motherhood would quite simply be out of the question. Damaged goods? Now here was a perfect tiny baby boy wrapped in the white shawl Connie had crotched for him, coming home from hospital with her. Her cup was overflowing.

\*\*\*

A month or so after the birth of Jamie, as everyone called him, Clara was noticing changes in her daughter Kitty. She was just three years old and up until now had been a lively, chatty, bright child. Recently, she was falling asleep on the sofa in the middle of the day, which was unheard of for her. Clara also noticed that Kitty now had a growing pallor which was replacing her rosy cheeks. She asked Bruce if he had noticed.

'I have, Clara, yes,' he replied. 'I've noticed she no longer wants to spend hours in my workshop. She's coughing a bit too.'

They both decided that she probably had a nasty virus, even though it was mid-summer. Best to leave it a couple of weeks, Bruce had suggested, and if she is no better after that then it would be a trip to the doctor.

Clara was not given to displays of much affection for her daughter, mainly because she did not actually feel a huge amount of love towards her. From the first day she realised she was pregnant Clara had thought of the child as an interruption. Yes, she had grown fond of Kitty and tended diligently to all her needs, but the special self-giving love almost always accompanying the love of mother to her child was missing. Clara acknowledged this in herself, and often worried about why she did not feel much maternal love running through her veins.

Within the fortnight they had given the situation for observing Kitty, Clara noticed that Kitty had bruises on various parts of her body. As neither of them had noticed Kitty knocking herself or having a fall or a bump recently, Bruce and Clara concluded that they were spontaneous bruises. Each knew individually the implications of these medical signs, but neither voiced it to the other, hoping a wrong conclusion had been drawn.

Clara would look at Kitty as she slept fitfully and think how beautiful she was, and how she could not bear anything to happen to her.

She phoned the doctor, explained Kitty's symptoms, and he sent them immediately up to the local hospital for blood tests. Within forty-eight hours, Clara had a telephone call from Great Ormond Street Hospital no less asking both parents to bring Kitty up the following day. The Secretary said ominously,

'The consultant says please don't delay. This is an urgent case.'

Neither Clara nor Bruce needed to ask any more. They heard the warning message from the consultant and had already prepared themselves for the worst. This was a very speedy appointment and many people often had to wait weeks for one. Clara and Bruce were not misguided in their fear.

The consultant, a young and pleasant-looking man with rimless spectacles and a balding head opened his door and first bent down on his haunches and shook hands playfully with Kitty, who was in her pushchair.

'Hello. You must be Kitty. What a lovely little bear you have! My son has one like that but his is blue. I'm Dr Roy.'

Only after he had focused all his attention on Kitty for a few minutes did he then turn to Bruce and Clara and welcome them, indicating them to sit down.

'Mr and Mrs Connors. Thank you for coming at such short notice.'

The consultant looked at his notes, buying time, and then back up at Clara and Bruce. 'It's no good my beating about the bush. I'm afraid there is no easy way for me to tell you this. From your daughter's blood tests I can see that unfortunately she is very ill. She has lymphoblastic leukaemia. I'm afraid this is a very aggressive form of leukaemia in children and will need immediate treatment. I'm sorry to have to tell it to you so bluntly, but that's it in a nutshell.'

Clara and Bruce gasped at the same time. Then, uncharacteristically, Clara burst into tears.

'Oh no, *no!* What does this mean? How ill is she? How are you going to treat her? I *can't* lose her. I *can't.*'

Even amidst this tragic news, Bruce could not help but wonder, and in a sense, marvel, at this sudden display of love and panic in Clara. Kitty looked up and thrust her bear towards Clara.

'Mama. Have bear. Don't cry, Mama.'

Clara swiftly undid Kitty's harness and lifted her out of the pushchair and held her close, rocking her continuously throughout the consultation. Kitty was enveloped by a sudden tsunami of love from her mother.

Bruce knew he must focus on everything the consultant was saying as Clara was on the verge of disintegrating. The consultant outlined the various characteristics of the condition, together with treatment options, adding,

'We will have Kitty into hospital for two or three days initially to run a series of tests. As Kitty is now nearly five her best option is for us to find a bone marrow donor so that she can have a transplant.' He paused.

'We don't call it a transplant. We call it a "rescue" which it is.'

He asked if Kitty had any siblings? No. Any cousins? Bruce paused and explained the situation, knowing full well that it would be impossible for either Jack or little James to be a donor. No bloodline.

'She has two cousins, but the older one, Jack, has some very serious congenital conditions. My other sister has just given birth to a son, but he is only six weeks old.'

The Consultant took in this information and made a note.

'Parents are less likely to be compatible, but still often a better bet to look at them initially than searching outside for a donor. That can be a very lengthy process, and,' Dr Roy paused before continuing. 'And time is not on Kitty's side, I regret to say. Think about whether either of you would want to be tested for compatibility and let me know when you bring Kitty up for hospitalization. We may be lucky with one or other of you.'

Bruce was silent as they walked towards the car. This was the most important gift anyone could give Kitty now, and a vivid reminder of what he was genetically unable to do for her.

Clara and Bruce held each other into the night, mulling over the situation. Clara would without doubt be willing to donate bone marrow if her bloods were found to be compatible. Bruce eventually spoke out about what was on both their minds: whether to approach Oliver to see if he would be willing.

'It's a big "ask",' said Clara. 'We've told him to be as little involved as possible with his daughter.' (There, she had said it). 'And now we are asking him to have his bloods tested and possibly go through the lengthy and complicated procedure it would involve if he was found to be compatible…'

'We — I — will have to swallow any mixed feelings and pride, Clara,' replied Bruce. 'Because otherwise our daughter will die. We'll have to rely on Oliver's generosity.'

The next day Clara left to go and see Oliver and Connie. She had a present for the baby which should have been delivered when he was first born, but it wasn't much of a priority in Clara's mind even before Kitty started becoming ill. She was struck again by how innately selfish she was not to have bothered to pay Connie a visit to congratulate her on the birth, and she made a vow, there and then, that she would mend her ways.

She made appropriate noises over James, who she could say sincerely was a very sweet baby. Oliver and Connie both noticed straight away that Clara looked pale and haunted.

'Clara, are you OK?' asked Oliver.

Once again, Clara unexpectedly burst into a torrent of tears, and in between sobs told Oliver and Connie the whole story, ending with a plea from her heart that Oliver might help. Oliver looked across at Connie. Oliver was quiet for a minute, then spoke.

'Connie?'

'You must have the test done, Oliver. Of course you must.'

'I knew you'd say that Connie,' he said softly. Oliver didn't have to think any further.

338

'Yes, Clara. I'll have it done. Of course I will. What father wouldn't? It goes without question.'

'It goes without question because you are both full of the milk of human kindness,' said Clara passionately. 'I can't thank you enough.'

'No thanks required. She's my daughter, Clara, isn't she?'

Connie said nothing but picked her baby up and held him closely. This discussion felt quite painful and she would have to pray that she would be kept free from resentment. She had so far, and after all, she now had a precious son so how could she possibly mind about Oliver doing the best he could to save Kitty? This was sweet Kitty they were talking about, who she had nursed, treasured and loved from day one, and prayed over before she was born.

## Chapter 29

Bruce had a dilemma. He wanted to give the very best chance to his sick daughter, but he realised this would mean a good deal of exposure for him. He would have to give a reason why Oliver was having the blood test out of the blue. He and Clara discussed whether they should come clean with the young consultant about the paternity of Kitty.

Clara and Bruce arrived two days later with Kitty, who was to stay in hospital for her tests. Both parents were to have their counselling and blood tests as well. Dr Roy had explained that before they took the blood tests, parents were strongly advised to have an hour with the hospital counsellor to make sure they knew all the implications were one of them a match for Kitty's "rescue". The counsellor, who was also a qualified psychotherapist and bereavement counsellor, always saw parents separately and then afterwards, together.

Clara and Bruce both blanched when they heard the counsellor also had bereavement skills. That sounded like brutal information about which they did not wish to know.

Bruce stayed with Kitty on the ward while Clara went to the counsellor. They had a straightforward session, with the counsellor explaining all the implications of becoming a bone marrow donor and the journey both the donor and the receiver would go through. It sounded frightening for Kitty, but Clara had no fear for herself. All that mattered now to her was saving her daughter and being there for her. In Clara's heart, she felt that donating her bone marrow for her daughter might be a way of making amends for the lack of maternal instinct she had felt up until now. But it seemed that had all changed and almost overnight, because of Kitty's prognosis, Clara's instincts to love and protect her were now working overtime.

The counsellor found Clara Connors had an intelligent and realistic approach to what was happening and Clara proceeded to the haematology department for her blood test.

Bruce intended to go through with the blood test for the sake of protocol. He was not sure how to explain why Oliver would need the test. Perhaps he could be a brother, cousin, a blood relation of some kind? Bruce was uncertain what Oliver would think of that idea. His gut told him it would meet with a negative reaction.

He knocked at the Counsellor's door, which was ajar, went in and came face-to-face with Dr Sonia Hamilton.

Yes, she had the same reddish hair, still parted at the side, even the same or similar large, black-rimmed glasses. Nothing much had changed visibly about Dr Hamilton in five years. Bruce was rendered speechless from the shock of seeing her again. He remembered that he had never explained the facts behind Clara's pregnancy and had acted in what he saw now was a rather cowardly way by not telling Dr Hamilton the truth. She, for her part, had slightly reluctantly, but also rather angrily, drawn a thick red line diagonally across her notes on Bruce Connors. although it remained for her a case of unfinished business.

Sonia Hamilton was equally surprised to see Bruce.

'Right — Bruce — isn't it? It's been a long time. I have often wondered about you.' She paused and mentally assessed the way forward. 'Now. Where do we start? Tell me about your daughter, first of all.'

Something in Bruce made him quite suddenly and unexpectedly blurt out the whole truth to Dr Hamilton. Maybe it was the memory of how he had been able to unburden himself to her in their previous sessions about his dysfunctional family. She had helped Bruce unravel some of his childhood memories of abuse. Maybe he suddenly felt a huge push simply to tell her the truth. His first sentence came out in a loud, clear voice, without hesitation.

'She is not my blood daughter, Dr Hamilton.'

Dr. Hamilton remembered in a flash how Bruce's doctor had broken patient confidentiality regarding the expected Connors baby, how she had felt sad, no, much more than that — hurt — that Bruce had not confided in her about it. She had wrongly assumed that his impotence must therefore have become a thing of the past for Bruce. She had found his stories of his father's abuse to his children utterly tragic and her heart had become engaged in what she regarded as a surprisingly unprofessional manner.

Bruce told Dr Hamilton everything: about Oliver, finding his dying father, meeting Connie, the funeral of his father, sister Sadie's appearance with little Jack and how his impotence had resolved spontaneously after his father had died. He told her how he loved Kitty as his own, and the heartache both he and Clara felt at the mind-numbing diagnosis of lymphoblastic leukaemia, which he knew was aggressive and requiring immediate treatment if Kitty was to live.

Throughout the twenty minutes of his story, Dr Hamilton did not interrupt. Finally, Bruce finished by saying,

'Clara and I would like to keep the information about Kitty's paternity secret, but Oliver is a willing donor of his bone marrow if he is a genetic match.'

'I can easily arrange that for you,' said Dr Hamilton without hesitation.

'Thank you.' Bruce paused. 'I am very pleased to find you here, Dr Hamilton. I didn't know you counselled in this field as well as in the sexual and behavioural clinic.'

'I undertook a further training course to be fully qualified in it,' replied Dr Hamilton. 'One can have enough of hearing about sex all the time.'

They both laughed and the atmosphere lightened.

'I will be with you all the way through, Bruce. You have had more than your fair share of suffering one way and another. I will respect your confidentiality and do everything I can to make sure both yourselves and Oliver's decision is protected.'

Bruce got up from his chair and on impulse took Dr Hamilton's hand and kissed it.

'I can't express how grateful I am to you.'

'Bruce,' said Sonia Hamilton. 'I am very pleased that your problem has resolved itself. It was a case of the father eating sour grapes and the children's teeth being set on edge.'

Were Oliver Lockwood there, he would undoubtedly have added 'Ezekiel 18, v.1-2!'

Bruce smiled. 'You were a significant part in my release, Dr Hamilton, and for that I am eternally grateful.'

\*\*\*

Little Kitty was as brave as brave over all the needles being stuck in her arm. When she had a blood test, Bear had one too. When she had a cannula inserted into her arm, the nurse rigged up a mini pretend cannula for Bear. Connie had prayed over the little bear when she had been making it, and the soft white toy that Clara had once tossed away dismissively was now, washed and sanitized, an essential part of Kitty's armoury in dealing with her cancer. The nurses went beyond the extra mile to keep her as pain-free and as relaxed as possible and Bruce and Clara were touched and proud at how well Kitty coped with everything.

Dr Hamilton rang Oliver and explained briefly that she was fully in the picture regarding the "paternity issues" and said she would accompany Oliver down to the haematology department herself. She would arrange an appointment for him and the whole thing would be regarded as completely confidential. She would personally collect the results from the laboratory herself.

She rang Oliver again the next day explaining that as there was no time to lose over Kitty, she had managed to squeeze him an appointment the following day. Dr Hamilton would meet him in the waiting room at the haematology department and he would identify her by her large, black-rimmed glasses. She also explained that they would need to have a conversation in her room as Mr and Mrs Connors had also done about the situation.

Once back in Dr Hamilton's counselling room, Oliver began by saying how grateful he was for everything she had done. With a wave of the hand, Dr Hamilton acknowledged him, then dismissed his thanks and proceeded down the tried and tested route of explanation about the possible implications for Oliver if his bone marrow proved satisfactory.

Oliver listened without a qualm. He had never been frightened of physical pain and was very familiar with hospitals from his parish days of visiting sick parishioners. However, he feared for his little daughter's life, and subsequently for Clara's pain, and he knew this was something he might be able to do for them both. In his heart he had always felt the grief of having by necessity to be an absent father, even though the birth of his son had softened the pain considerably.

As they were talking, Dr Hamilton was forming an impression of Oliver and assessing in her mind how this man would cope with the situation in which he found himself. He had handed over his daughter at birth, had not been allowed much contact with her since, until he was needed to make this magnanimous gesture. Like most people who encountered Oliver Lockwood, Sonia Hamilton sensed something special in him and was confident that, whatever the outcome, he would be emotionally competent to deal with it.

However, she had not bargained on the trauma that was to follow.

\*\*\*

The results were due back the following morning, and Sonia Hamilton went down to the laboratory to collect them as promised.

Bruce waited anxiously at home for the phone call from her. Clara was still at the hospital with Kitty, whose tests were ongoing. Dr Hamilton had promised to let them all know the results by noon. The phone did not ring, however, despite Bruce practically sitting on top of it ready to take it at its first bell. Clara kept looking out for Dr Hamilton to come into the isolation unit. Oliver kept himself busy at the church army, and Connie, in between feeding Jamie, was painting the skirting board of their bathroom ready for redecoration.

By three-thirty, Bruce could wait no longer and telephoned Dr Hamilton.

'Ah, yes. Bruce. My apologies for not getting back to you. I've asked for a rerun of your tests, just to be sure.'

'Is there a problem?' asked Bruce.

'I'll speak to you all later,' replied Dr Hamilton noncommittally.

Bruce was perplexed but decided to take what she had said at face value. Perhaps it was a hopeful sign that there was a near-match and she wanted to be certain before telling them the good news.

At five o'clock Dr Hamilton walked into Kitty's ward. After saying hello to Kitty and talking to Bear, which Kitty had thrust in her face in welcome despite being hitched up to the cannula, Dr Hamilton asked Clara to phone her husband. She would stay late to see them and would phone Oliver as she wanted to see them all together.

'Is it good news?' asked Clara anxiously. 'Have you found a match in Oliver or me for Kitty? *Please* say yes!'

'You will have to wait just a little longer,' replied Dr Hamilton. 'I think it only fair to let all of you know at the same time.'

She walked away briskly to avoid any further questioning.

Clara was rather put out. She was, after all, Kitty's mother, and therefore had a right to know whether the other men were there or not. Didn't she? She knew, however, that she would do whatever it took to secure her daughter's future, so she swallowed feelings of resentment and any argument that might have been brewing inside her.

Both men arrived by six p.m. precisely. Sonia Hamilton had decided that she would take as much time as was needed over this, even if it meant cancelling her bridge class that evening. She looked at Bruce and Oliver sitting in front of her. Bruce was twisting his hands nervously and was obviously on edge. Oliver, on the other hand, appeared calm and composed. He knew that he was psychologically ready for the bone marrow transplant if Kitty needed it. He liked the fact that the procedure was called "the rescue". That was a positive statement.

Clara arrived minutes later, flushed from the heat of the ward. Oliver immediately asked how Kitty was, to which she replied, 'Very brave.' They then all looked expectantly at Dr Hamilton, who was looking serious.

'The good news is that one of you is a surprisingly good match for Kitty,' she said.

'*Wonderful!*' said Clara immediately.

'As you know I have run the tests twice to make sure the results are correct. Blood groups can provide unequivocal evidence when a male is *not* the father of a particular child. I also asked the lab to run me an additional test for human leukocyte antigens, the results of which can back up and confirm the results of the blood test, and it also gives me additional information. She paused, looked down at her notes, then continued,

'From the results of your blood tests, it is clear that the father of Kitty is *not* Oliver.'

'*What?*' said Clara and Bruce in unison.

'The genetic father of Kitty Connors is in fact Bruce Connors.'

# Chapter 30

Dr Hamilton went on to talk about the blood groups of Kitty, Bruce and Oliver, explaining the impossibility of an "O" type blood group male, which Oliver was, being the father of Kitty, who was AB group type, with Clara being an A group type.

'I'm sure you must have covered Mendelian Inheritance at some stage in your schooling,' she continued, avoiding eye contact, realising that what she was saying would be impossibly difficult for all of them to deal with. She continued speaking, hiding her feelings behind the scientific data.

'Bruce is in the B blood group, which indicates he is the father, and the more sophisticated analysis of the bloods makes it clear that Bruce is in the twenty-five percent category of compatibility for a bone marrow transplant with his daughter.'

That was unusual, Dr Hamilton was saying, and it was very good news. None of them heard her. The three of them were reeling with the shock of the findings and unable to process any of the further information. They were each locked in their own worlds of bewilderment and disbelief. Finally, it was Bruce who found the courage to ask the question for them all.

'Dr Hamilton. You know my problem. It is not possible for me to have made Clara pregnant. These tests must be wrong.'

'Well, Bruce, that is where *you* are wrong. Many people have been caught out thinking that it is only through full-blown intercourse and all that entails that a child can be conceived. There are stages in lovemaking where…'

'*Stop!*' said Oliver, signalling with his hand. 'This conversation must be between Clara and Bruce only. I absolutely do not wish to hear the finer details of how Kitty was conceived. This is no longer *any* of my business. I must go. Bruce, Clara, I will be in touch, but meanwhile I have my wife and son waiting for me. I suppose I should congratulate you, Bruce, but all I can feel at this moment is that I have lost a daughter.'

Oliver left unceremoniously and in deep shock, shutting the door firmly behind him. He walked home through the streets of London to Wandsworth. It took him over an hour, but he didn't notice time passing. He was filled with grief over the child he had prayed for, cared for and loved from her conception. It was he who had persuaded Clara to keep the baby, had adhered to his promise to stay away, had treasured every brief glimpse of her and held her close to his heart always. Now she had been wrenched away and it felt like a gaping wound. It also meant he had no reason to keep any ties with Clara whatsoever now, and that suddenly felt hard.

Oliver was a man of faith and had often shone a light out to others without knowing it. People spoke of an "aura" around his presence, indicating his burning spiritual passion for his Lord. Just now, though, Oliver cursed out loud as he marched briskly forward.

'What are you playing at, God? How can you do this? Haven't I been faithful? Haven't I been fair? I've had it with you!'

He walked on, feeling himself descending into a very dark place, where he stayed for many minutes. Such was the depth of Oliver's faith, though, that within a little while he was modifying his language and asking God why He had forsaken him. He knew those were the words that Jesus had used when he was dying on the cross. *Had God forsaken his Son? Not for a second,* reflected Oliver. He had rescued him from the dead to witness that it was possible to have new life. This belief was the bedrock of Oliver's faith.

These thoughts began to calm Oliver and by the time he reached home, he was thinking more rationally. Connie was there with Jamie in her arms and she greeted him with a torrent of questions.

'Hello Oli darling. I've been thinking about you and praying for your meeting. You've been a long time. What about the results? Were they good? Will there be new bone marrow for Kitty from one of you?'

'Yes, there will, Connie.'

'Then that's a wonderful answer to prayer,' she said.

'Is it?' replied Oliver.

He took the baby and held him close. He gazed at his beautiful little head and smoothed his dark brown hair. The baby held Oliver's gaze and was very nearly smiling at five weeks old.

'Well of course it is!' said Connie. Kitty has a much better chance of survival now, doesn't she? Are you the match, Oli?'

Oliver sat down and the weight of his sorrow and confusion spilled over. He handed his son back to Connie, who put him in his carry cot, seeing that Oliver needed her undivided attention. The baby was quiet and calm.

Oliver recounted the scenario to Connie, telling her how he was not Kitty's father and that the blood tests had proved that Bruce was. Connie was silent. She could not reach her own thoughts, let alone deal with them in any way yet. Her only concern was for Oliver and his distress. She had never seen him like this.

They both sat down on the sofa. Connie held Oliver in her arms and said nothing. They sat there for many minutes, she stroking his head. Eventually, Oliver looked at Connie and said, 'Thank God I have you. Thank God.'

'Oli, I don't know if this is the right thing to say just now,' Connie said gently. 'But you know we'll have more children and we can go on loving Kitty. We'll pray every day for her full recovery, and we'll pray for Jamie and our future family. All will be well, my darling.'

'Connie, I love you so much,' said Oliver, and folded her into his arms.

'Shall we pray?' said Connie.

'No, not at the moment,' replied Oliver kissing her. 'Just for now, I've got a better idea.'

Dr Hamilton explained more to Bruce and Clara about the bone marrow transplant. Bruce readily agreed that it must take place and that he was happy to be called whenever necessary to donate his stem cells. They were both in total shock about the news of Bruce's paternity. Neither of them had the emotional space at this stage to consider the feelings the knowledge might have stirred up in Oliver. They were both too absorbed with trying to process this latest earth-shattering news.

They did not talk about it immediately but walked back to the ward in silence to see Kitty and focus entirely on her. Later, both acknowledged that this was the best displacement activity they could have had, as Kitty was being prepared for her first course of chemotherapy when they saw her, and she was clutching Bear very tightly. Clara had been warned that the treatment of Kitty's type of acute leukaemia would be long and gruelling and the bone marrow transplant — the "rescue" would only take place after high doses of chemotherapy had been administered. Her decline would be rapid if neither treatment was available.

It was only after Kitty had fallen asleep that evening, that Bruce and Clara set off for home, agreeing that they would return to the hospital very early the next morning. During the car journey home, Bruce began to talk.

'Clara, I don't know what to say. I'm overwhelmed that Kitty is my child. Nothing in the world could make my heart sing like this news, but — Oh Clara — the poor darling — all that chemotherapy — her beautiful hair falling out — months of pain and—'

'*Stop now*, Bruce. We've been told the prognosis is good with bone marrow replacement and donating your stem cells will give her the best possible chance. We really must stay positive for Kitty. Isn't it good news for you, though Bruce, that you're her father?'

'It's the most wonderful news in the world, Clara. You know I've loved Kitty as my own. She's been the most amazing gift to me, especially as I thought I'd never be able to father a child. I couldn't love Kitty more if I tried but—' he groped for the right words. '—I suppose knowing that there is a blood tie between us is — is life-changing.'

Bruce wiped his eyes and Clara put her hand on his knee and left it there for the rest of the journey. Neither spoke.

The following morning, in between holding Kitty's hand at her bedside, playing with Bear, talking to nurses and generally supporting her daughter, Clara began to examine her feelings. It was all so complex and strange to know that Oliver now had no legitimate part whatever in her emotions. It had always been bittersweet to realise that the result of their wonderful if brief liaison had resulted in Kitty, and she knew she would have to work hard to let that go. It had been part of her psyche for five years. Forming a new pattern of thinking would be a challenge.

But there was also a sense of the most overwhelming gratitude (Connie would have attributed it to God) — that finally she could relinquish the guilt, the deception, the feelings of duplicity and the agony of holding the knowledge as a secret so that Kitty would never find out who was her real father.

Still neither Bruce nor Clara yet had the head or heart space to give a passing thought for Oliver in all this.

## Chapter 31

Coincidentally bishop Hermes was visiting Great Ormond Street Hospital a few weeks later. One of the clergies of his diocese — Simon Chapman — had an eight-year-old son with a severe head injury from a freak accident on his scooter involving a car mounting the pavement. The damaged boy had pulled through — just — but sadly was likely to be left with brain damage which would need his parents to attend to him for the rest of his life. The bishop knew the family well. Simon Chapman had a parish in the east end of London. It was a tough and all-consuming job which Simon managed with dynamism and energy. The diocese was busy building a ramp to replace the front steps of his vicarage and widening the entrance so that the boy could be wheeled in when the time came. This was on the bishop's instructions, no expense spared.

Kitty was still in hospital having her final round of chemotherapy before receiving the stem cell transplant that Bruce was due to donate the following morning. Clara had left her sleeping daughter briefly to buy a sandwich from the canteen.

'Clara, isn't it? Clara Connors? Well I never! I remember you clearly. You came to my doorstep when you were nearly due to give birth. I seem to remember you were asking the whereabouts of Oliver Lockwood?'

Clara was at her most vulnerable. Bruce was recovering from his stem cell donation. Kitty was looking wan and ill from many weeks of intensive chemotherapy and was about to receive the stem cell transplant. The bishop had a kind face and one that invited trust.

'Have you got time for a quick cup of tea?' asked the bishop, seeing that Clara was clearly very distressed.

'Oh, thank you. Well, just a quick one. I don't want Kitty to wake and find me gone.'

'Kitty!' the Bishop exclaimed. 'So you did call her Kitty? My wife *will* be pleased! Do you remember the conversation on my doorstep? How lovely to see you. But what ails your daughter?'

Clara told the Bishop about Kitty's leukaemia and her treatment. The bishop had remembered from *that* conversation five years ago now that Oliver had made Clara pregnant, and as a result he, Oliver, had resigned himself from his post as theatre Chaplain.

'How wonderful that you have found a bone marrow donator,' said the bishop.

'Yes, it's my husband. It's more usual for a sibling to have a match, but Bruce's stem cells are a good match. He has the procedure tomorrow.'

'Bruce? *Bruce?*' said the bishop, remembering the whole saga. 'Oh yes, of course, of course.' He quickly covered himself. Clara stared at him.

'You know, don't you — about Oliver? I remember he told me he had spoken to you about it.'

The bishop looked at the ground.

'I do, my dear, but my lips have remained sealed, ever since, even from my wife,' he replied. 'How is Oliver Lockwood?'

'To be honest I haven't been in touch with him since we heard. I'm afraid I've been very caught up with Kitty. He hasn't contacted me either. Perhaps we all thought it best to let sleeping dogs lie.'

'I've heard wonderful reports of Oliver Lockwood. I have my spies you know! His excellent work at the church army is widely recognized. He befriended a troubled lad, I believe and I'm told Oliver gave a brilliant defence on behalf of the boy.'

'Yes. He's a wonderful man,' said Clara slightly wistfully.

'Well, I must go. I'll come and visit Kitty if I may when I next come and see my colleague. Would that be in order?'

'We'd love that,' said Clara, and meant it. Clara vowed she must do something about Oliver and felt a pang of shame that she had not found out how he was in all this. The next day she ordered a posy of tiny pink roses with forget-me-nots, small but exquisite, and had them delivered to Oliver, with a card that read,

*"Thank you for everything, lovely Uncle Oliver. Lots of love, Kitty xx".*

# Chapter 32
## ONE YEAR LATER

Sadie Connors and her son Jack were happy enough with their solitary life in the caravan in the Highlands of Scotland. Jack attended a school which was suitable for his needs, although Sadie had to drive nearly thirty miles each way every day. Sadie herself had no social life to speak of, but she knew she was doing the right thing for Jack, although she had to admit that Jack was beginning to feel the isolation as he grew up.

Mother and son had travelled down to London three times in two years to visit Robbie, who was always delighted to see them. At the same time, they visited Kitty, whose lovely hair had all fallen out with the intense chemotherapy but who had received her father's stem cells, and her body was satisfactorily building new bone marrow and slowly healing itself. The consultant was cautiously optimistic about Kitty's prognosis although there was a long and gruelling road ahead regarding her further treatment. So far she had been doing well and much to Bruce and Clara's delight was regaining both her energy and the beginnings of rosiness in her cheeks. Clara did not leave Kitty's side and her belated devotion to her was, as Bruce commented rather poetically, "a perfect example of the purity of maternal love". He was thrilled to see such a huge turnaround of attitude in Clara towards her daughter, even if it had taken a potentially terminal illness to prompt it.

Sadie and Jack also visited Connie and Oliver when they came down south. Connie was delighted to show off her beautiful son, and readily let Jack hold him and give him his bottle. Jack was always overjoyed to see his two cousins and was very gentle with the baby.

Both Bruce and Connie tried to persuade Sadie to come and live nearer them, but Sadie was always adamant that her job in life was to protect Jack from the hurtful and wicked comments that people could make as they stared at him without understanding or empathy. Bruce had gently tried to say that perhaps a better way for him now he was growing up, would be to let him work out some survival strategies of his own. Bruce was sensitive, however, not to push the point, as Sadie was such a generous and unselfish mother and maybe she knew best.

Sadie and Jack planned to come down to London again when Robbie was released from prison in a few weeks' time. Bruce and Clara had remained touched by the story of how Robbie had defended their twisted and deformed little nephew against the foul mouth of Surly Stuart. Robbie had paid for it in full with a prison sentence, so Clara and Bruce had decided that they would go along to the gates of Wandsworth Prison too so that Robbie was welcomed back into the world by the entire family.

A few days before the day of Robbie's release, Oliver discovered that a large parcel had been delivered to the reception area of the church army hostel for him. He carried it back to the flat to share the opening of it with Connie. He cut the string round the parcel. Inside was a thick brown paper bag which he dimly recognized. Stuck to the outside of it was a brief note:

*"Once a Priest, always a Priest.*

I will be in touch. God be with you

Rt Rev Timothy Hermes".

Oliver undid the parcel and there, folded exactly as he had left them, were his priestly robes. The sight of them brought a lump to his throat. Connie had not seen them before.

'What does this mean, Oli? Why would he have given these back to you now?'

'I've no idea,' replied Oliver, 'Clara told me she had spoken to him at Great Ormond Street Hospital. He was the bishop I confided in about Clara's pregnancy,' said Oliver. 'I wonder if Clara said any more.'

He hung the robes out in the air to get rid of the musty smell.

That evening Connie persuaded Oliver to put his robes on to see what they looked like. She was taken aback.

'Oh Oliver, I really do feel I am married to a priest now! I feel a bit scared by them.'

'That's why I didn't wear them much in the parish, just mainly only on Sundays when I was officiating. The robes speak of separation, don't they? But they're also a symbol of a holy calling, aren't they, Con? That's why I felt compelled to give them back. I had broken the sixth commandment.'

Connie went up to him and put her hands on his cheeks tenderly.

'Ssh, Oli. That is all finished with. You asked for forgiveness and you will have received it. You are one of the holiest men I know, with or without your robes.'

'No, Connie. You're wrong. Right from when we first met, I knew I had brushed up against my angel,' he said smiling. 'I swear it.'

Connie laughed.

'Well, we certainly have a mutual admiration society here! Methinks a pedestal is a dangerously high place for us to put each other on. The only way is down! But why has the bishop chosen to send your robes back now, I wonder?'

'I think I'll have to give him a ring,' replied Oliver. 'I'm curious about it too.'

\*\*\*

Oliver rang the bishop the following morning. After pleasantries were exchanged, the bishop spoke.

'Oliver, I want to put a proposition to you. Please let me finish before you say anything.

'One of my clergy — Simon Chapman — you may know him — runs a dynamic parish in the east end of London. It's a well-known church which is very lively, all-inclusive and generous in outlook. Simon has done a wonderful job there. Sadly, his son has been in Great Ormond Street Hospital and has severe brain damage. Simon and Julie, his wife, are now looking after him at home but they have three other younger children. The workload at the church, together with family demands and the ongoing needs of their disabled son, have proved too much. Simon handed in his notice a month ago and the parish is now vacant.'

Oliver held his breath and waited.

'Oliver, I would like to offer you this living. I can think of no one better to rise to the challenge. You served your time in your first parish. Good as the folk were, they were not exactly forward looking, if I remember rightly. You then had a totally different experience as theatre chaplain, and I know you have overcome all sorts of matters of conscience. The work you have been doing in the church army has been magnificent. I keep my ear to the ground, Oliver, and I know you have a pastoral heart. Please consider this carefully. It is yours if you want it. I have talked to the parochial church council about you and they are very excited.'

Eventually Oliver spoke.

'I am very humbled over this, bishop. Can I think about it and talk it over with my wife and come back to you on it with some questions?'

'Of course, Oliver, I would want nothing less. Just one more point. It has a very large, rambling vicarage with seven bedrooms and an equally large garden, which is unusual for the east end. The house is in good repair. It has recently been done up for the Chapmans and has a ramp going up to the front and back doors. It was put in for the disabled boy. Sadly, he won't be able to use it, but it might be useful for a pram or something.'

*** 

Connie was hugely excited. She saw that it was time Oliver had a change, and the parish sounded just right for him. She didn't ask about the house, and Oliver thought he would wait before he described it to her. He wanted to be sure that if they took the parish on, it was for the right reasons. He knew too many clergy who were overly concerned about accommodation. It had never been on Oliver's list of priorities.

They spent a long time talking about the implications, looking up where the church was on the map, praying about the future and listening to the still small voice inside that might be leading them.

The next day they drove up to the east end to gain a sense of what the area was like, how the church was positioned and so on.

Oliver was warming to the idea, although he knew it would be gut-wrenching to leave the church army.

By the next morning, they had both come to the conclusion that this was, in their language, a "calling" that they could not, did not want to, refuse. It was then that Oliver told Connie about the house.

'Oh Oli. How wonderful. We must give Robbie a home. Maybe use a couple of the rooms to make him a bedsit upstairs with a kitchen.'

'And maybe we can persuade Sadie to come and live with us. After all, we're used to community life, aren't we?' said Oliver.

'And it's even got ramps put in for a disabled chair,' said Connie excitedly. 'This has got to be God's handiwork!'

'There's one proviso,' smiled Oliver 'We've got to make sure we leave enough room for our four children!'

'Only four?' laughed Connie. 'Half a dozen more like! If Robbie was agreeable, he could perhaps help with Jack?'

'I might be able to rope him in to help with the youth club,' said Oliver. 'He'll need to be occupied and he's got a way with youngsters.'

'We're going to say yes, aren't we Oli?'

'I must meet the PCC first. They might not like the look of me.'

'Impossible!' said Connie. 'Not like Oli-Locki? Whoever heard of such a thing!'

'Might you just a wee bit biased?' smiled Oliver.

## Chapter 33

On a bright morning two weeks later, Oliver, Connie and the baby, with Bruce, Clara and Kitty, (who was swathed in a blanket), together with Sadie and joyful Jack, waited at ten thirty a.m. precisely for the formidable gates of Wandsworth Prison to open. Robbie knew that Oliver was going to meet him but had no idea that the entire family would turn up.

A small door inset in the main gates opened. Out stepped Robbie carrying a small rucksack and screwing up his eyes in the sunlight. He was much thinner and paler than before and had completely shaved his head.

'Robbie,' cried Jack. 'Robbie, where's your hair?'

*'Robbie, Robbie, had a dare,*

*Got a razor, shaved his hair!*

'It's all the rage,' said Robbie, smiling broadly to see Jack. 'I'm a skinhead now.' His eyes alighted on Kitty in her chair.

'Look! Kitty's in fashion too. When d'you shave your head like mine, Kitty? I like it!'

Kitty laughed.

'Kitty's not an ugly duckling now. Kitty's a skinhead like Robbie!' she said delightedly, punching the air.

In less than two minutes, Robbie had worked his magic on Kitty. Bruce and Clara were overcome with joy. It had been a tough few months.

Oliver shook a large bunch of keys in the air.

'Come on everyone. We're going to see our new home. There's room for you, Sadie, and you, Jack, and of course Robbie!'

'And me, and me!' cried Kitty.

Bruce and Clara smiled at her. This was their little girl emerging from the shadows of her illness.

'You can visit us as often as you like, Kitty. Isn't that right, Clara?' Oliver asked.

'Absolutely,' replied Clara with a smile.

'Lucky Kitty!' said Bruce, bending to stroke the soft golden down that was beginning to appear on her head, and smiling up at Oliver.

The twisted threads of pain and suffering that had marked their lives finally seemed to have unravelled. In their place was the promise of a kinder future, with the threads this very day beginning to interweave to create a bright new pattern for them all.